NEVER
NEVER

Never Never

David Gaffney

Tindal Street Press

First published in September 2008
by Tindal Street Press Ltd
217 The Custard Factory, Gibb Street,
Birmingham, B9 4AA
www.tindalstreet.co.uk

A CIP catalogue reference for this book is available
from the British Library

ISBN 978 0 955647 60 4

Typeset by Country Setting, Kingsdown, Kent
Printed and bound in Great Britain by Clays Ltd, St Ives PLC

FSC
Mixed Sources
Product group from well-managed
forests and other controlled sources
Cert no. SGS - COC - 2061
www.fsc.org
© 1996 Forest Stewardship Council

For Susan

One

One

Apartfromtheobvious wants to get it over with and kill him today, but Magnum is only interested in her lolly. Jerks her hand to her chin to catch a tumbling shard of chocolate.

Slade's 'How Does It Feel?' wafts in from the kitchen cassette.

The man groans, straining at the cables that bind him to the radiator.

Many years from now there will be new horizons, sings Noddy Holder.

Underneath the poorly recorded songs you can hear a family thumping about and in the middle of the bass solo his mother's crinkly voice tells him to get out of the way of the bloody screen. Remembers his wrist hurting as he aimed the microphone at the TV.

Another groan from the man. Apartfromtheobvious swings his head around, glares. A thin stain of blood covers the man's face and upper neck, darker blotches on his forehead.

Slade clunks into Sparks. The tracks on the tape finish abruptly, mid-bar, even mid-syllable, and to get the songs to repeat he has bounced them from tape to tape several times, degrading the sound quality even more.

The man is twitching. Why does he twitch? Apartfromtheobvious can't get the hang of hurting. Doesn't know what he is doing. An amateur. Not usually violent (apart from that one time, when he was provoked) and it shows. The man is very much alive despite being bashed on the head with an electric guitar and having a heavy sewing machine dropped on his chest. The how to kill people page on the internet is no help. He doesn't have any of the equipment and the methods seem so messy.

He goes to the window. Saab slumping into mud on the reservoir bank. Meant it to go into the middle but couldn't push it any further. Take some explaining. Locals will notice right away. Don't miss a trick. It will be *Where has Apartfromtheobvious gone? Whose is the car by the reservoir? Where has the woman gone?*

They all call him Apartfromtheobvious. All of the people around there. Comes from when he first moved in. They knew he was hiding, knew he was running, scarpering out of debt, and one night in the pub one of the sheepfuckers asked if he was all right and he answered, Yes, apart from the obvious, and the men in the pub laughed and said, That's good, *apart from the obvious*, that's a good one that is. And they carried on calling him it, called him it all the time. Like it was his name. It was *Get one in for Apartfromtheobvious, Here's Apartfromtheobvious*, crunching the words together, and the more they called him that the better the joke got so in the end everyone in the village, even Magnum, knew him only by that name.

Apartfromtheobvious strides across to the man on the floor. 'He's quieter than before.'

Magnum chews the last nub of chocolate off the Magnum stick and tosses it on to the table. 'But not dead,' she says. 'Quiet isn't dead,' and adds, a little scornfully he thinks, 'What you did isn't going to kill him.'

Apartfromtheobvious goes quiet for a long time, thinking. From the kitchen Noddy clunks back and keeps asking them how it feels.

'What about a plastic bag over his head?' he asks.

I

Eric slid the piece of paper in front of her so that she could see what he was writing. *Keep her involved. Make it so she owns the problem and the problem-solving process.*

'What about the three grand to the bank?'

Showing a row of perfect teeth, she said, 'Well. I bought this lease on a nail-bar. Franchise really. For my, er . . .' her lips slithered apart into a smile '. . . companion. Aye, my friend. We were fine for a bit, but then he starts asking me for this nail-bar. He'd pay me back. It was about honour, he said. But soon I noticed it was always muggins shelling out – holidays, meals, the lot.'

They gazed at the heap of her bills as if it were an embarrassing growth he was about to remove. A faint rustling came from a cockroach trap on the floor; inside the cardboard tube an insect was swaying slowly from side to side, making light smacking noises as it strained to remove its feet from the syrupy floor. Tempted by the faked smell of a sexual partner, it was trapped and dying. Cleator Moor Money Advice Shop was in the St Cuthbert's Centre, a converted church shared with the community samba band, K'chaa!!, the chittering of whose percussion instruments was continuous, piercing the partition walls of the old church like needles.

Nothing seemed to be working. What had gone wrong? He'd been understanding, empathetic, non-judgemental, just as he had learned in front of a thousand flip charts with a thousand bespectacled cardiganed training officers. He had listed Doreen's debts. He had numbered them. He had written the amount owed next to each creditor's name and made a total at the bottom. And now she was crying again.

Doreen wasn't from Cleator Moor. She was from one of the more flowery bits of Cumbria, the Eden Valley. Blonde, perfect body, perfect car, perfect house, she was Eden Valley through and through. He couldn't imagine why she had no husband, or permanent boyfriend. Just the dying traces of this last relationship: the man who had cheated her, landed her in debt.

'So Doreen. Fifty-five debts, a hundred and twenty thousand pounds in total, and no one has sent you so much as a warning letter?'

'No. I've kept up to date.'

'How?'

'Well, see the HTC Bank and Newland Trust? I used these accounts to pay the cards. I scrounge along, bouncing one off the other, and between the rigs and the reels I manage. I have been foolish, innocent, and I will use the term –' she hesitated, then frowned at him with a nervous kind of intensity '– reckless.' She stared fixedly ahead.

'What we need to do,' he said, 'is find out how much you can afford to pay off all these debts.' He looked at her. She was at the wrong end of her thirties and although she was pretty – sexy even – she had a kind of cake-shop lady's face; stern, with a jaw that looked set ready to spring open as if she were always about to shout.

'So, what do you do?'

'I'm a clerk in an office. I get about nine hundred a month. I live round here now. Council. Just me and my son, but he's at college.'

Eric tried not to look surprised that she had a son so

old. And to fall so far, from a mansion in Eden Valley to the B&Q pergola land of a Cleator Moor council estate.

'Where's he studying?'

'Newcastle.'

Newcastle Poly it would be. There weren't many escape routes out of Cleator Moor. The sons and daughters of Cleator Moor families had the choice of Sellafield (the nuclear reprocessing plant), Bateson Thermometers, Scrugham's fish factory, or Gillespie's timber yard, and if at age sixteen you didn't scuttle like a woodlouse for the damp dark security offered beneath these local monoliths, you went to college, like Doreen's son – and Eric, and the rest of the advice shop staff. And you always went to Newcastle because although it was a hundred winding B-road miles away, it seemed spiritually closer than Manchester, a hundred and forty to the south.

Eric rummaged through a stack of old papers, searching for unused white space. Recycling mania. Making notes on sweet wrappers. He tugged out a memo headed 'Cumbria County Council Funding Review New Lead Officer Appointed' and began to scribble Doreen's income and outgoings on the reverse. After essentials, there was £50 left over. He wrote this at the bottom of the statement and adjusted the sheet in front of her so she could see the figures. She stared at them. The chaos of her finances reduced to two columns of numbers. Tears and sleepless nights. It was all so simple.

Eric explained that the figure of £50 was all that was left each month to repay the creditors listed on the first sheet. They looked at the first sheet. The list of creditors filled a side of A4. They stared at the total: £120,000. All those creditors. Each believing in its own uniqueness; each believing that it alone had a special relationship with Doreen. Always the last to know. And the names: Newland *Trust*, Market *Trust*, North West *Trust*.

'What other choices have I got?'

Eric said, 'Well, some.' He stroked his finger down the list of finance houses and her eyes followed. 'But what's for certain is you can't carry on like this.'

Once she was an Eden Valley wife. And now she had nothing. Nothing but a debt of £120,000. Nothing to lose. While Eric had a mortgage of £90,000 on a lovely house, a loan of £5,000 on a not so lovely car and dozens of different credit accounts all at differing stages of distress.

Eric's debts *were* becoming a problem now. He hid most of the letters from Charlotte; she knew nothing about it. He had experienced many methods of debt enforcement from the wrong end: bailiffs, attachments, he had been through the lot. He could now say with confidence that he knew the game from both sides.

Doreen stood up slowly. The strong winter sun, filtered through the Good Shepherd stained window, shone directly into her face, the margarine-yellow robes giving her a sickly jaundiced look. She screwed up her eyes. In this harsh light, her pretty face suddenly looked all built of folds, a muddle of curves, tired, complicated. The debts were taking their toll.

'Listen,' Eric said, 'watch out for that debt to Shopaloan. He's door-to-door, isn't he?'

'Yes. Local. These lot, round here, he's leeched off them all for donkeys, they tell me.'

'Don't pay him. His company are having some trouble' (they were under investigation for harassment) 'so he shouldn't come on too hard. He's scrubbing out debts every day. Uncollectable, illegal, the lot.'

'Funny thing is, it was him suggested I see you. Said he'd been the wrong side of you so often he knew that you would work it out for me with these other companies.'

'So he thinks you'll keep paying him?'

'I won't?'

'Not going through me you won't. You go through me
they each get the same. Once we've broken it down all they
get is shrapnel.'

'Mr Friday'll be none too chuffed.'

Eric shrugged. Mr Friday *was* Shopaloan; a slimy runt,
skimpy moustache bisecting a ratty face.

'So, is that the end, have I got to cut them up?'

'Cut?' Eric said.

'All the cards, all –' she looked down at her bag '– my
little babies?'

Babies. *That word needs a lot of unwrapping,* the
others would say when he related the interview to them
later.

'Well, it's not for me to say at this stage. It's your
decision.'

'Strikes me you may as well fill your boots first.'

'Well, I'm just the peacekeeping force. I come in when
the killing's over, to look after the ceasefire, so to speak.'

She hooked her hand over the door handle. 'One other
thing; should I move my microwave, my CD and stuff into
the loft, hide them?'

He looked at her. She was one of those people for
whom dishonesty was like breathing and she assumed,
with attractive candour, that everyone was as crooked as
she.

'There won't be any need to do that. You've not done
anything wrong, you know.'

Her face sagged with disappointment. 'Oh.'

Doreen's high heels made a clocking sound as she disappeared out of the old church. Eric scooped up the papers
and carried them against his chest towards the main office.
It was in what used to be one of the side chapels and en-
closed by a screen supported by paired Ionic columns. The
old chapel on the other side was rented by K'chaa!!, the
samba band. God knows why they needed so much space.

Through the Annunciation window he watched Doreen's ancient Allegro bursting the puddles as it juddered out of the old churchyard into the road, then he began to write up the interview: non-judgemental, non-subjective, avoiding stereotyping and personal prejudice. Using a few cryptic sentences which only he would be able to understand, he scribbled down a history of Doreen's problems, an account of the interview, a record of the actions he would take, made a date to revisit the case, entered this date in his diary, clipped Doreen's financial statement to the case sheet and slid both sheets of paper into a brown cardboard folder on which he scrawled *Jackson* in black marker pen. He added a copy of her credit reference record, copies of letters from her creditors, then tossed the bulging folder on to the pile of other noticeably slimmer folders on the floor under his desk.

He had begun work on his monthly expenses claim when Pedro held out the phone to him.

It was Charlotte. 'Scooter got fatter.'

'Are you sure?' Eric wondered whether this was the real reason for the call.

'His belly just drags.'

'Maybe his fur got longer.'

'Would you get your father to have a look at him?'

'You know he doesn't like to deal with small animals. He says it's sentimental, like a doll's hospital.' Give him a cow with mastitis and he was happy.

Charlotte was silent.

'Was there something else? Only –'

'It's probably nothing. We've had a strange letter.'

'What's it say?' Eric supposed it was another letter from a debt-collection company. Charlotte had opened letters about his debts before and had been confused by them, always certain they were a practical joke, never suspecting that he could in reality owe any money.

'Just one word.'

'What's the word?'

'Coerce.'

'What's *coerce*?' Eric said the word as if it were a foreign term.

'Making you do something.'

'I know what coerce means. I mean what's the context?'

'There is no context.'

'Where is it written? At the top of the letter? Is there a dear sir, yours sincerely, what is it exactly?'

'He's just cut the word out and stuck it on.'

'He? Is it signed?'

'No.'

'Why do you assume it's a he?'

'I don't know.'

'Stuck on like ransom notes?'

'Yes.'

'Each letter separate?'

'No.' She paused, presumably examining it. 'It looks like one complete word cut out of a book.'

'What did it arrive in? A brown envelope? A white one? Is it on headed paper? What?'

'It's stuck on the back of a photograph.'

There was a hole where there should have been speech and the hole seemed to suck Eric into the phone. A photograph. His heart jumped. He had not been entirely faithful to Charlotte over the past years so who knew what documentary evidence of his philandering the tide may have brought in.

'A photograph of what?'

'It's a photograph of a caravan.'

Eric breathed a sigh of relief: caravans meant nothing to him. He asked her what sort of caravan it was.

'Eric, what do I know about caravans? How would I know what kind? Who do you know who would send you

this sort of thing? Is it a woman? Do you stay in this caravan with her? Do you *coerce* her, West Cumbria?'

Charlotte often called him *West Cumbria* when she was ·
annoyed, as if all of his faults, all of his failings, could be
summed up by the name of the place that had borne him.
Eric stared at the phone, at the numbers on the dial. He
felt he should deny all the accusations but he was at a loss.
The truth was he had no idea who would send him a photograph of a caravan with the word *coerce* stuck on the
back. He looked up at the shabby stained-glass windows
that pierced the upper parts of the church walls. Well Done
Thou Good and Faithful Servant was in need of attention.
The church was listed and they couldn't afford a proper
period repair job so the man receiving the sword from a
kingly looking fella had his face obscured by an opaque
web of curly edged Sellotape. Eric wondered what his own
problems would look like depicted in the form of stained
glass, imagining himself as a brightly coloured elf pursued
by dark brown debt-collecting monks gripping abacuses.

'Charley –' he began to say, but he couldn't think of
anything.

The photograph of the caravan would wait till he got
home.

Eric continued scratching numbers into the boxes on his
expenses form. To squeeze an extra few pounds out of the
advice shop's budget he invented his expenses, concocting
elaborate journeys to clients in unlikely and inaccessible
areas of Cumbria, seminars which incurred extra parking
and mileage, and extra evening meetings to incur meals
allowances. All this helped to bolster his measly salary. But
the art of good expenses fiddling was making the figures
credible. He worried that someone, somewhere would be
able to tell the figures were made up. True, he made an
effort to vary the totals, so that they weren't all round
figures or anything obvious. But it occurred to him that no

round figures at all, ever, would be a dead giveaway, so he began to include a few a straight thirties and forties and even some fifty ps. Nevertheless, even after all of this creative effort, there still seemed to be a lot of fives and sevens in the final figures and he had heard of something called 'number preference' which could be identified in fabricated statistics.

Later, as he passed through the waiting area, he found Pedro and the new worker, Marjorie, sitting in a niche that had once held a statue.

'What you have to do is reframe it,' Pedro was saying to her. Marjorie was shaking her head incredulously at Pedro as he spoke. 'Reframe it,' he continued, 'and put the whole thing in a new light. You're going to be a welfare rights appeal officer for a time. It's not what you wanted, but it's experience and once you get your solicitor training it will prove to be useful. Put it in a frame that says *I'm going to get as much out of this as I can.*' Pedro pursed his lips and narrowed his eyes and Marjorie nodded. Marjorie was tall with a round face, a head shaved virtually hairless and plump lips set into a serious expression. Eric sat down next to her. She looked at him, blinked, then snapped her head away as if she had taken it all in and been instantly bored. But Eric was fascinated. In seconds he had been seduced by her insouciant attitude of defiance. The way she wore her clothes, the way she sat, the way she stared at him, the way she didn't say anything to him at all. But mostly by the tiny self-inflicted ballpoint tattoo of the word *thrill* on the back of her wrist. He looked at her long legs sheathed in black nylon and she caught his gaze and scowled back, impaling him with eyes of saturated blue. Pedro had to nudge him twice to get his attention.

'Bernard is worried,' Pedro said.

'What's he worried about?'

'The figures.'

The figures. The figures were something only Bernard knew about; the others knew that the figures were important, that they had something to do with how they got their salaries every month, that if Bernard was worried they should be worried too, but that was the extent of their knowledge. Bernard liked figures, spreadsheets, tables. He had no circuits for the detection of boredom.

'How do you know he's worried?'

'He was looking at the figures and I saw him doing that thing with his mouth.'

'Oh.' Eric pulled the sides of his mouth down. 'The mouth. That's bad.' When Bernard did the thing with his mouth they all knew it was serious.

Just then Bernard scuttled out of the office, bent over a sheaf of papers, doing the thing with his mouth. Bernard was a semi-retired (long-term sick) accountant, who acted as the advice centre's volunteer treasurer and finance manager and also ran K'chaa!! in the space next door. You could tell by the way he walked that he had just finished a big drumming session: the shuffling rhythms sank deep into his consciousness and manifested themselves in the texture of his walk, the patterns of his speech.

'They've put their head honcho on to us,' Bernard said. 'Mr Lowe from County Council Funding. He will drop in to see us the day after tomorrow. He wants us to update him on the changes to sickness benefits and also he's gonna tell us about the council funding review. Oh, and mate? This came for you.' An envelope coloured deep red on which was scrawled in splodgy turquoise ink, *Eric Mcfarlane, Advice Shop, somewhere in Cleator Moor.*

Eric recognized the handwriting. He took the letter over to his desk and, with trembling fingers, ripped it open.

Reading her name, touching a piece of paper she had also touched, made his joints tingle and slacken like the beginnings of flu.

Eric, the note said, *I think that now is the time. Remember Brainbloodvolume? Julie.*

Brainbloodvolume? He had no idea what this meant. But this was Julie. This was a note from Julie. After all these years. He looked at the phone number for a long time then dialled. He got a tattooist's in Manchester and they fetched Julie right away.

'Hi!' She sounded quick, breathless. 'Don't speak, just listen. The next train from Whitehaven to Manchester is eleven-thirty. I'll meet you at Piccadilly Station. See you.'

Eric put down the phone. He had been given no choice; he picked up his bag and left for Whitehaven Station.

2

A long rattlebanging train took him from Cumbria to Manchester and then he was standing on the station concourse, scouring a thousand faces. He spotted Julie's large angular nose – her attack brand she called it, a feature Eric found immensely erotic – poking like a blade through the dark quills of her hair. Catching his eye, she pulled her dark eyebrows down low, focusing a fierce intense stare on him. Then her face erupted into a grin and she shrieked and skip-hopped over into his arms.

'I've only got an hour,' she said into his hair. 'I'm on a lunch-break. But I just had to see you today. This evening I fly to Amsterdam – for the weekend – but I thought, you know, today's the day I should see Eric McFarlane.'

An eight-hour round trip for fifty minutes with Julie. Extreme, but worth it.

On the way to her flat, Julie said nothing; just gripped Eric's hand tight and kept looking back at him and laughing as he trailed along behind her.

From hills and silence to concrete, mess and mayhem. Eric loved the city. He squinted into every shop window and savoured every sign, every poster, every item of street furniture. Maiden, More O'Ferral, JCDecault; unignorable images, angry colours. The visceral grunt of a passing car's stereo said *city* to him over and over. Drum and bass, jungle, speed-ambient house, he had no idea. Hooded and puffa-ed figures hovered on every corner, staring at them. A woman was sitting on the street, begging, wearing a lampshade on her head with eyeholes cut into it and a mouth and nose drawn on the front.

They stopped at the window of a second-hand shop, at a display of old comics. They looked at the comics, saying nothing. He felt for her hand but it wasn't there and he looked to see she was twirling her fingers in the downy slope of her neck, smiling and looking down at her feet. He touched her elbow, and she looked at him, then pointed at a *Hulk* comic. She told him in a low voice about a Marvel comic artist whose remains were mixed with printer's ink for a special edition. There wouldn't be much of him in each copy but it still felt to her like he was there, on the page, in the solid green of the Hulk's body, in the black skies over the cityscapes. Eric wasn't sure if this was funny, ironic or profound so made a noise that would pass for a laugh, or a sad sigh, or a wowed coo of amazement, but Julie said nothing else. A pedestrian crossing beeped, a burglar alarm trilled in the mid-distance, a plane rumbled across the sky, buses whined and moaned their way up Oldham Street.

Julie's flat was above the Shudehill tattooist's where she worked and once they were alone she said she didn't want to speak to him at all. She didn't want to catch up, didn't want any of that. All that could wait. She wanted to look at him, that was all, and he to look at her. She didn't even want them to touch each other. Gaze was everything.

'I want a memory of your eyes on every inch of me, and mine on every inch of you,' she said.

So that's what they did. Took off their clothes and looked at each other.

Afterwards, Eric stood for a time outside the tattooist's, watching Julie meet and greet the customers, explaining to them the various scarring and mutilation options on offer, while the last word she said to him rang in his head: *Brainbloodvolume*. The word resounded across the years yet right now, for Eric, it had lost all its meaning.

Eric put the rest of his afternoon in Manchester to good use. He called in at the office of the North West Money Advice Group and registered to work as an adviser on the BBC debt helpline. He visited Manchester County Court and confirmed his attendance at his administration order hearing in a couple of weeks, a useful legal procedure which would help sort out a few of his debts. But he had an urgent need for more cash; a payment to one of his more persistent creditors was required by the next day and Julie had given him a useful contact: the landlord of her tattoo parlour who, as well as drug dealing, pub managing, taxi driving, gym owning and general violence and criminality, offered loans – ultra-short-term, ultra-expensive and ultra-illegal. So Eric took a bus to the council overspill estate where he lived, a grey stifling place where human leftovers had been tipped over the sides of the city, banished to live outside its walls in vast cheap storage units.

The man wore a big thick gold chain round his neck, incongruous against his Adidas top, and enormous luminous orange trainers with translucent bubbles on the sides like the newly evolving eyes of some primitive creature. The gold chain resembled a mayoral chain of honour; it was as if he was mayor of the overspill. The overspill mayor told Eric that if he paid the money back in two weeks, plus the thick end of another thou for interest, he would be a dog with two dicks. He didn't say what sort of animal he would be if Eric didn't pay it back at all. The man seemed to like Eric. It amused him that this kid from Cumbria looked like *such a fucking student, such an indie-cunt*. He kept calling him *Damon-out-of-Blur*.

*

On the train back Eric thought about Julie. He had been dreaming of her for years and finally, out of the blue, she had appeared. There still existed a longing between them – a desire, a bond, a knowingness, something perfectly ripened – but there was also an absence, as if a constant pleasant low hum he hadn't known was there had clicked off. His job was to switch it back on again.

3

The next evening when Eric got home from the advice shop he found that Scooter had got even fatter. Charlotte was crouched on her haunches peering at the oddly rounded cat. Next to her was a box of her old vinyl 45s, a few choice titles on the top: Dead Boys' 'Sonic Reducer', the Adverts' 'Gary Gilmore's Eyes', the Radiators from Space's 'Psychotic Reaction', the Lurkers' 'Ain't Got a Clue'.

'What you doing with all these singles?'

'I need the room. These games take up so much space.' She nodded at a GamesWorkshop bag, the angular shape of more computer games pressing out from within. 'And I never play these records any more.' She turned her eyes, the bright bubbles of brown glass flecked with green he had fallen in love with, to him.

'But these are classics,' Eric said. '"Outdoor Miner" by Wire, Swell Maps' "Read About Seymour", "She Is Beyond Good and Evil" by the Pop Group. And here – "Don't Dictate", Penetration. You used to love that. I mean how can you think of throwing this stuff out? This stuff is you. Us.'

Charlotte gave Eric an exasperated look from under her swing of brown hair. 'We grow up – some of us, Eric. Listen, I'm worried about Scooter. He's not supposed to be like that – so suddenly explodingly fat. Will you ring your dad at St Bees? Like you said?'

'Yesterday, by the way –' Eric began to explain. It had been the early hours of the morning when Eric returned from Manchester and he had forgotten to let Charlotte know where he was. She hadn't spoken to him that night nor in the morning.

'Never mind about that,' said Charlotte. She pulled something from the back pocket of her jeans and pushed it into his hand. It was the picture of the caravan. He had completely forgotten. Charlotte watched him, hands on hips, waiting for his assessment.

'This it then? What you were upset about yesterday?'

He bent his head over the picture and creased his brow, scanning every inch, as if in the style of the caravan's carriage, in its shape, he would find some sort of code he could understand. He tried to date the picture; it looked current. He tried to place it geographically; the caravan looked as if it was in a showroom rather than on a holiday park.

Charlotte snatched the picture out of his hands and slapped it on to the phone table. 'Who do you know who would pull a trick like this? Because I've never stayed in a caravan in my life. Not even when I was a kid. My mother would have died rather than stay in one of these. I mean, where would she even hang her dresses, what would she wear?'

'I don't think it's anything, Charley, I honestly don't. Let's have a look at the other mail we've had.'

Charlotte put out her bottom lip and blew her fringe off her face. 'It's just a load of finance stuff, I opened one by mistake, sorry. Seemed to say you owed money so that can't be right. Will you make sure you sort it out to-morrow?'

Her fringe flopped prettily on to her brow and she made a monkey face at him, one of the faces he liked, where lines appeared at the top of her nose.

When he grunted assent, she pulled out a large box with the legend *Crystal Amulet Mountain* on the side and took it through to the living room to liaise with the Mac.

He could see a red heading on one of the letters. That was always bad. There was a bailiff's letterhead on the other, which was worse. How can life be so urgent and so pointless all at the same time? He tore them open. The bailiff's letter was nothing to worry about; it was from Copeland District Council bailiffs. Full of threats, but Eric happened to know that they didn't even own a van and they had never uplifted goods from any domestic home in Cumbria. He could safely ignore it. The red-headed letter was from Anubis Securities, one of Eric's more persistent and troublesome creditors. Something in Latin was written at the top of the letter: perhaps dead languages frighten debtors.

The letter began curiously:

> *Dear Mr McFarlane,*
>   *Where did we go wrong?*

Had they gone wrong as well? Eric had thought it was just him. They thanked him for the £4,000, a sum of money Eric had borrowed off one of his other credit cards, but were unimpressed by Eric's effort. Thanked him for four grand like it was four quid. The rest of the arrears – another £5,678 – was still owing and if they remained unpaid the entire debt of £35,000 would become payable. If they hadn't heard from Eric in seven days they would enforce their county court order.

Eric felt for the cash he now held in his pocket, the cash he'd borrowed in Manchester. But he had a few other pressing priorities before he could hand this over to Anubis. He thought back to the dodgy overspill mayor bloke, his big round baby face.

He took the letter into the back room and sat at the dining table opposite the Mac, where Charlotte tapped and clacked away, frowning at the screen, the cellophane wrappers of *Crystal Amulet Mountain* all over the floor. He put the letter in front of him, placed his elbows on the table, sank his cheeks into his fists and looked at it.

Enforce the county court order.

Anubis were in a weak position, and they knew it. It's tough to drag money out of debtors who don't want to pay. So they were playing a game. *Take you to court. Sue you. Send you a summons. Gum you to death with a sick sheep.* But that was their atomic weapon, the worst they could do, reserved for only extreme situations. So they laid it on extra-thick, made out that court was the most horrible experience you could ever have. Whereas, in fact, the issue of a summons was the last action they wanted to take. Because once they'd done it, they couldn't threaten to do it any more. And if they did it, the judge at court would order one pound a month or some other minuscule contribution, and Anubis would get fuck all.

So they preferred to stretch out the bit before court; letters, phone calls, calling at the door, more letters, more phone calls, more calling, more calling at your door, maybe a call at the work address, anything. Like some fragile sort of foreplay, some squarehead pretending he liked his earlobes sucked when he just wants to stick it in and get it over quick. And, with most debtors, dragging out the process worked. But not with Eric. Because all day he worked on the debtor's side. So they could forget getting any money off Eric. They could massage him, suck his toes, kiss his shoulders for as long as they liked. It would make no impression, produce no arousal, make no juices flow. Eventually his belligerent, vain, over-attentive lover would forget what she was there for.

Except in this case, the letter went on: *The court order*

will be enforced by the charging order we have acquired on the property owned by the debtor at 32 The Loop Road, Whitehaven. And according to the letter the court hearing was in a couple of weeks. He rubbed his thumb over the picture on the letterhead, a human figure with the head of a jackal. This stepped things up. Anubis already had their court order, he'd forgotten that fact. He'd lost track of where all his creditors were up to, he had acquired so many, and tended to throw creditors' letters straight into the bin. A charging order was a good tactic. It meant he could lose the house. Eric crumpled the letter and threw it on to the table in frustration. This was getting serious.

How had he ended up with Anubis, anyway? They were scum-sucking sock-puppets, the lowest of all finance houses. He'd always made a point of avoiding them. Those other bastards had sold it on. Didn't want to get their hands dirty. He would have to visit Anubis, professionally. A diplomatic visit to ease relations between his clients and the collectors. He would learn more about their methods, find out what he was up against.

Charlotte picked up a bottle of wine and pointed the base at Eric. 'I can't understand how these companies think you owe them money. And you a debt counsellor. It's funny, in fact.' Her fingernails tweezered away at the metal sleeve around the cork.

'They've got their figures fucked up, I think. Don't worry. Reframe it.'

Charlotte looked at him. 'Reframe?'

'Something Pedro says.'

Charlotte sniffed. 'I prefer a bleed. No edges. You see what you see, no artificial borders.' Charlotte was in graphic design. She was always explaining technical printing terms. He thought of the caravan picture, the grass bleeding over the edges, water running off the sides of a flat earth. Thought of the blood that the debt companies wanted from him and of all the credit companies that in his professional capacity he'd bled, bled white, and of the way his relationship with Charlotte bled him dry of all his resources.

Money was always a worry to Eric. He never had any – ever. Charlotte was a consultant – that's how she described herself – and this meant that she did odd little pieces of work for companies: helping them set up databases, designing newsletters, producing flyers, laying out annual reports. She did some of it at home, on her Mac, and some of the time she went to the company and worked in their offices. She liked that better. It seemed more like going to work and she said that it made her more disciplined. However, despite the fact that she always seemed to be working on something or other, Eric never saw the results of any of the money she earned. Cheques came sporadically and sometimes Eric saw the invoices that had been attached to them: some were for large amounts – one had been for £5,000. But she squirrelled them away and always said that they were spoken for within the mysterious accounting system she held on the Mac. 'If it weren't for the taxman and the overheads, I would be doing well,' she would explain. 'I never spend money on anything.'

But she did. She kept buying computer games and the packaging – big boxes the size of cereal packets – lay all over the house. Each box bore pictures of beautiful and violent individuals, whose mission, presumably, was to rid the world of evil invaders. The Mac was a third person living with them, a strange quiet brooding lodger who, while keeping himself to himself, exerted great power over the structure of their lives. 'She's spending the evening in with Mac,' Eric would explain to friends.

Eric picked up a sponge and used it to brush the morning toast crumbs from the kitchen surface into his palm, cupped at the edge of the table. Charlotte's head was in the fridge. 'There's nothing in again.' She pulled her head

25

out and looked at Eric, who was stood holding the toast crumbs in his hand. 'Donatello's?'

Charlotte came from a family where her father had paid for everything and her mother's money was for herself, and she was always telling Eric about her glamorous mother.

'My mother had a different dress every weekend, Eric. Beautiful gowns. Cocktail dresses. A new one every week. Can you imagine that? When she and my dad were ready to go out they looked like film stars. They would go to the Talk of the Town. They knew film stars; boxers, racing drivers, crooners, those sorts of people. This was when we were in London. It all seemed so romantic. My mother never saw or handled any money. My father would open up accounts for her at stores in town. Any money she earned herself was her own. She never knew what a bill was.'

Although this arrangement was never spoken of or formally agreed as a system for running their lives, Eric had fallen into this way of working too and he tried his best to pay the mortgage, the car loan, the insurance, the fuel bills, the water bills, the phone bills (part of these were claimed against Charlotte's business, but he never saw any result from that) and any joint leisure activities. It was a lot of money to find each month and hence Eric had become increasingly reliant on credit and the fraudulent use of his various accounts. But Charlotte didn't know about any of this. So she'd always insist they ate out. Even when he had no money, nothing in the bank at all. Well, at least *he* knew he had no money. Charlotte thought he was always flush. Because each time she suggested they go for a curry or an Italian or a Chinese he'd say OK even though he didn't really want to. Well, he wanted to in that it saved cooking and it was better than sitting in the house, but he didn't like to think of the money spent. Five pounds for a starter – five pounds! Eating out at least two or three times a week. Yet despite his anxiety about their spending, Eric never said anything. He didn't want his debts to crash down on her as well. Charlotte had no idea his earnings were just over a thousand pounds a month. She received cheques for that amount regularly; he had seen them.

Watching her hunched over a ledger, doing her books, a twist of hair in her mouth, he often wondered where the punk Charlotte had gone. The Charlotte who loved chaos, gigs, noise and smell and dirt and sweat, who stage-dived at 999 and lost her shoes at the Upstarts, who hoovered drugs, slept where she fell and lived only for feedback and strobes and cider. The girl who had left Greg Torkington, lead singer of Hoovercock, for Eric, humble roadie for Tubular Bondage.

Eric scraped the crumbs off his palm into the bin. 'I'm not very hungry.'

Charlotte's face tightened. She took off her shoe, squeezed her foot. Then she went upstairs to get ready and Eric sat looking at the Mac. Multicoloured fish swam across the screen eating specks of food.

'Plastic bag?' Magnum snorts. 'A plastic bag over his head will leave a trail. Say there were secret numbers on every bag; that way they could work out the day and time it was given out. The shop-girl would remember us: *They seemed edgy, something odd about them, wrong clothes for time of year*, that sort of thing. It's the small things. You've got to –' she crosses her legs smartly '– have a bit about you if you're going to get away with this.'

Apartfromtheobvious sits down, puts his feet up on what he calls the coffee table, a huge dining table the landlord sawed off to knee height. It is piled high with newspapers, catalogues, partially completed job applications and rejection letters; sedimentary layers of hope, rejection, despair. Last rejection letter has been torn into inch-sized pieces and the shreds form a jagged paper peak that shifts every time he raises his voice, which is quite often.

'How did that bloke Nilsen kill people?' Magnum asks.

'Strangulation. Then sawed them up, boiled them and flushed the bits down the drain.'

Magnum shudders. 'Christ. I don't fancy that.'

'It was the sludge in the drains caught him out. *Human porridge*, the papers called it. He was the one that used to listen to "O Superman" while he did them.'

'I'm not surprised – ah ah ah ah ah ah over and over; drive you mad as shite.'

'Before he offed his victims, they drank Bacardi and Coke together. Always.'

Sudden thought. 'I know, what about we get him pissed? So pissed he dies. We could pour it down his throat. Alcohol is a poison.'

'There's half a bottle of Thunderbird, but that's not going to kill him. And I was expecting to have a drink tonight.'

He leaps up, spins round to face her, thrusting his face into hers. 'We've had him here for hours, bloody hours we've had him here and we're just pissing it up the wall!' He moves his face closer, so their noses almost touch. 'Are you listening? Pissing it up the wall!'

She jerks away from him with a sharp cry and her breath begins to come in short fast pants like someone madly pumping at a bicycle tyre. One of what she calls her attacks. Turning out to be like the other one. Her shoulders lift and fall like stumpy wings, breasts shuddering beneath the short cotton blouse. Brown stain on her belly where a flake of chocolate has melted. But she isn't bad, not bad at all for her age. Seeing her like this gives him a nice feeling like someone is crinkling crêpe paper inside his head. He takes her chin in his fingers as if it were the muzzle of a dog and strokes it absent-mindedly, lowers his voice to a whisper.

'It's him, Magnum.' Jerks a hand at the man who is pulling at his wrist cables and pointing his small grey eyes at them. 'I wish we didn't have him. I don't want him any more.'

'When you call me Magnum it means you don't want me to eat the lollies. You think I'll get heavy.'

'It's a pet name.'

'You buy them. You buy them for me then you make fun.'

'The bloke: I'm just not sure I've done the right thing.'

'Don't worry,' she tells him, and takes hold of his hands and pushes them together as if to make him pray. 'We'll just have to keep at it. We'll soon polish him off.'

Polish him off. He is new at this and eager to succeed. But they don't even have the right vocabulary.

4

Eric heard the doorbell ring and Charlotte pad down the hall. There was a change in sound – the soft whoosh of tyres from the main road – and he felt cold air prickling his bare arms through the anaesthetizing fug of the central heating. A polite low tenor voice burred between Charlotte's harsh questions, then she called out, 'Eric, it's the assistant bank manager of the Cumberland and Borders Bank.'

The assistant manager of the Cumberland and Borders Bank had a big, neckless oblong of a body shaped for nothing but blocking doorways. He was somewhere in his sixties with a big wide red face and white hair tinged with yellow. He was holding a trilby hat in his hand. There was a feather in it you could catch a fish with. He gazed into the house wistfully and, when Eric asked him if he wanted to come in, he said in a fruity Cumbrian accent, 'Aye, lad, aye, lad. I'd like that. Just a few words, like, about the account and that.'

He stood in the middle of the room looking around him all the time. His eyes came to rest on Charlotte's glass cabinet, her collection of lumpy Carlton Ware pottery. Eric thought of all the money Charlotte had spent on her pottery collection while he paid the bills and ran up the overdraft to the Cumberland and Borders Bank. Yet he loved to see her rummaging at bric-à-brac stalls, tapping cups against her teeth to assess their density.

The assistant bank manager spoke. 'People will collect all sorts of things. Eh, Mr McFarlane?' he said, pointing his trilby hat at the cabinet. 'I had a bank customer once who collected nails; new nails, old nails, rusty nails, all different sizes as well. I went to visit him and he had all the nails on little shelves.' He sighed and shook his big square head. 'I suppose it kept him busy. I had someone once who collected –'

Eric interrupted him. 'Have you called for any special reason?'

The assistant manager looked at the black director's chair and Eric nodded for him to sit, which he did. 'I have, yes, aye. There is a reason, and it's this. As I say, people collect things and it looks like you like to collect –' he opened up a brown plastic briefcase and drew out a ring binder which he opened on his lap '– cheque books. You have four of our cheque books at the moment, each with twenty-two unused cheques in it. You have a cheque guarantee card of a hundred pounds too, I think, haven't you, Eric – can I call you Eric?'

'Aye, sure, course you can.'

'If you think about it, someone with that number of cheques and a guarantee card could spend a lot of money.'

'Eight thousand eight hundred pounds.'

The assistant manager looked surprised. 'Is that right? I hadn't worked it out.' He looked up at the ceiling. 'Yes, I suppose you're right. And I suppose as a bank, if the card number was on the back, we'd have to pay it, wouldn't we?'

Eric said, 'I dunno.'

'I think we would, yes. I've looked into it in fact – to-day. I asked one of our legal people – you know the type; they love to get into all the in and outs and ifs and buts of things like this. I can't say I really understand all the acts and legal precedents myself, it was all done on honesty, trust before, in the past, you know –' he tapped his chest '– when people like me started out in banking. You knew a family, you lent money to them, you got it back. That's how it worked.' He shook his head and sucked in his lower lip. 'It's not the way nowadays. There's the courts and, I don't know, you don't seem to get to know the people – the customers – any more.' He lowered his eyebrows. 'They're all just numbers on a screen.'

'That's the way things are,' Eric agreed.

'I don't know what you do for a living,' he said, sinking lower into the chair, 'but I'll bet you have to work on computers all day as well.'

'It's getting that way.'

'Aye, there's no human touch.'

He crossed one foot over the other and touched the laces with his hand. For a moment Eric worried that he was about to remove his shoes. Instead, he rolled a shoelace between his long flat fingers as he spoke. He had pearly fingernails, clean, manicured.

'So it's the matter of your account.' He thinned his eyes. 'Let's see. Aye.' He found a sheet of paper. 'Three thousand two hundred and seventy-one pounds sixty-seven pence overdrawn.'

Eric's head moved back as if it had been struck. 'No. It can't be.'

'That's what it says,' the assistant manager said. 'The last transaction was, let's see, Donatello's bistro, a cheque for thirty-five pounds, and then we bounced a direct debit to another finance company – that unfortunately made a referral charge of forty-five pounds – and the balance now stands at around the three thousand mark.'

Eric saw the assistant bank manager's eyes darting about the room and read his thoughts. 'The house is Charlotte's, my . . .' he searched for a word, as he always did '. . . co-habitee.'

The man adjusted his feet and began to twiddle with the lace of his other shoe.

'I feel I can talk to you, you being white-collar. You see, Mr McFarlane, I've had accounts like these before. As you know, some people think banks don't matter. They don't realize that banks are people. That's all they are. Just a lot of people doing things. They are not buildings, not machines in the wall, but people with homes and children and –' he hesitated '– cohabitees. I can see that you understand.' His large square face tilted towards the floor. 'When I have accounts like these –' He pulled his face up, interrupting himself. 'You see I'm in a structure – a hierarchy. They draw it for us like a hanging mobile with little threads between every box.' He smiled at the picture, and they both looked up at the ceiling rose, imagining the dangling boxes. He pointed at the air in front of him just above his head. 'That's the manager at the top, in London, then below that there are other boxes with names in for each area. One here might be for the North West Regional Manager, for example. Then there are boxes under those boxes. You have your own box if you are very senior; if you're a minor player you share your box with a few others. I'm down here somewhere.' He pointed towards the carpet. 'So from the top –' he pointed to the ceiling '– the messages go down through the boxes.' And he pointed to the floor.

'Now don't get me wrong, Eric, I'm not right at the bottom, there are other workers – the people you see on the front desk for example. How it works is this. I get it from the senior manager who gets it from regional. He says to me, "Why do you run accounts like these? Why do you let them borrow so much money?" But I tell them that you can't stop people having money, money to live on. It's not as if they're driving about in big cars. He says to me, "Right then, Howard, bounce everything, bounce the lot, everything that comes in, bounce it. Get Johnny Debtor's attention. And charge them for the pleasure, charge them high, put them right in the shit, right in so they can't see out."' He sucked in his lips. 'They talk straight, some of them. So sometimes, to be honest that's what I did. I bounced things. Bounced mortgages, bounced car payments and Christ, do you know, it worked. They were running in off the street, begging me for help. But,' he paused and gave a weary smile to Eric, 'I didn't like that approach.'

Then, without changing the shape of his smile, he locked his eyes on to Eric's. 'You shifted all your direct debits and standing orders a while ago though, didn't you?'

'I don't know. I guess so. I must have cancelled them. I honestly can't remember.'

'Yes, you cancelled them before the account got messy. It's funny, it's almost as if you cancelled them on purpose, almost as if you *knew*, knew how the bank would behave. I said to my boss, that can't be the case, it's a coincidence, no one would deliberately do that. "Well," he said, "check it out, Howard." After the direct debits were cancelled a lot of cheques came in. And we had to honour those, Eric, because they had the card number on the back, didn't they?'

'Does that make a difference? The number on the back?'

'A big difference, yes it does. Means we have to pay it. Even if there's no money there. We've got to pay out. We've been had, so to speak.'

Eric sighed and shook his head sadly. 'You know, someone could take advantage of that system, someone dishonest. You should look into changing that system.'

The bank manager bobbed his head up and down and placed his fingertips together as if he were praying. 'So that's my position. Can you see where I am from where you are?'

'I can see where you are now, yes.'

'Aye. So I'm here. And he, the manager, is saying it's a bad loan and it's a bad lending decision. And I have to give him that. But I've got something he hasn't got.'

Eric looked at the man's big head hanging forward. 'What's that?'

'I've got faith. Faith in nature. I know in here –' he thumped his chest '– that people want to pay. They don't like debt. When I started in this game the only individuals with bank accounts were the local doctor, solicitor, head-master, vicar. Nobody else. So you took a cheque from the likes of them, you didn't need a number on the back, you knew the person. It was like a personal letter, a promise letter. You knew that the cheque would be honoured. And honour is the right word. It was an honour to be paid by a cheque from one of the professional classes, all written in beautiful handwriting. You wanted to keep it. It was bet-ter than money; it was personalized money, like money made specially for you with your name on it. Nowadays, even the lot from Scrugham's fish factory have bank accounts. *Weekly paid people.* Aye. They're paid weekly, it goes into the bank and every Friday they come and get it all out again. People from terraced houses. And then the regional manager comes along and he says to me . . .' Eric looked up at the ceiling, imagining the regional manager climbing out of his oblong box and sliding down the connecting thread into the assistant bank manager's box. '"You're not selling enough," he says. "You should be mov-ing more product. Loans, insurance, second mortgages, personal pensions." I say to the region that's not what bank-ing is about in this area. It's about helping people. They haven't got the money to be buying things.' The assistant bank manager had begun to mumble, as if he were talking in his sleep. His head lolled forward, he looked tired now. He was holding his trilby hat by his fingertip and swinging

35

it lightly as he spoke. 'Maureen, that's my wife, says I should retire early. The young ones coming up under me, aye, they're eager, they'll be tough as well. Now I know I've kept you a bit and I'm sorry for that. But what I want is to have a look at your cheque card.'

Eric knew that when the man got hold of the cheque card he would keep it. Yet he was finished with this account. His system for the past few months had been to save up cheque books from accounts he was ready to leave. He had left many banks in the past. In fact he had at one time been with every high street bank in West Cumbria and now had his salary and his direct debits with the Lothian and Borders. As a cover he feigned financial incompetence and always promised faithfully that the money necessary to rectify the account would be with the bank the following day – in cash. Of course it never was. He would give it a couple of weeks and then he would write to the bank offering them 50 per cent of the whole sum due as full and final settlement. He told them the money was coming from a kindly concerned auntie who had inadvertently seen a bank statement; she hadn't been able to live with the thought of a family member in debt. The bank usually accepted and then he would apply for a personal loan from his new account to pay off the old overdraft. This usually worked, but it couldn't work for much longer. He knew now that he couldn't save the house by merely juggling a few accounts. Something more was needed. He had taken it to the edge. Now he must go over.

He went upstairs and returned with the card. The assistant bank manager took the card between his pearly nailed fingers and tucked it smartly into a ticket-pocket on the front of his jacket.

PLAY NEAR POWER LINES

We'd left Spangles and her mum, and were *happily-rolling-along-the-road*, guinea pigs softly tooting in the back, when the snow started to *really-hammer-down*, and Dad said the road, a single tracker, often got clogged up and we would have to turn round, so he swung the car on to *what-turned-out-to-be-a-frozen-pond*. 'Where were the bloody signs?' he complained, but as Spangles says, 'THE EMPTY SIGNPOST SHOWS THE WAY.'

There was a loud crack and the car tilted forward. We were stuck. I worried if guinea pigs could swim. Dad jumped out, hopping and vibrating with distress, jerking about this way and that, then said to me, 'Stay there,' and ran off back to the house belonging to Spangles, to get help. This was so embarrassing. It was growing dark and I could hear the guinea pigs tooting and I hunkered down to keep warm. I thought I was going to die. Spangles says, 'LIFE WITHOUT RISK IS MEANINGLESS,' but I was still scared.

The so-called 'sick pigs' Dad had rushed us out to examine, taking me with him on another of his *well-you-never-know-you-might-find-it-interesting-you-might-want-to-follow-me-into-the-family-business-after-all* projects, turned out to be *guinea* pigs, and the woman who owned them turned out to be the mother of the GORGEOUS SEXY WONDERFUL Spangles, from my year at school. Dad disappeared for ages looking at the sick pigs, leaving me alone with Spangles, who had black hair that hung in berserk abandoned bunches and watched me with a reproachful stare.

'You got a few spots going on there, honey,' Spangles said, after a time.

The only sound in the room was the shush of her purple skirt against her black school tights as she crossed and re-crossed her legs.

'I suppose,' I said, touching a large one on my chin.

She told me about a documentary she'd seen about getting rid of spots. 'In this film these scrag-skinny models said that the best, the really, really best thing for your skin is the slime stuff from –' she made her mouth wide, mock screaming '– slugs. Or snails, but slugs were better, which is a shame because snails are cuter – you could imagine them having friends and, like, a social life, whereas slugs are real loners. Anyway, the slugs crawled about on this kid's face leaving their horrible slime and the spots melted away – they showed it in slow motion, this spot shrivelling up. Looked gross as a matter of fact.'

She examined a glitter-polished fingernail.

'Why can't you just collect the slime and bottle it?'

'Well, the stuff in the slime is only active for like half a split second or something when it oozes out of the slug's arse.' She enjoyed the word oozes, enjoyed my face as she said it.

The thought sent judders through me and we sat in silence again for a long time. As is often the case, *I-couldn't-come-up-with-a-single-contribution-to-the-conversation.*

'Christ almighty,' she cried out. 'What language do they speak in outer-nerdgolia? I must enrol in a class,' and left the room without saying goodbye.

I was dazzled.

And so I ended up on a frozen pond, freezing to death, snow settling all over the car – and I didn't dare move in case I tipped the car right into the pond, because my whole body would freeze and my arms would break off like when the science teacher dipped a blade of grass into dry ice and it snapped as if it were glass.

The car tilted again, there was a groan from the ice, then stillness. 'TO LIVE FOR EVER IS TO DIE EVERY DAY,' Spangles says, but this was getting scarier and scarier.

Then a pair of trembling white dots resolved into the headlights of a four-by-four, and Spangles' mother attached a tow rope and tugged the car off the ice and on to the road.

'All right, kidda, you'll be all right,' she said, as she draped a thick coat over me and handed me a flask. Then she stood for a time and looked out over the pond. 'To be taken by water,' she said and shuddered. 'I sometimes wonder what it would be like. What you'd feel. They say a numbness, then nothing, like being swallowed by giant grey cloud.'

Spangles was in the car and when my eyes met hers she made a wanker movement with her hand.

Later that week I was stood outside geography with Brissy and Dink, doing the same usual nothing, when Spangles herself wandered over.

'Hey you,' she said. 'Is your dad some sort of stunt driver?'

'Yeh. For Camberwick Green,' Brissy chipped in.

I hadn't noticed Spangles around school before the *night-of-the-frozen-pond*, but since then I'd thought about little else. She was *the-sexiest-girl-in-the-school*, with a sort of thread-bare glamour, like a circus performer. While other girls cooed over Donny and David, she obsessed about a weird American band called the New York Dolls, who looked like a bunch of cross-dressing bricklayers. Spangles had *immersed-herself-in-the-new-punk-gimmick* and dressed accordingly.

Unbelievable luck that Dad took me to her house to treat some imaginary sick pigs and then drove us on to a frozen pond. She would never forget me now: I'd been cool in the jaws of peril, and she had witnessed it.

· I laughed. 'My dad's an idiot.'

'You're telling me,' she said. 'How's the little guinea pigs? I hated them. The twitchy cute noses, the pissy smell. Utterly vile creatures. I was glad when they got ill. And they were always shagging – one of them would get on the other one's back and move like this. Euggh.'

'They're dead,' I lied. 'I put them in the pressure cooker. To see what would happen.'

Brissy and Dink sniggered.

'Guts everywhere. My mother was a bit upset cos she was due to cook in it later.'

Spangles didn't smile. She looked at me for a long time. Then she pulled out a folded piece of A4 paper. 'I've been watching you,' she said, 'and I wanted you to read this and let me know what you think. It's all, like, what I've been thinking lately. It's about stuff and that. Life. It's like about the volume of blood in your brain, that kind of thing. All über-organic. I've got it written down in my head. You seem, like, deep, like a profound sort of person who has, maybe, a rich interior life. I connect with that. I connect with that powerfully. It's like, PLAY NEAR POWER LINES people, you know what I'm saying?'

And she stalked off up the corridor.

Brissy and Dink were making hissing noises trying to suppress their laughter.

'*Rich interior life*,' Brissy repeated.

'*Über-organic*,' said Dink.

'PLAY NEAR POWER LINES,' Brissy drawled.

'I tell you what though,' Dink said. 'You are in there with that weird laal lass. She's a reet nutter, but, well, she's got tits and an arse. Why not?'

We fell silent for a time. We were busy thinking about the way she had imitated the guinea pigs shagging, thrusting her hips in and out.

'Anyway. Sex,' Brissy said finally. 'What is it for? To facilitate the accumulation of advantageous mutations.'

'Good line,' Dink said. 'Does it work?'

'No,' he said sadly. 'Nothing works.'

5

A round waitress with a fierce expression brought the starters. Charlotte speared a mushroom and dabbed it in the sauce. Eric took a bite from his garlic bread.

'I'm worried about this caravan thing,' he said, loading his fork with a deep-fried mushroom and dipping it into the bowl of tartare sauce. Charlotte filled their glasses with the watery red wine Donatello served in ceramic jugs and sat back in her chair.

'I'm thinking: Greg,' Eric said.

'Gregory? Are you? What's Gregory got to do with caravans?'

'I don't know. It's not caravans, it's just – the idea of that mad cider-punk rearing his head again is disturbing.'

Eric met Charlotte when her husband, Greg Torkington, was lead singer of punk noisniks, Hoovercock, and Eric was roadying for Hoovercock's support band, Tubular Bondage. Eric had been on stage duty at Whitehaven Civic Hall during Hoovercock's set, leaning on the speaker stack, coolly eyeing the seething mosh pit, watching out for fights, potential stage divers or crowd surfing, the usual herd madness, making sure he himself represented an impossible-to-impress roadie displaying no enjoyment in the music. It came to Hoovercock's 'big' hit, 'Death to the Dead' (76 in the indie charts) and as usual at this point Greg ripped his shirt off and slashed his chest with the scrunt of a broken light bulb and the audience went mental. Bare-chested Greg, streaked in blood, flailed about, haranguing the audience and band, madly spitting and screaming. It was then that Eric noticed one face in the audience looking utterly bored by the whole thing and he immediately liked her. If he'd known this sexy plastic-bin-linered, pink-national-health-spec-wearing, Poly Styrene lookalike was married to Greg he'd have ignored her – everyone knew Gregory Torkington was dangerously un-hinged and lacked the normal human aversion to physical violence. But when Charlotte caught Eric staring she stared back and bobbed out her tongue and they both laughed, and after the gig she grabbed him and pulled him into the back of Hoovercock's Commer van.

Eric realized that something was wrong when the van sped off back down the road to Hoovercock's base in Barrow-in-Furness and she made him hide under a pile of coats before chucking him out at traffic lights in Millom. It was a long walk home.

The waitress picked up the starter plates, hovering a little as if about to say something.

'When Greg found out about our affair, he –'

'Eric, don't call it an affair.'

'Well, isn't that what we had?'

'People don't say *affair* any more, West Cumbria.' There she was, calling him West Cumbria again. 'The word affair supposes a medieval fear of institutions, like you have to creep round the back of them and whisper in dark corners. You know that I think living together is just as important as being married.'

'But you were married to Greg.'

'Well . . .' She waved a hand as if chasing a fly. 'It's the word *affair*.'

'I just had that phone call – remember?'

'Yes, I remember. And it was stupid, meaningless. It

42

can't have anything to do with the caravan picture. It was years ago.'

Eric put down his glass and leaned over towards Charlotte to whisper: 'Do you remember what he said?' Charlotte gave him a patient half-smile with her head on one side. She had heard this before. 'He said, "I'm gonna rip your fucking liver out and eat it."'

'Yes, I remember. Well that's just the sort of thing people say when they are angry.'

'It's not the sort of thing I would say.'

Charlotte looked at him for a long time then said, 'Well, maybe you'd be a better person if you did say that to someone who had hurt you.'

'Maybe I wouldn't say it. Maybe I would do it.'

'Greg is fine now. It's his new wife you'd want to worry about. I've seen Sandra Melon carrying a sheep under each arm.'

The waitress plonked Eric's pasta in front of him. 'You're one of the Cleator Moor McFarlanes, aren't you?'

Charlotte emitted a long sigh. In West Cumbria everybody knew you.

'Yes,' Eric said.

'You do the debt stuff. At the St Cuthbert's Centre.'

'Aye.'

'You'll know about my mate. She's one of yours.'

'Oh,' Eric said, 'I can't talk about my clients.'

'No, it's all right, she tells me everything. Debt: the family's riddled with it. She's out of her mind with that Shopaloan bloke. You know them, off the high street?'

Eric knew Shopaloan well. The man who had sent Doreen to him, who'd been bleeding Doreen and the rest of the estate dry. Eric would happily hook him up like a veal calf, slit a smile in his throat and drink from the gush.

'Remember the incident? She must have told you. He gave her a real hard time. She called the police. I don't know exactly what happened but all the neighbours were talking about it. She's been post-viral ever since.'

Eric had forgotten the client and remembered only vaguely that there had been an incident. He knew, however, that Shopaloan was in trouble and he was helping get him there.

'I just hope she hasn't paid him.'

Charlotte made wide eyes at him.

'Anyway,' Eric said, 'I can't talk about cases in public, like I said.' The waitress nodded. She thought that Eric must have got half of Cleator Moor's debts written off by now. Eric said he didn't know about that. The waitress could tell them a few more stories about Mr Friday and Shopaloan, but they declined her offer and she left them to their food.

Charlotte watched the waitress's retreating back. 'You must make those companies so angry.'

'Must I?'

'How would you feel if your entire business was pole-axed by yappy upstarts in a derelict church?'

They ate silently for a time. Eric picked bitterly at the baked-hard edges of his cannelloni.

Then Charlotte said, 'We are going to have to do something about the living room, West Cumbria.' She was twisting a long lock of hair around her fingers at the back of her head as she spoke.

'The living room? What do you mean?'

'It's the furniture. It looks plonked. We need to spend some money on it.'

Eric knew that he would agree to buy new furniture. He always did. It would be the bathroom all over again. What he thought would be a simple trip to B&Q had turned into a freelance designer building them what he called a *wet-room* (this meant that the shower was open to the room and that water splashed everywhere). There was a low prison-style toilet and a big curving glass screen in the middle. A twist of blue neon shone over the door. The whole thing was done in rough crimson tiles and it was like walking around in a quarry. It had cost £20,000 and was one of the credit agreements secured to the house Eric was worried about repaying. But he loved the house, he really did. The way the light hit the walls, the way the fireplaces were crooked, the way the ceiling bulged. The varnished floorboards, their knotty eyes gazing up at the rag-printed ceiling. He remembered Charlotte up a ladder, rag-rolling pale orange paint over the ceiling, her face speckled with orange lost-orphan freckles, and later, her breasts rolling out of Eric's old shirt as they made love on the floor, she underneath, admiring the tricky cornicing work which had required a fine brush (and which Charlotte had taken charge of) as he moved on her, enjoying her paint-smeared bare skin beneath the harsh decorating lights.

32, The Loop Road, Whitehaven.

Their common love of the house was the connective tissue that kept the relationship together. They were in love with it. It was everything for them, like an only child for an introverted couple. They would hold lengthy conversations about the house because it was easier to talk about the house than talk about themselves. And if ever they became bored and their lives felt becalmed ('We're living in cement,' Charlotte would say), it was easier to change the house than it was to change each other. They could move furniture, make their surroundings look different from week to week, and they would never need to go to the trouble of altering their lives.

'We can go and look at some stuff tomorrow,' he said.

She nodded. 'You know, Eric, my mother used to have her furniture sent over from America. And this was in the days when no one did that sort of thing. It was all high-tech for the time, Bauhaus-type designs. Her and Dad, they lived in like a space-age bachelor pad. Waking up in our house was like waking up in *Play for Today*.'

As Charlotte drove back, Eric watched the spangled lights of Whitehaven disappear when they climbed the hill to their home, and he thought of Greg, blood streaming down his light-bulb lacerated bare chest at the Hoover-cock gig, Greg his enemy, Greg 'I'm gonna rip your fucking liver out and eat it' Torkington.

6

Her breasts. Marjorie, the new worker, had brushed his bicep with her right breast when leaving the advice shop last night. He took that as a sign. Women use their breasts like antennae, sending out messages, picking up vibrations.

So he had to be at work early. It was Marjorie's first interview with a real client and he wanted to be the one to help her out.

The car was smothered in ice so as soon as the engine coughed into life he twisted the heater knob to windscreen and waited. Cars tooled by with tiny scraped slits in the windscreen ice, their owners peering out like tank drivers, predatory animals. Eric drove like a creature preyed upon and always scraped his entire windscreen clear.

He picked a cassette case from the passenger-side floor and began to hack off the ice with the edge. He imagined he was making an ice sculpture of Marjorie, like in *Edward Scissorhands* when Johnny Depp flash-razors an iceblock into a thoughtful, intelligent angel, and he could picture Marjorie tippy-toe dancing in the tumbling ice shavings as they drifted down like Lux flakes. With the edge of the cassette box he described in the frosted windscreen how he would tweak the ice into the precise curve of her small breasts.

But why wasn't Julie dancing in the streaming flakes?

Who was this impostor? In his mind he pushed Marjorie away and replaced her with Julie, but Julie's dancing was awkward, clumsy, unconvincing. The real Julie was not yet installed correctly in his head. It would come, he assured himself, it would come.

Scraping the ice was useless so he went into the house for a jug of hot water.

He was watching the rod of water barrelling into the jug when he heard movements behind him and turned to see two balding men in brown suits. They had moustaches. They were in their fifties and their stomachs and eyes bulged at him aggressively.

'Mr McFarlane?'

Eric returned his attention to the jug and waited as it filled. He twirled off the tap and turned towards them, the jug of boiling water in his hand. 'Excuse me, gentlemen.' The men stood aside and he passed between them and outside to the car. The men followed him. He drizzled the steamy water over the front windscreen and watched as it froze into a flowery pattern.

'You can crack your windscreen that way,' one of the men pointed out, throwing his colleague a vulpine smile. 'Saw it happen to a friend.'

Eric turned to them.

The first man said, 'Is that your computer inside?' The other one added, 'And your pottery collection? Looks worth something, that. Even to my untrained eye.'

'Not mine,' Eric said. 'Nothing to do with me.'

'All goods of the debtor –' the man said.

'And those of a spouse are taken to be jointly owned,' the other one chirped.

'Would you say –'

'Mr McFarlane –'

'That the computer and the pottery were items –'

'Absolutely essential for normal domestic life?'

Eric could see that the men had been reading the items off a list. He knew it was too late.

'And how did you effect your entry, gentlemen?' Eric said.

'We did not have to force entry. The door was open so we walked in.'

'Once we've crossed the threshold –'

'As you well know –'

'We can break in on the next visit.'

'Like Dracula.'

'If you know your vampire lore.'

He wiggled his fingers at Eric, pushed his mouth out, making an ugly spout in the middle of his face, and did ghosty noises. 'Woowoooowooo. Are you frightened?'

Eric ignored him and got back into his car.

The bailiff crouched and shoved a thin crinkly sheet of paper through Eric's open window. 'You may continue to have use of the goods, Mr McFarlane. But if payment isn't received in fourteen days a van will arrive to remove the goods for sale at auction.'

And the bailiffs waddled off towards their car.

Fuck, fuck, fuck, fuck. The Mac and the pottery!

He noticed something underneath him on the seat and pulled out a piece of crumpled card. Another photo of a caravan, this time a tiny one, ancient looking, standing on a concrete drive in front of what looked like a council house.

He looked all around him. The neighbour opposite was scouring the icy crust off her car with a frying-pan spatula, a determined expression on her face. Otherwise the street was empty. What was he expecting to see? A trail, footprints, something. He didn't know. He flipped over the photo. On the reverse was pasted another word.

calculated

7

On his way to the advice shop he passed the various offices of creditors he spent his life upsetting: Nat-West, Royal Bank, Barclays. On Cleator Moor High Street he noticed that the offices of Shopaloan were closed. Good. That bastard flogging overpriced duvets and sheets to dole-ites, on loans with APRs of three hundred plus. Another loan company out of business was a good thing as far as Eric was concerned. It made him happy. So happy he put his favourite Fall tape on, and foghorned along to 'City Hobgoblins'. At a roundabout he watched the coagulating stream of cars. As he edged out, making it known he wanted to join the stream, an old teardrop-shaped car stopped. Something out of the 1960s by the looks of it. A dark red colour – russet. Its driver, a young man in a sharp haircut, waved him out. Eric pulled into the mainstream and waved a thank you and the driver smiled sarcastically and shook his head from side to side. Inside Eric cursed him. Letting him in was such arrogance; as if he controlled the road and decided when people could and couldn't go. And the car was so cool, so desirable.

Eric pulled in to a space outside the St Cuthbert's Centre and listened to the tick tick tick of the cooling engine for a few moments while looking at the sagging, clumsily painted banner that hung over the entrance to the old church –

CLEATOR MOOR MONEY ADVICE SHOP – SORT IT HERE.
He wondered if he was wasting his life. The old sandstone
church with its stained-glass windows, now protected by
heavy metal grilles, was once the hub of the community. In
many ways it still was, but for different reasons. Possibly,
Eric thought, he was a new kind of priest. He watched the
lights go on in the office, noticed a queue beginning to
form at the side door. The other priests would be waiting
for him. The money advice shop was staffed by three full-
time salaried advisers funded by a combination of lottery
good causes money, grants from Cumbria County and
Copeland District councils, and even a charitable contribution from Sellafield nuclear plant. In the 1980s, when it
was established, a time of soaring unemployment and a
blistering class war fought in the pit towns of Yorkshire and
at the printing presses of Wapping, the advice worker's job
was to make sure the growing ranks of unemployed received the welfare benefits to which they were entitled – and
some to which they weren't. The benefit system was at that
time full of fascinating wormholes through which you could
wriggle and winkle out an extra few quid for your client's
family. There were dietary additions, laundry additions,
single payments for one-off items, all kinds of tailor-made
social security benefits. But these benefit perks were rapidly
culled when Thatcher realized the system was leaking more
money than a public–private partnership. So when the unemployment figures became embarrassing, she decided to
hide them under some nicer-looking numbers, and into the
sick and disabled bin they went; after all, no one could say
it was the government's fault that so many people got sick.
Job centres encouraged it. Not feeling too clever? Maybe
we should sign you off, shove you on to invalidity. More
money for you, less hassle for us. And the welfare advice services grew along with the size of the textbooks explaining
the ever more complicated laws as layer upon layer of new

rules were laid on top of the old ones, creating a contraption as pointlessly complex and dazzlingly incomprehensible as Harrison's first working sea clock. And the work of this new industry? Helping people claim more state benefits, arguing the toss about whether a person was too sick to work and getting people's debts written off. Eric was on the debt side.

He went in. Water pattered into a bucket in the middle of the waiting room. Another roof leak. Eric peered into the bucket. Half full. He looked up at the church ceiling. Pinholes of light shone down like stars. The waiting area was in what used to be the apse of the old church. A segmented arch divided it from the main body of the building where the office and interview rooms were. Within the apse a straight-sided pediment supported by fluted Ionic pillars formed a centrepiece, around which they had arranged display boards for their posters:

CLAIM IT NOW!

KNOW YOUR RIGHTS!

SICK OR DISABLED?
YOU MIGHT BE ENTITLED TO MORE MONEY!

HARASSED BY YOUR CREDITORS?
DEBTS WRITTEN OFF – APPLY NOW!

Always the exclamation marks and the merry tone adopted to sell the public what was already theirs.

He riffled through his messages, the daily data of panic fed to him intravenously by his clients. The North West Money Advice Group about the BBC helpline he was working on in Manchester in a couple of weeks; Doreen: ring her urgently (it wouldn't be urgent, it would be a pointless letter from one of her creditors or a pleading phone call from her bank); and a couple of his regular debt-soaked chancers.

There was a message to return a call to a potential new client, and when he did, the voice on the other end of the phone was a surprise.

'Mr McFarlane? It's Mr Friday from Shopaloan. I don't know if you remember me. We spoke in connection with an, er, mutual acquaintance shall we say, a mutual customer so to speak. You remember, it was a lady with debts, a couple of which were debts to my company, Shopaloan. In fact you have advised a few of my customers, I seem to remember. Well, it's me who needs advice now.'

There was a long silence. Eric couldn't think of anything to say. A creditor had never rung him for advice before and this concept caused so many issues to fire off in his head it rendered him speechless.

'It's rather embarrassing, actually,' Mr Friday continued, 'what I'm calling for. It's about debts, but in a rather different way.'

'What way's that then, Mr Friday?'

'Now that Shopaloan is no longer trading I find myself on harder times and unfortunately not always able to make good my contracts with various other finance companies.'

Eric smiled, stifled a laugh.

'Do you need advice on your own debt problems, Mr Friday?'

'Yes. Well, you were so effective when we were on opposite sides so to speak . . .'

'Of course, Mr Friday. I can see you in a couple of weeks.'

'What? No sooner?'

Eric did have a˙few appointments free before then but he thought it would do Mr Friday good to wait a little while.

'That's fucking beautiful,' he said to the room after he'd put down the phone. 'Now the debt companies want advice on their debts.' Eric pictured the grim little debt collector, his worm of a moustache, his screw of curly hair, and he looked forward to finding out how Mr Friday felt to be on the other side. He wished he could recall the incident the fat fierce waitress from Donatello's had begun to relate; maybe there was something on the computer about it. He opened his client database and searched through the hundreds of phantom lives in binary code, but there was nothing about the Shopaloan incident. He did find a total of every account Eric had forced Shopaloan to write off over the years and it was a surprisingly large amount.

A crumple of gravel outside made him look up. Through the clear lower half of the Our Lord, Mary and Martha window he watched a car nose into the advice shop car park. The vehicle was unmistakable. The russet teardrop, the sarcastic headshaker. Not your average voluntary sector type of car – a 2 CV or a VW Polo – this was a trendy, arty, city type of car. The writing on the front said Saab. It was the sort of old car that had a distinctive face, its features held in a perpetual Gary Glitter shock expression, the mouth a small arched grille under cunning beady headlamps.

A tall man with a crumpled linen jacket and shiny tie climbed out. He reached into the passenger seat and pulled out a black courier bag with Mo'Wax written on the side. Most visitors to the advice shop carried tatty rucksacks – this man was a city person.

Bennett Lowe said, with the courtesy that goes with immense self-confidence, that he'd have a black coffee and drifted into one of the interview rooms which had been constructed out of an old side-aisle. They followed him in and arranged themselves around him in a circle.

'For those who've never met me,' he began, after his eyes had done a languid tour of all their faces, 'I'm the development officer from Cumbria County Council Funding. Names in bureaucracies, however, always mean the opposite of what they say. When, in South Africa, the government introduced a law to prevent black people from going to college they called it the Expansion of Education Act. So when they told me I was to develop advice services in Cumbria I knew that it meant I was to wield the axe.'

At this point the door opened and Marjorie entered the room. Bennett Lowe looked up, flapped a hand towards a chair and continued, eyeing Marjorie as she slowly took her seat.

'So I'm here to find out what you do. This is what I want. I want to know why you exist. I want to know what you are for. I know there are poor people in Cleator Moor. I want to know what difference you make to their lives, how much difference and how many lives you touch. We pay you eighty thousand pounds a year to give advice to Cleator Moor residents. But that doesn't mean we'll pay you to spend all day supporting some old biddy with her bills.' He looked to the side for a beat, as if considering something, then continued, 'You land your grant and it's ice-cream Mars all round; but then what? I'll be honest.' He gave an expansive shrug, palms up. 'I don't like hippies. All these advice centres were set up in the eighties when advice, law centres, *rights* –' he made a peace sign as he said this and adopted a low drawly hippie voice '– were a big thing. I'm not interested in that at all. So, I'm on your back. I'm breathing down your neck. I spend money I get from the council tax payers. Council tax payers from round here. People who can't afford to pay the council tax. And I don't like to think that they might give you their money so that you can sit about being righteous.'

Bennett had long sideboards cut to sharp points and angled towards the front of his face so that they looked like pincers holding his lips, a mouth held perpetually in quotation marks. His speech was made with the ghost of a smirk on his face; he used words as bullets and he enjoyed watching them penetrate the liberal lefty advice workers' soft unprotected flesh.

Pedro's leather jacket creaked and they all looked at him. Eric hoped he wouldn't conform to type and say something counselly about *framing* or *supporting*.

'Mr Lowe,' he croaked. 'Round here, in Cleator Moor, they live on benefit. They have debts, they deal with loan sharks. That's their reality. We give them something. We help. We rake in money from the benefit system. We show them how to use the law to *their* advantage. We empower people to deal with their own problems.'

At the word *empower* Bennett Lowe took a swig from his unmilked Nescafé. He was the sort of person who would drink black coffee even if he didn't like it.

Pedro was walking him through the advice worker's stations of the cross: empowerment, empathy, non-judgementalism, equal access. Yet Bennett Lowe showed no expression while Pedro talked. He registered no emotion, didn't nod, didn't shake, in fact there was no sign he had heard any utterance at all. With his silence he controlled them utterly.

Eric looked at the other advice workers: Pedro, his long hair gathered up in a ponytail, in the biker jacket he never removed; Bernard in lumpy off-road sandals and baggy-kneed trousers that crawled out from under a misshapen woolly jumper; and the new girl, Marjorie. Most noticeable about Marjorie was her stillness. Not even the dark fuzzy trainers at the end of her crossed legs stirred, and her hands rested motionless, overlapped on her sheer black stockings like shadow-play bird's wings.

Bennett continued: 'Take the Riley case.' The advice workers looked at each other. Last winter old Mr Riley's boiler had packed in and the council lost the work card. His body had been found rotted in his armchair – TV remote still in his hand, the *Whitehaven News* said – and the advice shop got the family £5,000 in compensation.

'Does it help other council tax payers for Cumbria County Council to lose five grand? Whatever happened to –' he spread his hands and widened his eyes '– simple misfortune? Is there no such thing as bad luck any more? Somebody is always responsible, somebody always has to pay.' Bennett shot them an alligator smile, showing odd overlapping teeth that somehow made him less of a threat.

'Mr Lowe,' Bernard said, after jabbing a couple of quick coughs towards him, 'the Riley family would have hired a solicitor if it wasn't for us and half of the compensation would have been creamed off.'

People like Bennett Lowe were rare in Cleator Moor. Cleator Moor was a small town of mostly Catholics, exported from Ireland in unloved shoals to work in the iron-ore mines of the 1930s and 1940s. Short red-faced middle-aged men in ties, V-necked jumpers, sports jackets and trilby hats. The bookies, the Knights of St Columba social club, Mass on a Sunday. Bennett Lowe seemed separate from all that West Cumbrian stuff. You got the feeling that he spent a lot of time in cities, cities at night. The question in the front of Eric's mind was: why does someone like Bennett Lowe come to West Cumbria to work and live? Sure, the council had a picture of a mountain and a lake on its recruitment adverts, but he didn't seem the type to need the countryside to relax. What did he know about advice work, its dead patches, its natural callousness, and all day long nothing to look at but the sucked and spat-out faces of the poor?

Bennett Lowe asked, by way of ending, if anyone else had anything to say.

'Yes,' Pedro said. 'You asked when we spoke on the phone if we could give you an update on the new social security rules for claiming sick benefits?'

'Oh yes,' Bennett said, and sat back into his chair.

'Well, to do this I need to tell you about our treasurer

here, Bernard. Bernard devotes his life to voluntary work. The Cleator Moor community couldn't manage without him. I can't begin to list all the groups Bernard is part of, all the boards, the trusts, the organizations. And he runs K'Chaa!!, the community samba band which you will have seen at Cleator Moor and Whitehaven events. But Bernard is on the sick. Can't work any more. He suffers from anxiety and mild depression. Also, arthritis and back problems; can't lift, can't carry, can't stand for long periods, can't sit for long periods, can't bend, can't stretch, can't kneel.'

Bernard nodded in agreement. 'Not that I need to kneel. But you never know, I might get religion.'

'And now,' Pedro continued, 'The Department of Stealth and Social Insecurity have waded in. Sure, they said, Bernard can't work at his old job. But there must be other things he can do. Look at that fella in the wheelchair who writes about space. But at the top end of his fifties Bernard isn't suddenly going to land a job as a bestselling author of popular science books. Call centre work, they suggested. But it's computers. He would need retraining. But suddenly everything is going to be all right. A new test is being introduced – the fit-for-work test. It works like this.' Pedro picked up a black top hat he'd been hiding behind his chair and from it produced a carton. 'First you need a litre of milk.' He placed the milk on the table. Then he held the top hat out to senior funding officer Bennett Lowe, as if he were making a prize draw, and asked him to pull out the next item. It was a paperback copy of Burroughs' *Naked Lunch*. 'A book,' Pedro announced and placed it on top of the carton of milk. Next was a woolly hat, which he wafted in Bennett's face. 'Baseball, bowler, top, trilby, any kind will do.' The final item produced from Pedro's hat was a giant cardboard 50 pence piece.

Pedro arranged all the items on the floor. 'This is everything you need to test Bernard's ability to work.' Pedro held each item up in turn. 'Can he bend and pick up a coin? Can he raise his arm to put on a hat? Can he lift a carton of milk or a paperback book?' Silence. Coughs, chair scrapes, titters, mutters. Then he pulled a food blender from his bag. 'Do you know what this is, Mr Lowe? I had to fight for two years – through three appeals and an oral commissioner's hearing – to squeeze twenty-nine pounds ninety-nine from the benefit agency for this blender for my client who has throat cancer. Can't eat normal food, has to be liquified. Well, this is what we think of this new test.' He placed the book, the hat and the cardboard coin into the blender. He ripped open the milk carton and poured it in on top and, leaving the lid off, switched it on. There was a loud nasal whine and a plume of grey milk, puréed paperback and woolly hat rose up and splattered them all, Bennett Lowe included, with a heat-soured retch-inducing fit-for-work soup.

Bennett stood up, brushing milk droplets off his suit. 'Very radical, very amusing,' he said, and suddenly turned to Marjorie, who was wiping milk from her face with a tissue. 'We've met, haven't we? Listen. I'm making a fundraising presentation this afternoon – it would be useful if you could attend.' Then he looked over towards Pedro. 'Thanks for the presentation, by the way. Very creative. I hope that approach will help the council understand the case for continuing investment.' And Bennett Lowe headed off through the old church and into the car park, where he stood for a time looking at the building, his eyes screwed up, and writing things into a notebook.

Pedro said that he had acid for blood.

Bernard pushed his glasses up his face with an extended third finger. 'They pile us high and sell us cheap.'

It was like a scene from *Here Come the Double Deckers*, a kid's programme Eric watched as a pyjamaed child on Saturday mornings. Some kids lived on a bus and had adventures. The bus was always under threat by some stiff bureaucrat who didn't like 'the kids' and didn't want 'the kids' to have any 'fun'. Some bypass, factory or car park was always about to be built on the site where the bus stood and the kids fought against it, always winning out.

Eric surveyed the room. The Double Deckers had energy, creativity, youth and good looks. The group assembled today in the advice shop waiting room had none of these things in any great quantity. If Bennett Lowe was their enemy, they had better knuckle down.

8

Eric was supervising Marjorie's first welfare benefits appeal case, which was an interesting one, because the client was Bernard. As Pedro had so eloquently expressed to Bennett Lowe, through the medium of sour milk, Bernard was suspected by the Benefit Agency to be *fit for work* and in danger of losing his incapacity benefit, so who better to advise him than Marjorie, Cleator Moor Money Advice Shop's brand new welfare rights appeal officer. Bernard Roberts was indeed involved in every committee, every voluntary group and every good cause in West Cumbria. The operatic society, the recyclers who pulled trailers around town behind tricycles, the Ramblers Association, the Citizen's Panel who advised Copeland District Council on policy, West Cumbrians Against Nuclear Power, the MIND Creative Writing Group, the Friends of Whitehaven Museum, the Save Florence Mine Visitor Centre Campaign: he seemed to have time for everyone's problems, but never enough time to sort out his own. His voluntary work took up more time than most people's full-time jobs. His health problems had begun in his job as an accountant for the fish factory – stress, anxiety, mild depression – and there was no doubt that, despite all the extra-curricular activity Bernard engaged in, Bernard was not physically or mentally fit enough to hold down a normal job. But demonstrating this to the Department of Stealth and Social

Insecurity was going to be difficult. Marjorie had a task on her hands.

Bernard's case notes hit the desk with a thump. 'The medical is the week after next,' he said. 'I was hoping you would attend with me, in a supporting role?'

Marjorie allowed a small grimace to show on her face, then quickly removed it.

'Of course,' she said. 'I guess it's OK to represent a member of our own staff, Eric?'

'We are the only advice shop in Cleator Moor,' said Eric, 'so Bernard has no other options.'

Marjorie snapped the photocopied sheets out of the envelope and riffled through the pages. 'Just as I thought; the original IB50 contains a fair bit of contradictory information – that's not your fault, Bernard. It's how the form has been designed. See here –' She angled the booklet so that he could see and indicated an elegant line of handwriting with a tapered milky-coloured nail, which for some reason made Eric think of frozen semen, 'They've given you three points here when you should have had ten and – look here – where it talks about standing for long periods, you've ticked the box that says can stand for three to four hours but then in the extra information box you've put that you have to move about and stretch every ten minutes. They should have picked up on that. And then there is the anxiety, stress, and – arthritis too, wasn't it?'

'Yes,' he said, sadly.

'And all of these different symptoms, though some of them are mild, together make you unfit for any sort of work, Bernard. I take it the DHSS don't know about you running the samba band classes for K'chaa!! and working here as volunteer treasurer and all of your other community work? Those activities don't help to persuade them that you are too sick to work, you know?'

'I'm not doing anything illegal. It's just, I can't do paid

work, I've tried. But look at how much I do for the community. I'm a pillar.'

'Yes, Bernard, I know. We simply need to spend some time preparing our presentation. I'm fairly confident we can make something out of it.'

Marjorie was putting on a good performance, considering she had confided in Eric that she didn't know the name of one social security benefit before last night when she sat up with the *National Welfare Benefits Handbook*. But Bernard looked worried.

'I'm not comfortable,' he said, 'about lying or exaggerating my condition.'

Marjorie stood up. 'It's not a case of lying, Bernard. Sometimes, the forms are inadequately constructed: they don't properly reflect the truth, your truth. So you have to add things, change things around a bit, to allow the truth to come out. Leave it with me, as I said, and we'll do what we can.'

Bernard looked at her for a long time, his mouth prim and censorious.

'It says here that before you scop a body into a lake you should eviscerate it. That way it never comes up.' Magnum is sitting at the computer.

Apartfromtheobvious looks over. 'What's eviscerate?'

'Take out the guts.'

Grey-eyed man pulls at his wires, makes squeaking noises. 'Be like doing a chicken.'

'Put them in a plastic bag and stick them up his arse.' He laughs, an ish-ish-ish sound.

'Listen to the rest. This is exactly what we need to know. This site is gold dust. Right, these are your basic weapons: one, the knife edge of your hands; two, fingers folded at the second joint or knuckle; three, the protruding knuckle of your second finger; four, the heel of your hand; five, your boot; six, your elbows; seven, your knees; and eight, your teeth.'

Apartfromtheobvious looks at his hands, bends them at the knuckles. Makes a chopping motion, slicing at the arm of the sofa, winces. 'What does it say about boots?'

'It says . . . let's see.' She scrolls through the text. 'Kick him in the temple; there's a large artery there. Kick him there and he won't get up.'

'We've already hit him there.'

'You hit him on the *back* of the head.'

'I've hit him on the front as well, plenty of times.'

'The other thing it says about is screaming. You have to scream when you are killing him.'

'Why?'

'Screaming has two purposes,' she reads, 'one, to frighten and confuse your enemy; two, to allow you to take a deep breath which, in turn, will put more oxygen in your blood-stream.'

'That's if you are having a fight. We've got him tied up. We don't need to scream.'

'I think you should scream. Try it now, right in his face.'

Apartfromtheobvious goes up close to the grey-eyed man, puts his face into his, screams 'Aaaaaah!' Man jerks violently, eyelids snap open, shakes all over.

'See. It frightened him. But it wasn't loud enough. You are going to have to work on making it louder. Now. The next thing is balance. If you make him lose his balance you will kill him with your next move. It tells you how to stand.'

'I keep telling you, this is for fighting; we've got him wrapped round the fucking radiator!'

'Listen to it, Party. It's good advice. Anyway, he might escape and then you would have to fight him.'

It annoyed him that she called him Party for short. It was worse than the whole thing, somehow.

'But he can hear this advice as well,' he says. 'So if he does escape he'll be using the same tricks.'

Magnum comes across from the computer and pulls Apartfromtheobvious up straight. 'Feet spread, it says, to about shoulder level.' She kicks his feet apart as if about to do a body search. 'Right foot about a foot ahead of the other.' Pulls his leg forward. 'Both arms bent at the elbows, parallel to each other – what does that mean?'

He shows her.

'Now, stand on the balls of your feet.'

Raises himself slightly.

'Then bend your waist a little.'

Bends low like a boxer, crouching.

Magnum steps back and looks at him. 'Yes, that's better. You've been standing all wrong.'

Apartfromtheobvious sighs, pushes past her. Sits at the computer and scrolls down the text. 'This is what we need,' he says. 'Vulnerable parts of the body. Let's see. Here. The eyes. Use your fingers in a V-shape and attack the eyes in a gouging motion.' He stabs a V-sign at the computer screen. 'And listen. The nose is extremely vulnerable. A strike with the knife edge of the hand along the bridge will cause break-age, sharp pain, temporary blindness and, if the blow is hard enough, death. And a blow with the heel of your hand to the nose in an upward motion will shove the bone up into the brain.'

From the kitchen cassette, Splinter bursts in rudely on the fade-out of 'Mother Earth', and 'Costafine Town' begins for the twentieth time that day.

He reads about how if you cup your hands in a clapping motion over your enemy's ears the vibrations burst the ear-drums and cause bleeding in the brain, about the vulner-ability of the groin area (get it with your knee, hard, and he'll buckle over very fast), about how a direct blow to a large nerve that branches off the spinal cord and comes very close to the skin at the kidneys will cause death. He is sickened by the matter-of-factness of the language, the washing-machine manual instruction. It talked about the soft bodies of people. How to stop soft bodies from being warm, how to stop flesh from pulsing, eyes from glittering, lips from moistening. All makes him very depressed.

He watches Magnum fit together her baked-bean jigsaw, holding the orange flakes of card up to her face before jam-ming them together on the tray.

Grey Eyes is asleep. The faint wrinkles that hinge his jaw writhe as he grinds his teeth.

9

On their way to Bennett Lowe's fund-raising session, a figure dressed as a lemon handed Marjorie a Jif lemon-juice squirter and thrust a 'How to Make Pancakes' leaflet into Eric's hand.

Eric opened the leaflet and stopped still.

'What's up?' Marjorie asked him. 'It'll be Shrove Tuesday next week, that's all.'

He quickly folded the leaflet. 'Nothing, nothing.'

He glanced back at the lemon, its face painted into a gaping lopsided laugh. It waved a white padded glove at him and its yellow foam-rubber body rocked from side to side.

Inside the leaflet was another caravan picture, a big streamlined American model. A word pasted on the back: *harass*.

Eric looked at the lemon again and again it waved its fat white hands at him. Eric tried to drag up some sort of appropriate gesture and came up with a throat-slitting movement with his finger, a movement supposed to convey the meaning *stop*. The lemon man put his hands on his round yellow belly and made shuddering motions of uncontrolled laughter.

Eric and Marjorie marched away from the shopping square. As they passed Gillespie's timber yard the squealing of the circular saw made his heart beat faster; for some reason, he associated the shrieking of the saw with the lemon man. He pictured the man inside the suit with his mouth expanded in Munch-style anguish. Outside Scrugham's fish factory, a huddle of women in white wellingtons and white coats were standing, smoking. Eric wondered whether they should run into the fish factory to hide from the lemon. He had never been in the fish factory before and knew nothing about what went on in there, only that it had curved corners where the floors met the walls, to make it easier to clean. He turned to look back and there was the lemon man, following them, swinging his big hands, his feet incongruous in Green Flash trainers.

Marjorie followed Eric's eyes. 'That lemon person. He's not doing anything, not giving out the leaflets. I think he's following us.'

'No,' Eric said.

'OK. We'll see. Let's take a short cut.'

They took a short cut and they took another short cut. Marjorie seemed to have an entirely different mental model of the town from anybody else's, and the routes she chose were wild, feral, bizarre, involving holes in fences, gaps in hedges and secret paths across bleak patches of litter-strewn wasteland where straggly bushes formed ideal Saturday night body-dumps. She landed them eventually on the White Stuff, a slab of solidified ashes the colour of steam-cleaned bone that hulked behind Bateson Thermometers. The slag had been excreted years ago from the iron-ore smelting plant and the company promised to grass it over but never did. Marjorie stopped in the middle of the White Stuff, made a cap's peak with her hand and squinted out.

'He's still there.'

Eric followed her gaze. There was the lemon man, luminous yellow against the bleached white ash.

Marjorie pulled a face and bit her lower lip. 'I don't like this. I'm going to ask this dickhead what he thinks he is up to.'

'Don't,' Eric said. She looked at him. 'He is probably just a local nutter.' There was indeed a local, a huge six-foot-something bloke, who roamed the fields and lonins on his own, and it was generally understood that he wasn't right in the head.

'Or maybe it's an ex-client,' he added. 'Let's just get to the meeting.'

She shook her head, watching him narrowly.

They took a lonin down past the Blackship, a poisonous brown stream once used for iron-ore waste, which ran along concrete troughs and then crossed between two grassy ridges in wooden boxes on concrete stilts, tight-ropes for daredevil kids. The lemon man followed them, waving every time they stopped to look.

Bennett Lowe arrived at the training session late and from his Mo'Wax bag took out a pile of A4 papers in different colours. He then spent some time setting up a laptop computer and a portable projector.

Eric picked up one of Bennett's handouts and noticed as he held it that his hand was trembling. He couldn't pull his mind off the lemon man. He was certain he would be waiting for him outside. His head ached, a pounding in his frontal lobes, and his heart hammered in his chest. The lemon man had knocked his mind into another place entirely, disturbed him more than he thought. He ran through the possibilities. Greg Torkington?

I'm gonna rip your fucking liver out and eat it.

He tried to concentrate on Bennett's performance. He wanted to find out all about fund-raising. He didn't know why exactly – there was a vague thought that one day he might become a hotshot fund-raiser for a charity. He drifted off, however, as Bennett spoke and Bennett's mouth became a blurry smear, his voice a distant booming.

He thought of the caravan pictures and the lemon man.

Was this the start of something? He tried to imagine someone slipping a photograph through his door, to picture the man's facial expression: would he chuckle without mirth under his breath, a skinny grin distorting his face? Would he say something quietly such as *There, you bastard*, or *That'll show you*? Would he be afraid? Would he twist his head over his shoulder, hungrily scouring the street for witnesses, before trotting edgily up the path? Would he park his car on the next street? Would he arrive on a bus or on foot? Would he wait in the bushes for Eric and Charlotte to leave? Would he pay someone to do the job, a casual whistling kid sauntering up the path, unaware of the dark motive? Are we all capable of persecuting another human being in this way? He tried to imagine a man alone in a dirty room, cackling over a stack of caravan photos. He couldn't.

Bennett was now speaking quietly. He commanded attention without the need to project. His face contorted as he emphasized different aspects of fund-raising. The laptop was projected on to a screen and words spun towards you, headings fluttered into focus, graphs and lines and squares moved up and down, side to side, like scenery sliding away within a proscenium arch. But despite the visual acrobatics the subject matter was difficult to grasp. Bennett's sentences were clotted with terms which nobody understood: drop-dead dates, going upstream for an answer, pigs in pythons, uninstalling, transitioning, brand damage, hitting auks, front-filling, cascading, having a scratchy-peely session, intermittent issues, strawing people up, undocumented behaviour, emotional cross-tabbing, shrink-wrapping – and finally he had stated that what the voluntary sector needed to do was really stuff the crust.

Yet, despite all this, Marjorie seemed interested. Eric's main purpose in attending this meeting had been to spend some time with Marjorie. He looked at her legs, her sheer black stockings incongruous with Converse trainers, and her arms, covered with tiny fluffy hairs that stood erect in the chilly hall, and the little home-cut ballpoint tattoo on her wrist. He had dropped the ball in every interaction so far, but maybe tonight would be different. They might wander out of the meeting and pop into the pub for one, one which could turn to several.

Marjorie caught Eric looking and winked at him. Eric smiled back, a frozen tangle in his stomach. Seeing Marjorie, feeling Julie.

'Grants will be made,' Bennett was explaining, 'under the heading *Improving the quality of life of people and communities in the UK disadvantaged by poverty.* So. Tell me what you want.'

One man wanted £2,000 for a new computer. A woman next to him wanted £1,000 to build an access ramp for the disabled. Another man wanted £5,000 for a development worker. Throughout all of these contributions Bennett shook his head. 'No, no, no. Too small. All too small. Think big. The money is out there. It's all about persuasion, business plans, match funding. If some other agency, some reputable body has already said that it will fund part of your project then other funders will kick in with the rest. What about –' he paused, swivelled his head around the group '– five hundred thousand for a brand new service, a service to do something new for the community, to take the community on to a new level entirely?'

Mumblings of *No chance, What's the point?*

'You know what? You are more likely to succeed with a big idea bid like that than you are with any of the other little bids. That's what we shall concentrate on today – how to raise large amounts of money for big projects. These are the main points to make.' He pointed his remote and a large phrase slid on to the screen:

NO PERSONAL GAIN OR PROFIT

'No personal gain or profit,' Bennett said without looking back at the display. 'No one should be making anything out of the project.' Another point of the remote and words appeared out of dust particles, in a reverse explosion:

NOT POLITICAL

'Don't ask for funding if the main aim of your group is to overthrow the government, or Cumbria County Council for that matter.'

Click. Skyscraper-shaped stretched-out letters shrank to read:

WRITTEN CONSTITUTION,
WITH PURPOSES FOR THE PUBLIC GOOD

Click. There were several different headings.

'Finally,' Bennett said, closing the meeting, 'get some figures from –' he picked an imaginary fruit off an invisible tree '– anywhere you like, and use the numbers to justify your cause, to prove the need for the service.' He held the imaginary fruit in front of him, eyeing it narrowly. 'Everybody loves figures, proof. Find a gap, a need, and you are the scientist who's found a hole in the ozone layer. The money is yours.'

He smiled, thanked his audience and ran his tongue across his overlapping teeth as if in an effort to straighten them.

But Eric hadn't been able concentrate on the last few minutes of Bennett's presentation. Because, in the window just behind Bennett's head, the lemon had been bobbing about, waving in at him, all the way through.

Afterwards, while discussing with the man from the CAB a change in the law relating to bankruptcy, Eric watched Marjorie talking and laughing with Bennett. They were by the tea-making stuff and he watched her stick her finger into the centre of the sugar bowl, wiggle it, remove it dusted white, then slide it into her mouth past the knuckle, almost as far as the base of her finger, before sliding it out slowly, sugarless and damp.

'What do you think of him. Of Bennett?' he asked her as they left.

'I think –' she looked quizzically to the side for a few beats as if sniffing the air for something '– he is riding on the rims. And that's interesting, I don't think many people notice that about Bennett. I think he hides that very well.'

The lemon could be seen approaching over the White Stuff. 'Here comes our fruity friend again,' Marjorie said.

'Yes. You carry on,' Eric told Marjorie. 'I'm going to sort this out.' He stepped behind a bush. He waited. He waited for a long time. Then, loud breathing and the flopping of the trainers. The lemon came into view. Eric jumped out and stood in front of him. Whether it was the costume or the person inside, the figure was tall. Eric's face was level with the lemon's chest. The lemon put its gloves in the air as if to say, *Fair cop*. Eric took a step back. 'What the fuck is your game?'

The lemon shrugged. Eric couldn't see a join where the head came off. It was the kind of costume you crawled into. He wanted to say, *You want a piece of me* or *You picked the wrong guy, mister*, but he couldn't find those sorts of words.

I'm going to rip your fucking liver out and eat it.

Eric wasn't normally violent, but the fact that the man was in a costume gave him courage. He lifted his hand and gripped the man's arm, pulling him close. The suit stank of the accrued stale sweat of a succession of desperate lemon impersonators.

'Don't mess with me. You . . . just don't mess.' Eric tightened his grip. He could hear the man's breathing, rasping and fast, feel his pulse through what must have been his upper arm.

'Say something. Can't you say something?'

The man didn't flinch as Eric gripped him tighter. Then suddenly he let go and pushed him away. The man wobbled, the weight of the costume sent him backwards, and when he hit the ground he began to roll. Eric ran after him. He was rolling towards the Blackship and, though the water was only two foot deep, Eric felt a sudden fear that the man might hit his head and drown. He caught up with the lemon just as it landed with its face in the rust-coloured water.

Eric grabbed its shoulders with two hands. 'Speak to me, you bastard. Are you OK?'

The lemon lifted its fat white paws and made as if to wipe tears from its eyes.

'Just keep away from me,' Eric shouted, and birds rose from a field near by with a soft explosion of beating wings.

Two

IO

Manchester. The time of Oasis. Untucked citrus shirts, Kickers, Adidas Gazelles, every bloke Liam-and-Noeled up to the bushy eyebrows. Eric walked slowly down the road from Piccadilly towards Manchester County Court, where the hearing of his application for an administration order was due. This hearing would sort out a few more of his debts, but it was by no means the final solution. Later was the BBC late-night debt phone-in to share his debt tricks with an anxious debt-ridden nation. But the main feature of this Manchester trip was his second meeting with Julie: an encounter he hoped would be an improvement on the first, two weeks earlier. This time he needed to see her eyelashes dip when she said his name, feel the walls of his throat fill up with blood, sense the world about him swirl into a blur. He needed to hear again the soft drone, the low deep-stretched hum that had continually caressed them all those years ago, that he hadn't realized was there till someone switched it off.

Liquid office blocks shimmered in the glossy black sides of taxis. He craned his head to look at the tall buildings. Sliding his eyes down their length, he noticed each block was garlanded at its base with knots of office workers standing in shirtsleeves, smoking. Sentries. You wondered what they did.

He was asked several times for money by uglylovely street types. He wished that there were more people like this in Cumbria. He loved what he thought of as the dark dangerous side of the city: the dirty canals, the noisy traffic, the litter, the desolation, the panic. He adored everything about Manchester: the gasometers of North Manchester, the dual carriageways of East Manchester, the flatlands of South Manchester, where students, ex-students, wannabe students and half-been students lived. A few blocks brought him to the lower end of Oldham Street, where he passed through a tissue-thin wall between the hobgoblin poor, the humans in larval state, to St Anne's Square and Deansgate, where crisp-suited business and legal types swept him along to the legal district.

The district judge was sympathetic. This poor young man, now out of work, could not possibly afford to repay all his credit (£4,999 to be precise: exactly one pound under the county court limit for administration orders). The young man had clearly taken on the credit cards and store cards in the belief he would be able to repay them in full. Indeed, it was now so easy to obtain credit that the district judge would go so far as to say that the credit companies were partly responsible for Eric's plight. He ordered that Eric repay a total of £5 each month towards the entire £5,000 debt. However, he said, that's not the end of it; at that rate, it would take sixty-eight years to repay the total debt. *Sixty-eight years.* The district judge smiled at the words.

'Do you think that's a long time?' he asked the sole creditor who had bothered to turn up. The creditor did think it was a long time, too long, and couldn't Eric be forced to pay more? After all, Eric had enjoyed the money.

The district judge nodded and smiled. 'Well, I'll tell you what I am going to do.' He paused at that point, staring first at Eric and then at the creditor. 'I am going to make a part payment order – known as a composition. This means, Mr McFarlane, that you pay five pounds per month for three years only, that's thirty-six repayments, a total of one hundred and eighty pounds. The rest of the total debt – four thousand eight hundred and nineteen – is to be written off.' He threw a challenging look at the creditor, then told Eric, 'Should your circumstances change, Mr McFarlane, then I would expect to hear from you. It is always possible to arrange a higher repayment schedule should you fall on better times. And I do hope you find employment over the next three years. This is not a bankruptcy order, I might add, and the restrictions which apply to bankrupts do not apply to you. I would hope, however, that you do not take out any further credit as I don't expect to see you here again with debts you are unable to service. I wish you luck in the future. Good morning.'

That was it. And what was wrong with sorting out his debts in this way? It was a service Eric provided to his clients in Cumbria all the time. He was simply using his professional skills to alleviate his own poverty. There was nothing illegal about it. In fact, he had seven administration orders, at towns all over the country. He had borrowed nearly five grand on each order. The great inconvenience to Eric was sending off the monthly cheques. He had to keep up the payments so the courts and creditors didn't become suspicious, but the payments, combined with dozens of others, were becoming difficult to afford. Especially now, with Anubis on his back. He would have to come up with something creative to avoid paying those tight bastards.

After the court hearing he headed back into the centre. He visited Kendals, where he bought three Comme des Garçons shirts, each at between £90 and £150, then to Paul Smith, where he bought a jacket, then to Ted Baker for more shirts. Eric was on his Birmingham and Leicester Access card. Nearly maxed out, but he had a box-fresh card in his wallet too – newly received from an old student address in Newcastle, a Visa card with a £3,000 limit.

Laden down with shirts, he flopped into Mulligans and sank two pints of Guinness before he decided to go and see Julie. First, he put on a black shirt (expensive, some Belgian designer) and some Japanese-sounding trousers from Kendals. He flogged the rest of the stuff at an exchange shop for two hundred quid.

The Temple of Convenience had been constructed from an underground public toilet and in a dark corner where the cubicles used to be Eric could make out Julie, waiting for him. There was a hint of black in everything about the new Julie; hair the blackness of oblivion framing skin of nettle-sting-white, her cola mop sending out drops of darkness through the rest of her, putting the barely discernible wisp of a moustache above her upper lip, fine soft down on her arms and pretty flicks of near sideburns in front of her ears. And she only ever seemed to wear black, too. Tonight it was black nail varnish, long black skirt, black tights, long black boots, black one-armed gauzy shirt. Black six-buttoned gloves were draped over the back of the chair.

She stood up and smiled. Something inside Eric moved, something aching to live, beckoning.

'So, down here from Shane's Teeth yet again?'

Shane's Teeth was her name for Cleator Moor, the fag-end town of the Lake District; Shane MacGowan's teeth in Donny Osmond's face.

Her eyes were moist. Eric was quivering all over.

'An angel to minister truth to the uninformed.'

'Another crappy phoneline to satisfy the BBC's social conscience?'

He looked at her and she looked at him, and they laughed like children who'd got away with something. She looked and acted as she had all those years ago: sulky, belligerent, intense, with a larky smile that could erupt from nowhere.

But Eric was listening for the drone, and it still wasn't there. He was about to suggest they go back to her flat when a pair of sweaty hands slapped against his face, turning his world as completely black as Julie's attire.

'Down from gligmee-glogmee land to see big old me. Guess who, Eric.'

Eric didn't know.

'You ought to fucking know, my little Damon-out-of-Blur boy. I am the genie from the cunting lamp! You rubbed me out the bottle.'

The greasy hands slipped from Eric's face to his shoulders and Eric turned to find the overspill mayor standing behind him.

He looked at Eric for a long time, his eyes half-lidded, as if he were about to drop off. Then he said, 'I hear you've been a busy little fucker, Damon-boy, paying off all your wee loans – bosh, bosh, bosh. Not forgotten little me, have you? Two of our earth weeks, you said.'

Eric told him he didn't have the money.

'Well,' the overspill mayor said, sitting down next to Eric and casting an eye at Julie. 'If he can't pay, he can't pay, can he? You can't squeeze shit out of a bastard. But here's what. It's gonna cost me making this trip. My facility fee for a personal collect call is forty-nine ninety-five. That's what it is. Yeh. That's what my people say, the money people, the ones that work it out.'

Eric said, 'I don't know, it seems steep. You've come in from the overspill. Well, what would that cost to and from in a taxi?'

The overspill mayor smiled at Julie then at Eric, as one would at children struggling to solve a problem to which the answer was clearly evident.

'The question is, my little fucker indie-cunt friend, have you got the collection fee or have you not? Had you not got it, well, I don't know. No one's ever not had it before, actually.' He paused to look down at his Adidas top and flicked a piece of something off it. 'I don't really know what I would do. It's not written down anywhere, like in a policy or something. If we was to go for one of those charter marks, investors in people things, they'd probably criticize us for that. And I think they would be right. They would say, *Your policies and standards should be clear to all your users.* In fact they would say that this was a *complaint*, I suppose, and they would say, *How would you deal with a complaint from one of your users?*'

He picked up the heavy ashtray, turned it in his hands like a steering wheel. 'I'll be honest with you. The fee. To tell you the truth the amount is a sham. It's not a true figure. Forty-nine ninety-five. You see, I haven't got any five ps on me. I'm not a fucking cash register. The fee should be a flat fifty but the people, they say knock off five p and it will sound less. Does that work with you, Damon? The old something and ninety-five p trick? No? Me neither. But listen – I could talk marketing techniques all day with you guys.'

Eric didn't want to pay – he hated bank charges and could normally bluff his way out of them – the mayor was just an unusual kind of bank. But Julie got up. 'Stay there. I'm going to the cashpoint.'

When she was gone the overspill mayor settled back into his chair and said, 'You ever been to Cherries? That new lap-dancing club? Some lovely girls.'

'Not exactly my scene,' Eric said.

'Home fucking is killing prostitution, that's my motto. You know what I was thinking? Let me try this idea out on you. I reckon there's a niche market that nobody's opened up. People have certain tastes in women and I think they would pay to see their special type of women dance.'

'What?' Eric said. 'You mean, like, blonde lap-dancing clubs, brunette lap dancing?'

'Well, I was thinking a bit more specialist. Like, say, fat women. Cos some men like a bit of back on a girl. I think they'd pay to go to a fat lap-dancing club. Or you have a big club with different rooms like a fat room and an older birds' room, you know – dancers over forty – and maybe a room with Asian girls. Disabled women too. Some fellas like women with only one leg. Did you know that? Har har har. One-legged lap dancers. How fucking sick is that? Hur hur hur.' A perky V-shaped smile dimpled his baby-smooth cheeks. 'That Julie. She your girl? She could be a specialism all of her own, I'd say. No offence, like.'

Julie returned and from the plastic coin bag which served her as a purse she counted out £49.95p exactly, to the penny, handing it to the mayor, her eyes on Eric all the time.

When the overspill mayor had gone, she said, 'Don't mess with his head like that, Eric. I owe him a bit of back rent too. He's serious. Next time you are down here you're going to have to pay him in full – I don't care if you rob the money out of some kid's piggy bank – get it and give it to him. He's dangerous.'

They talked for a time – Eric filling her in on Charlotte, on the advice centre, on everything that had happened since – and soon there wasn't time to go back to hers because Eric had to start work on the BBC helpline.

Julie pressed a key to her flat into his hand. 'I know things seem different now. But what we say isn't important. The truth is pre-linguistic, nothing to do with language. Don't feel you need to speak, to tell. Or touch even.' She lowered her head towards him and whispered, 'It's all about –' and she tapped her brow '– Brainbloodvolume.'

The BBC researcher showed him to a desk in a room full of money advisers. The debt documentary had begun and when the helpline number went on screen the phones would go incandescent.

Eric clipped on his headphones. The first caller was an old man with a thick liquid voice. He had bought a conservatory and the company had said that he'd never have to pay a penny for it because they would show people round and for each one they would credit a payment to his account. It had sounded great.

'But,' the man said, lowering his voice, 'do you know, ever since I had the conservatory put in they have never shown anybody round? And now they are asking me to pay.'

Well, what do you expect, you stupid twat, Eric thought. But he didn't say that. He explained the law of contract and how, despite these promises, it looked as though the man was bound by law to pay back the company.

The man coughed in his thick liquidy way. 'I thought I'd have to pay. But I thought you ought to know what these buggers is doing. They're crucifying us.'

And he was gone. Eric couldn't help feeling furtive, an intruder, as he spoke with callers in their homes late at night. With a woman there was a definite sexual frisson and it was all Eric could do to stop himself from asking what she was wearing. He imagined the callers standing in cold hallways wearing dressing gowns and holding bowls of cornflakes. Their voices were still, bloodless; they seemed from a strange other race, reaching towards the mysteries of debt and money, mysteries with which he was cosily familiar.

The phone rang several more times, a succession of voices that seemed to leap in pain. Should I borrow to pay off credit cards? What happens if I get a court order? How do I get off the blacklist? He pushed out words, pushed out platitudes, pushed out advice, and at the other end they pulled it all in, hungry for it.

There was a break, then the phone rang again. 'Hello, BBC debtline, how can I help?'

A man's warbly voice, deep. 'Hello. You sound very small. That's interesting. Say something else.'

'This is the debtline.'

'I know. It's just you sounded smaller than I expected. Are you small?'

Eric was patient. 'I'm sorry, can't you hear me very well?'

'No I mean small, you sound like a small person.'

Eric paused, about to ask how someone can sound small, and thought better of it. 'What is your money problem?'

'You can't help, you fucking cunt.'

Eric had been warned that you'd get the odd hoax call. He played it calmly and dispassionately.

'Can we help you with a debt problem?'

'Eric, you can't help me with anything.'

The caller knew his name. Eric put his hand on the top of his head and ruffled his hair. His brow felt hot. Sweat was forming.

'Can I help you with debt problems or are you ringing about something else?'

'Eric, you are such a smarmy bastard. You are getting worse and worse.'

Eric was startled by the words. They came at him from nowhere like headlights round a country road. *Worse and worse*. Was he? Worse and worse at what? In what way worse? Suddenly he felt ill.

'Errrriccc.'

The name. He keeps with the name.

'Eric, I'm going to sort things out.'

Eric had had this sort of call before. But that was years ago. Surely not Gregory again? He tried to remember his voice.

'It's a long time ago,' Eric said, trying the voice out, to see if he could get it to commit to something specific.

'What's a long time ago?' There was a pause. 'You cunts never think about what you do, what you cause. You just do it, and keep on doing it, until everything's rotten, everything's dead.' His voice got higher and higher in pitch.

It was raspy now, from warbly to raspy. 'Carry on with the helplines, Eric,' the voice went on. 'You are gonna need help soon yourself and there's no helpline for what I'm going to do to you.'

The line went dead.

Eric's stomach churned with unarticulated emotion and his breath tasted metallic.

In the flat, Julie lit up a big fat joint to calm him down. It would soften the edges, she told him. Then she introduced him to the concept of non-contact sex. The advantage, she explained, is that it isn't cheating on Charlotte. It involved exchanging all items of clothing. He enjoyed the feel of her long black boots, her black gauzy shirt, her six-buttoned gloves.

'Before we evolved into land mammals,' Julie explained, 'there would have been no contact during sex – the egg and sperm would have fertilized in the water. All this internal bit is new.'

He looked at her on the sofa, wearing his black trousers, her size five heels slipping in and out of his size nine Vans, then looked down at his long legs in Julie's black tights, with his hairs peeping out. What had become of the two of them? What happened to the love they'd had when they were fourteen, a desire somehow warped into this?

Julie lit some stuff on silver paper and he smoked that too. It didn't merely soften; it melted every edge and dissolved the very centre of him. He became unaware of how to use his legs or support his body, and sank into a warm oblivion, a blackness, a nothingness, a melting world of fuzzy light and mushy sounds with no edges and no up or down.

REVOLT INTO SAMENESS

I lay on my bed and whispered her name. *Spangles*. Again – *Spangles*. Spangles was one special girl.

I unfolded the sheet of A4 she'd handed to me. One word, in the middle of the page, in tiny pink letters.

distil

I clutched the paper to my heart. Here was *the-girl-I-would-spend-forever-with.*

Distil!

She thought about the world in exactly the same way as I did. Tomorrow I would seek her out and ask her to go with me to the park. Or to the Wimpy in Whitehaven. Or the pictures – *Jaws 2* was on. Or a drink in the Derby Arms. Or I would ask her to come home with me. Or I would take her for a walk. Or . . . no. There was no point even thinking about it. No point at all.

I found a sheet of A4 paper like the piece she had written *distil* on, located a pen and spent the whole evening trying to think of one word to write down for her which would express *the-meaninglessness-and-joy-of-life-all-at-the-same-time.* I decided on purple ink, for the *death-and-suicide-associations*, and listed a few possibilities, even opened a dictionary at random, but nothing came out like *distil*.

When eventually I had decided, I printed my word carefully in the middle of the sheet of paper and folded it in the same way as she had.

The next day I dropped the sheet of paper into her pigeon-hole and waited.

On Friday I was hanging with Brissy and Dink doing the same old nothing – which according to Spangles was über-rebellious – 'REVOLT INTO SAMENESS,' she used to say – and Spangles herself appeared, said, 'Hi, come with me,' took my hand and led me off.

Silently she led me out of the school building. I laughed nervously, kept asking her where she was taking me, but she put her hand over my mouth and raised her finger to her lips.

Eventually we came to the woods that surrounded the school and she took me into a clearing. She rolled her sleeve up and showed me her forearm. There was my word, the word I had written on the piece of paper. Engraved on her skin. Around it her arm was etched with a web of pink and white gouges and encrusted with black scabs. A crimson bead of blood glistened.

'Permanent,' she said. 'I did it last night.'

'So, so . . . you liked my word?'

'It's perfect. It goes in here.' She tapped the side of her head. 'Mainline. Right side of the brain stuff. It's less of a structure and more of an absence? Like you can understand it but at the same time you can't?'

'Yes,' I said. I had no idea what she meant.

'How did you do it?'

'A pin and some ink out of a ballpoint.'

'Your mother seen it?'

She rolled down her sleeve. 'Mum doesn't give a fuck any more. Since Dad went, she – oh fuck, who cares? She's got money problems as well. Loan people come round. Since Dad left us, the Department of Stealth and Social Insecurity haven't manage to winkle anything out of him. So it's all fur knickers and no coat. We pay for everything with stamps – gas, electric, water and the telly. We pay the rates by giving a fella in a camel coat an electrical appliance every few months. I don't know what will happen to us, and I don't really care any more. Everything's so meaningless anyway, we'll all die and then what will this mean? This moment, this –' she waved her hand at the foliage around them '– bush, tree, this fragment of time, it's all just – I mean the world is spinning in space, a ball of rock, and we stand here talking about money and debts and relationships and parents and ink tattoos. I mean, what the fuck, honey!'

She sighed long and deep. She had a beautiful big nose and dark, dark hair.

'What was it Beckett said? Mankind –' she paused '– is a stain on the silence.'

'Have you seen Becko today?' I said. 'Only I thought he was off school with a broken arm.'

'Richard Becket? Him that stole the class gerbil? No, dickhead, Beckett the writer. You crack me up, hon. Come here.'

I leaned towards her and she kissed me long and hard, doing things with her tongue I never knew existed.

When she stopped kissing me I stood there, breathless, dazed. I hadn't kissed a girl properly before. I didn't know if I'd done it correctly. Gorgeous complicated flowers opened up within me. Streams of liquid gushed into a parched landscape. So much rushing, pounding. Like a million bursts of love. When she kissed me again I wondered why I didn't explode.

'What are you doing next week?' she said, panting.

'Nothing. I don't do anything.'

'Feed those guinea pigs?'

'I don't give a fuck about guinea pigs.'

'Crass and the Poison Girls are playing Maryport Civic Hall. You're coming with me.'

'How are we going to get to Maryport and back?' It was nearly twenty miles north up the coast.

'Maybe we won't come back. Maybe we won't go. Maybe we'll just be there without going or coming back. What is space anyway? What is being in one place or another?'

'Yeh, I guess,' I said.

'See you tomorrow,' she said. 'After school I'll take you to the Three Tuns.'

The Three Tuns was a notorious den of sin in Whitehaven, where hippies and off-duty policemen drank.

'OK.'

'Yeh, the Tuns is, like, great. You never been? I can't believe somebody creative like you hasn't been in the Tuns yet. You can get good stuff there.'

'Oh, right,' I said, not understanding what she meant.

'I mean, you've tried stuff before, haven't you?'

'Yeh, course,' I said.

'And I'm going to tell you my other secret plan.'

'Which is?'

'Brainbloodvolume, honey,' she said.

11

It was lunchtime the next day by the time Eric got back from Manchester; he'd already phoned in sick to allow him to spend the day recovering from the excesses of the day before. Charlotte was out and the unopened mail was scrunched up against the phone table by the door.

Eric was bursting for a piss but he picked up the letters and flicked through the wad. In between a Cumbria County Council letter and a missive from Anubis was another photograph. This time of a different kind of caravan. A Dormobile, one where the caravan had an engine and you could drive it about. This one flew a string of flapping shirts, so someone must have been staying in it. On the back of the photo was pasted one word:

demands

What the fuck did that mean?

Eric tore it into four squares. He piled the scraps on top of one another and strained to rip them into smaller pieces but the stack of card was too thick so he flung the shreds of photograph at the wall and was standing motionless when Scooter crept around the corner, dragging his grossly distended stomach over the polished floorboards. He was normally a pimp-roll, kiss-my-sweet-ass kind of cat – and to see him reduced to a Zimmer-frame shuffle was painful. He scooped up the cat and stroked it under its chin. It purred loudly, looked beseechingly at him. Taking the cat with him, Eric went into the front room with the rest of the mail. He was worried about the Anubis letter, a little less worried about the Cumbria County Council one, which had the smell of Bennett Lowe about it. He propped the letters on the fire surround; he wanted to be in the right mood before he read them. He opened two orders for his booklet on how to deal with debts – a four-page photocopy he sold for £25 a go – and a letter addressed to his other company, CreditFix, under the name of which he sold, for £90, a set of court forms and a short explanatory leaflet for distressed debtors.

He felt flattened, depleted. Why had he smoked the stuff on the silver paper? What was he thinking? He sucked a long drink of orange juice straight from the carton and tried to imagine what Julie was doing. He thought of her lips, the spark of pink lipstick incongruously luminous in her pale face. But for some reason her face kept morphing into Marjorie's.

In the bathroom he noticed something funny. His penis felt strange, sort of sore. It was an odd pinchy feeling. It hadn't felt odd when he had been on the train. He moved his fingers towards the tip and met something metallic and hard. He snatched his hand away as if he had been burnt and stared at himself in the £2,000 mirror, the sideways flattened star the architect had embedded into the tiles like an ice puddle. He looked at himself for a long time. His reflection would eventually speak, crack under pressure, tell him what horrible trick his other drugged self had played on him. Then, picking up courage, he lowered his head and lifted his penis to face him. A small gold ring stood there, jaunty, glittering.

Eric screamed and ran down the stairs into the living room. He then ran into the front room, then into the kitchen and then back upstairs again because he remembered he hadn't had his piss. He ran back into the bathroom and stood pointing it at the bowl. His hands trembled and he dared not look down again. When he was out of it. What had she given him to smoke? He knew, but didn't want to think about it. Never again. Julie, fucking Julie. How do I explain this to Charlotte? Oh my god, fuck, fuck, fuck, fuck. Eric couldn't relax to piss for what seemed like minutes and then, when it did come, it spritzed out at funny angles, like from a watering can, and he had to wipe urine off the special rough-hewn floor slabs, the crimson-tiled walls, and all around the stainless steel prison-style toilet bowl. He now remembered it had made a mess on the train but he had put it down to the rocking of the carriage. He didn't know what to do and was afraid to even touch it. So he went downstairs and lay on the sofa and stared up at the rag-rolled ceiling.

It was just past six when he woke to the sound of a key scraping at the door and he jumped up and ran to the hall where he found Charlotte poking the fragments of photograph with her shoe. 'What are all these pieces of card, Eric?' She bent and picked up one of the tiny squares. Eric had intended to hide this latest message from his unknown tormentor. Charlotte knelt on the floor and pieced together the picture. 'It's a caravanette,' she said, sitting back before her completed jigsaw. 'A caravan you drive.'

'I thought they were called Dormobiles.'

'We should tell the police about this. People can't go round putting things through our letter box.'

'What? Like people never put stuff through the door? Counselling for budgies, Dial a Chicken Kiev.'

Charlotte stared at the picture, her little finger between her teeth. She turned over each quarter of the image and arranged them so she could read the message on the back.

'Demands,' she half-whispered.

Eric stared out of the window. He was thinking about his pierced penis. Could he remove it himself? It would be similar to an earring. He had a stud in his left ear, which he was able to take in and out, so he should be able to manage this hoop. That's what he would do. He'd go up to the bathroom now and take it out.

'*Demands.*' Charlotte was thinking aloud. '*Coerce* and now *demands*. Is there a pattern?'

Charlotte had no idea about the many other caravans with similarly Delphic words stuck on the back that Eric had been hiding away from her over the past couple of weeks.

'Why should there be a pattern?' Eric put his hand on Charlotte's shoulder. 'Don't fuss about the stupid photos.' Charlotte got up from the floor, picked up an envelope from the hall table, put the pieces of photograph into it and placed the envelope in her handbag. She went into the back room, sat down at the Mac and began to play chess with the computer. Eric went into the front room and took down the letters from the fire surround. He tore open the letter from Cumbria County Council.

Dear Mr McFarlane,

As the principal funder of the Cleator Moor Money Advice Shop, I am writing to you about the financial security of the centre.

As you are aware, your management committee is responsible for the day-to-day management of your centre, both of its finances and of its personnel. However, should the agency fail to meet the current minimum standards of good practice for advice centres then I feel I must point out to each worker that their job would be under threat of redundancy.

Of course, the council hopes that the current review of advice services will only reassure us as to the excellent service provided by voluntary sector groups such as yours.

However, we would hope that you are fully aware of the possible consequences of a service review and will co-operate fully with the review and with all council staff concerned.

I look forward to working with you during this difficult period.

Yours sincerely
Bennett Lowe

The other letter was worse:

Dear Mr McFarlane,
ANUBIS SECURITIES –
UNAUTHORIZED BORROWING £35,000
ARREARS £5,678
You have consistently failed to make any effort to repay this debt.

Although we have a County Court Judgement for the above sum we have failed to recover the sum by means of Attachment of Earnings (apparently you are self-employed) or by bailiffs (apparently, even though your credit reference shows that you are a heavy credit user, you have no goods for a bailiff to take). Therefore we have obtained a Charging Order on your property.

As you failed to turn up at any of the court hearings of which you were given full and proper notice we are now notifying you yet again of our intention to ask the Court for an Order to sell your property.

An order for sale. And the hearing was in two days. He'd completely forgotten.

He examined the letterhead again. The jackal-headed man. Why? And he noticed a new motto: *Helping you see sense.* The new motto made this letter seem much worse than anything he had had before.

Those bastards.

In the dining room he sat down opposite Charlotte. The computer said, *Check.* Charlotte said, 'No you don't, you bastard,' and the computer bleeped. She was concentrating on the screen, her mouth open and the tip of her tongue touching her top front teeth as if she had been speaking but had stopped mid-word. Her brow was furrowed and her fingers were making circling movements in the fine down at the nape of her neck. He liked to watch her. Her fingertip on the mouse twitched and her hand made the odd tiny movement. Delicate. It reminded him of the concentration she used to apply when rolling joints on her Ramones album cover, back in the days before she was a businesswoman.

'Do you want some fat and jammy?' She nodded at the bottle of red wine next to the Mac. He shook his head. She turned from the chequered screen where 3D Chess pieces glided across the board with a swishing sound, and looked at the papers in Eric's hand.

'Just money stuff,' he explained. 'Oh, and one from the council about the funding crisis.'

'There's always a funding crisis. How's Bernard's mouth?'

'He's doing the thing.'

Eric put on a CD – Kraftwerk – bent down to Charlotte, gripped her hand and pulled her to a standing position. She reluctantly left the Mac and returned the embrace. He pulled her tightly to his chest. She rested her chin on his shoulder and they slowly padded around the room to Kraftwerk's synthesized strings and clipped bass lines, their feet describing small elliptical shapes on the carpet. Eric pulled her closer still and the ends of her hair brushed his nose. The smell – shampoo and hair wax, a pungent liquor of fruit and roots – aroused him. He licked her neck and got a dark liquorice taste of fermented sweat and moisturizer. He began to stiffen and the tip hurt. The hoop was killing him. But he would have to wait and remove it when Charlotte was out – he might need to scream. The thought made his shoulders tense up. To take his mind off sex, he thought of his debts again. Where could he get

£35,000? Or even just the arrears of £5,758? Anubis were right about using an order for sale. A demon tactic, he had to hand it to them.

He looked at the house, up at the cornicing. 32, The Loop Road was built in the years just after the First World War and had high ceilings at a time when space was used with throwaway generosity. None of the walls was straight and, if left unstopped, open doors swung slowly on their crooked hangings. Eric loved the house and didn't want to lose it. Cumbria wasn't the sort of place where you could rent a flat or a house. It wasn't like a city – students and thirty-somethings sharing spaces. Everybody was grown-up. He would be a child again if he were repossessed. And Charlotte would leave him. Then he would go mad, tank himself with Valium and keep twenty-five cats and a copy of every newspaper he'd ever bought.

He had always reassured Charlotte about money. *I know what I'm doing*, he had always said. *It's my job. I advise people on how to avoid losing houses – you don't think I'd lose ours, do you?* Well, it was looking pretty close at the moment.

Later, around eleven, Charlotte was still playing computer chess, now with the laptop in the front room, and Eric was using his cheque book to relax some of his more anxious credit card companies.

Charlotte said, without looking up, 'Are they your card bills?'

'Some of them, aye.'

'I hope you're not paying them all off, there's some of them not even up to the limit yet. I saw one with a thousand left to spend on it. How can you leave a thousand pounds lying there unspent? It's a sin. What I could do with a thousand pounds. You might as well fill your boots before you start paying it back.'

This was exactly the phrase Doreen Jackson had used. That was when Eric had the idea that would solve his debt problems utterly. He tossed down his pen and told Charlotte suddenly, 'I've got to go to the office. It's something important I should have done before tomorrow. About the funding crisis.'

'OK,' Charlotte said, as she took the computer's bishop with her pawn.

'Checkmate,' the machine said in its clear baritone. Eric wondered why the machine didn't speak like a robot.

'Yes, you fucking idiot,' she said to the computer, pouring another glass of Chilean red. 'Try me again.'

Eric's car dipped down from the rim of the hill and joined the long dark road away from Whitehaven. Below him, Cleator Moor was a rash of tiny lights under the shoulders of the fells, looking as though a giant crane had picked up a city council estate and dropped it into the centre of the national park, a scrap of urban decay in the middle of the countryside.

Shane's Teeth.

The St Cuthbert's Centre was in pitch darkness. There was nothing to compare to the darkness in Cumbria. It was unlike the dark in a city, where there was always a patch of light somewhere, or at the very least, the street lamps reflected back to you from the clouds. This was dark. Dark where you couldn't find your car, dark where you couldn't find the door to your house, dark where you wouldn't know if you were walking on the pavement or on the road, dark where as a child he was frightened to go up the two flights of stairs to his bedroom because the black landing window threw back monstrous misty faces.

But the advice shop wasn't quiet. There was a car outside, which Eric recognized: Bennett Lowe's Saab, the russet teardrop. Its orange headlamps gave out a slight glow from under the coy visors they wore like large false eyelashes.

Eric moved quietly through the walled area of the former churchyard (now cleared of gravestones and, he assumed, the attendant bodies) towards the door. Yes, the door was open. He went in silently. It was dark in the waiting area but Eric could hear noises coming from the office. Had Lowe sneaked in, no, *broken* in, to look at their papers, to get something on them to stitch them up? It didn't seem likely. No, not just Lowe, there were two voices. A woman's as well. There was a hatch between the office and the waiting room, an opening which priests had used to pass through the wine and hosts. It was open a crack at the bottom and, by genuflecting low, Eric could see into the office.

Marjorie and Bennett. Marjorie and Bennett! To Eric this somehow didn't seem fair. Their clothes were dishevelled and they were laughing.

She was sitting on the edge of Bernard's desk – Bernard's! Where every object was aligned and squared precisely, his high stack of papers seeming encased in a transparent cube.

Bennett began to move towards the door and Eric panicked. What if he were found? And which was worse? Found having an illicit moment in an office late at night or found watching someone else having an illicit moment in an office?

Found watching someone else.

How could he get out of it? He could pretend he'd just got there, but that would be awkward – they would suspect he had been there longer. He could sneak away, but he had come for a reason. He had to get a look at Doreen's file. Eric had devised a plan which he couldn't get off his mind.

He went behind the coat stand and assumed a coat-like position. After what seemed like an age, the door opened and a fan of light on the carpet got wider and longer reaching almost to the coat stand. *Turn off the light*, he said to himself, through gritted teeth. *Turn off the light.*

Bennett was first out of the room. 'Is there an alarm to set?'

'We haven't got one,' Marjorie said in a low smoky husk.

'Tut tut,' said Bennett, 'a minimum standard. That will have to go in my report.'

'Oh fuck off with your report,' Marjorie clucked.

They turned off the light and went through the apse and out the front door, Marjorie locking it behind her. Locking it, thought Eric. Fuck. He couldn't open it from this side. He was locked in. He looked at his watch. One-thirty. He waited until the wheels crunched out of the churchyard, then turned on the main light. Now. Doreen's file. He opened a drawer and pulled out the large brown folder stuffed with letters, bills and envelopes, and flicked through the papers until he came to what he was looking for. Doreen's credit reference file report. She was proud of the fact that she was still creditworthy although she had so much debt. The report was clean as far as he could see. Good. That's what he needed. He read every entry. It was scored zero to eight, eight being bad, a default or a court order, and zero being everything paid up to date. All zeros. Debts worth £120,000, no arrears and a perfect credit reference. Eric dropped the report, clenched his fist and shouted 'YES!' to the ceiling. His voice echoed off the cold walls.

He made a copy of the credit reference. The photocopied pages felt warm against his bare arm, comforting: he left them there for a few moments as they cooled.

Then he rang Charlotte.

'Listen to me,' she said right away. 'Scooter's getting worse. He sits there in his basket, in his own mess; it's horrible. He's all big, far too big. We must ring your dad. When will you be back?'

'I'm still at the advice shop. I'm locked in.'

Charlotte was silent for a time. Then she said, 'Why the fuck are you locked in?'

'I had to sort out some stuff for Central Funding.'

'How does that get you locked in, West Cumbria?'

'It's a long story.'

'Did you pin that caravan picture to the cork board?'

'The cork board?'

'I assumed you must have pinned it there for me to see.'

He had been in the house. The lemon man, the caravan man. But when? Either that afternoon while Eric was asleep on the sofa or in the last couple of hours while Charlotte was on her own.

'I stuck it up, yes,' Eric said. 'For you to see. I thought we'd collect them – for fun. What's it say on the back?'

'Didn't you look? The word on this one is *humiliation*.'

'Well, I know. Listen. Don't worry. I'll have to spend the night here.'

'Stupid,' she said, her voice clenched and trembling. Then she hung up.

He pulled a coat off the coat rack (the coat belonged to Bernard, who always left a spare coat on the rack), and lay on the floor using it as a blanket. He tried to think of Julie – Julie in his clothes, Julie laughing in the pub, Julie's nose, Julie's feet – but for some reason all he could picture was Marjorie's naked buttocks, stuck all over with Bernard's red and green paperclips, circling his mind like a planet about a sun.

He stands in the garden. Quiet. Just the wind and a low rumble from the open-cast mine. Magpies stabbing at bullet-hard bread, quick percussion of beaks like a fire crackling. Birds don't even shrug when Apartfromtheobvious passes near. Not even the animal world respects him. Claps his hands loud and the birds rise casually and alight on the droopy fence, aiming crafty eyes at him.

He peers up at the chimney. How would fire eat up the house? How would it ingest the contents, how would the walls fall, what evidence would be left?

Grey Eyes needs to be reduced to dust. What about the candle effect? That documentary about spontaneous human combustion. Human body smoulders slowly, nothing in the room burnt, just the person. In the documentary they wrapped a dead pig in a shawl, lit the shawl, and the fabric acted like a wick. The body, mostly fat, fed the wick. Bubbling skin, melting flesh, runny bones. Same with humans. Only the lower legs left because they are skinny. Bones to powder – not even a crematorium does this, they said.

Crick crack of magpies on bread. Frisbees a jagged shard of roof slate, but they dodge.

Magnum sifts through her baked-bean jigsaw. Pieces all the same. Orange sticky balls, odd black shadow round a few. What's the fucking point? He can't see it. She holds a bean-coloured edge piece poised over the tea tray. 'What you been doing out there?'

'Talking to the birds.'

'What if,' she says, 'we lock him in a room with birds? Wouldn't they eventually eat him, when they got hungry? Like in the Hitchcock film. That man's eyeballs hanging out?'

'No. I've got a killer idea. Just do what I say. First of all we need to take his trousers off.'

Locks an edge piece of bean into place, curls the back of her hand in front of her mouth and does a prim little cough. 'I can take care of that.'

She kneels in front of Grey Eyes. Man is sweating, sweating a lot, hair blackly wet at the front, brow gloopy and glowing. Magnum nips her lower lip between her teeth as she strains to tug his belt buckle open and then begins to slip each bronze Levi disc through its slit, a sly smile glimmering on her face. Tries to pull the pants off him but can't get them round his arse.

'You'll have to loosen him a bit, Party.'

'I don't know about –'

'You'll have to.'

So he takes one of the wires and unwraps it a bit – the grey-eyed man is shaking again.

Magnum says, 'Lift up a bit, sonny boy. Just want your trousers off. That's all. Shoes as well. And socks too. No, we can't leave socks on, can we? Not very sexy that, no sex appeal in a sock.' Tugs at the long drooping sock nose. Turns to see Party in leopard-print posing pouch (Magnum bought it from a Blackpool vending machine; it had been inside a plastic egg) and she says, 'What you doing? I didn't think you was into that sort of palaver.'

Apartfromtheobvious hands her his trousers, socks and shoes. 'These are for him, you fucking idiot. I'm no arse bandit.'

'You've got a semi. I can see it. There.' Prods him in the genitals.

'Will you fuck off? That's you giving me a semi, not him.'

'Where was the semi last night then, where was it then? When I was ravenous for a semi, or a demi, or anything.'

'We need to put my trousers, shoes and socks on him. Just do it.'

After a struggle they have him in Apartfromtheobvious's trousers and shoes.

'The trousers are a bit short on him, Party, a bit wide at the waist,' Mangum says doubtfully.

'Never mind that. Now we need something to put round his neck, something we can burn. Get that feathery thing you brought with you, the one you wear in the bedroom.'

'My boa!'

'Your boa, yes, your fucking boa. Get it.'

'Party, don't make me.'

Makes his face cornery and hard, the way he knows how to, the way he knows that with a tilt of his shoulder and a setting of his lips will remind her what he can do, remind her of his muscle, his speed, his determination. Will do what she is told.

Party splooshes petrol into a can, plunges the feather boa in.

Magnum watches. 'This had better be good,' she says.

'Going to be spectacular, Mags. Our very own fat little firework, our Yuletide log, warming us up for the next few nights.'

Grey Eyes whimpers when he sniffs petrol. Squeaking noises in rapid beats, Sooty and Sweep style.

Party puts his ear to Grey Eyes' mouth. 'What are you saying, Sooty?'

'Squeak squeak.'

'Yes . . .'

'Squeak.'

'Yes.'

'Squeak, squeak, squeak.'

'Yes . . . yes.'

'Squeal whimper squeak whimper.' Party nodding, nodding.

'You say that you don't want to be all burned up, Sooty?'

'He'll be fucking sooty then.'

'Hur, hur, hur.'

Grey Eyes makes long squeaks, then longer ones – Morse code.

'Where's Soo the panda, Sooty? Maybe Soo the panda can help you.' Party begins to coil the petrol-soaked feather boa about the man's upper body while the eyes, squirrel-arse grey, look up at him, anger-bright, moist.

'Sweep – you be sweep, Mags – Sweep, get the matches. Izzy wizzy let's get busy!'

Magnum squeaks two times, shrieks with laughter, disappears into the kitchen.

Likes it when they function as a team, when they have a giggle. Nice pittery feeling in his head, like someone putting their finger over a water spout, squeezing out fizzy spray.

He snicks on the lighter.

12

Butterscotch. That was the smell; a stench like rancid meat. Eric felt nauseous when Mr Friday leaned across the table and squeezed Eric's arm.

In a low voice, Mr Friday said, 'I loved her, you see. I do love her, but she's not really there.'

Eric unpincered his arm and edged over towards the filing cabinet. 'Has she left you, Mr Friday?'

'No, no. Not left me, but she's not there. She never goes out, never does anything. She's got this depression. It's a terrible thing. She's not the woman I married. I try my best, but she's a plank.'

Mr Friday, like most West Cumbrians, had the permanent expression and posture of someone walking in torrential rain – hunched over, shoulders squeezed together, head down and face contorted in pain as if he were being pulled backwards through a tight space. His eyes were tiny and deep set and he used them with quick darting movements, examining people when they weren't looking. Mr Friday was becoming a real heart-sink job.

Eric arranged the self-help materials in front of Mr Friday's face – a lined sheet of paper with *Financial Statement* written on the top, and a fat booklet whose cover showed cartoon bills, a cartoon man scratching his head and a think balloon saying, *Robbing Peter to pay Paul? If only I'd known about self-help for your debts before* – but

Mr Friday ignored him, continuing with his theme. He had with him a torn bit of cardboard box on which was daubed a list of words in thick pink ink and his blunt thumb moved slowly down the list of items as he spoke.

'It was her that got us into debt. Everything on the never-never. The suite, the nest of tables, the thing to clean venetian blinds – furry thing like a hand.' He lifted his arm and fluttered his fingers in the air like a pianist.

'Surely that wasn't expensive, Mr Friday?'

'Yes, Mr McFarlane, Eric, but the point is, things like the furry fingers were typical. She had to be up to the minute on gadgets.' His voice was quavery, thin, like the sound of a gnat. Mr Friday had a slim Clark Gable moustache which, because he constantly sucked butterscotch sweets, was always writhing about on his upper lip. His brown hair was so tightly curled it seemed to crackle with silent energy. There was something meagre and starved about his clothes, the way, apart from his ornately carved leather cowboy boots, they were functional only, without even a passing nod to fashion or style. His grey shapeless jogging bottoms told the world he had given up; if he couldn't compete he might as well be comfortable. The Shopaloan loan company, which he had established and now managed, specialized in high-interest loans to finance the purchase of low-quality household goods at inflated prices. The fierce round waitress had been right; Shopaloan was struggling – it had been told by the Office of Fair Trading not to take on any new business while its activities were investigated – and Mr Friday, his profits depleting by the day, was after help to sort out a large debt to a bank, several credit accounts and tax and VAT debts.

Eric wasn't concentrating on Mr Friday's story. He was thinking of his next appointment with Doreen and how Doreen was going to help him save his house, help him keep 32, The Loop Road out of the hands of Anubis and the county courts. He was planning how he was going to put his proposal to Doreen, the proposal he had formulated the night before, sleeping on the advice-shop floor. It was also in his mind that Mr Shopaloan was a creditor of Doreen's, a fact that made his advising them both very difficult.

'Mr Friday, I don't think that I can help. You are capable of negotiating with these companies yourself. In fact you have experience of the financial world. We need to concentrate our efforts on poorer, more disadvantaged clients.'

'Disadvantaged: what the hell am I if not disadvantaged? Wife laid up with depression, me up to the neck in debts, the business falling apart all around – and no help from the likes of debt counsellors and money advisers. *Disadvantaged.* I've always paid my way. In the real world as well, I might add. Not like this –' he wafted a hand at the room generally '– on bloody taxpayers' money. You've got to help me.' He paused, took a handkerchief from his pocket and wiped his brow. 'I'm sorry, I don't mean to curse, but I can't stop myself. Is it the incident with your lady client, is that what it is? Because that incident is in the hands of the police. Nothing has been proved, no witnesses are coming forward.'

Mr Friday's thumb was only halfway down his list and he had been there half an hour.

'I can't help you personally,' Eric said. 'But you can use the self-help pack. It will show you how to negotiate with your creditors.'

Mr Friday suddenly became quiet and sat back in his chair. He exhaled loudly, flapping his lips, and his eyes fell on the wall calendar. A frown passed across his face. 'When did you last have a holiday?'

Eric had been with Charlotte to Padua for the Giotto frescoes, but he couldn't explain this to Mr Friday. 'I went to Italy for a weekend,' he said.

'Italy. Well, that's more than we've done. And we've got our own place, a place in Fleetwood. What with the business on its last legs, I can't afford the time.'

Suddenly Mr Friday seemed far off, shrouded in a private conflict, a conflict of which Eric knew nothing.

'But we're gonna have to let it go,' Friday said.

Eric and Mr Friday looked at each other across the heap of papers in the middle of the desk.

'Well, it's a letter to Cumbria County Council about this, Mr McFarlane.' All of a sudden he wasn't angry; he seemed suddenly deflated and spoke dreamily, as if talking in his sleep. 'You're a public servant, a paid servant, *my* servant, and you're not doing it. You're not serving anybody at all.'

Eric couldn't let Mr Friday leave in this depressed mood. A complaint landing on Bennett Lowe's desk would be all they needed. He arranged his face to suggest strength, wisdom, and turned the smarm up to eleven. He felt he could communicate his years of experience with a downturn of the mouth and a slight curving of the eyebrow. 'Mr Friday, if I had the time and resource I would help you.' He pushed the self-help materials across the desk towards him. 'Ring me, Mr Friday. Ring me when you've read the pack. I honestly think that with some help on the phone and the pack we'll be able to sort it out.'

He watched the squat little debt collector through the window as he swaggered out of the churchyard, the spurs on the heels of his cowboy boots jingling as he went. Eric wondered about the incident involving Friday and his client, the serious incident, so serious the waitress said it had left Eric's client post-viral, whatever that meant.

Back in the main office, Marjorie strutted in, mid-rant.

'Those stupid bastards would find a dead dog fit for work.' Marjorie was in a smart grey suit and proper shiny shoes rather than her usual Fred Perry T-shirt, short skirt and trainers. 'Our evidence is that Bernard can't stand, can't sit for long periods, can't do repetitive movements and can't lift. And the medical officer finds him *fit to do light work*. It's un-fucking-believable.' Marjorie stalked up and down, flapping the medical officer's report on Bernard.

Pedro walked over. 'Do they know about him running the samba band and working for us as treasurer?'

Marjorie ignored him and he went back to his desk. 'They banished him behind a screen to get undressed. Then later they told him that he obviously had no problems bending over. And Bernard said, "How do you know that?" and they said, "Well, you must have bent over to undo your shoelaces." Bernard got angry. He asked them if they had a hidden camera. They said no, but if he went behind the screen with shoes on and came out with them off they could assume he bent over to undo them. And then the examining officer said to me –' Marjorie paused with her hands on her hips and head tilted. '"Sometimes it's difficult to distinguish between learned helplessness and malingering. I believe this is the former."'

Eric said, 'That was just the examination. Don't worry. You still have the appeal tribunal.'

Marjorie slammed the file down and walked over to the filing cabinet, scowling. 'The intermittent bad back decision. Does that apply?'

Eric see-sawed his hand. 'Ish. Persuasive, but I don't think binding.'

'It says here,' Marjorie went on, resting the sheets of paper on the open filing cabinet drawer and speaking with her back to them, 'that if you are unable to sustain work for long periods then *you are not fit*. That's Bernard exactly. You know, I wonder if they have other evidence. I think they've got something up their sleeves.'

Eric was studying Marjorie's bottom and the way the grey tailored trousers fitted her buttocks. Her outer haunches bulged beautifully like the front wings of a Porsche. She lifted one leg and rubbed her calf with the front of her shoe.

Eric was becoming obsessed with her. With Julie on his mind too, he couldn't understand how there was room for this new woman. Possibly he was trying to find that elusive hum again; maybe he thought he'd find it with Marjorie. He was trying everything he could think of to make Marjorie interested in him. Suspecting she was keen on music, he had left unusual or obscure CDs lying around on his desk; it turned out she knew nothing about music. Then he saw her reading a crime novel – he was driving past and she was sitting on a wall at a bus stop – and when she was out of the office he would pick up the book she had been reading and hungrily scour it as if in the text he would find some clue as to what went on in her mind. He looked at the pages, at the seriffed characters and the rivers of white running down the page through the words, as if he were studying the abandoned dwelling of some creature, the left-behind traces, the evidence of how it used to live. But when he dropped details from these books into conversations, it didn't work. She was coolly self-reliant; and this made her even more intriguing.

After a time sat staring at Bernard's file, Marjorie looked up and told Eric, 'I had a useful meeting last night with Bennett Lowe.'

Eric stared at her. He was hypnotized by her eyebrows, perfect little ticks over each eye, dark against her pale, lightly freckled skin. 'The county council funding guy?' he said. 'Was this a social meeting or a work meeting?'

'He wanted to talk about . . . funding and . . . stuff.'

'And was it fascinating? With Mr Lowe?'

'You know, he's OK,' she said, ignoring the question. 'We went for a drink in fact.'

'Sleeping with the enemy,' said Eric.

Marjorie's mouth fell open and her eyes widened. She fixed a stare on Eric the way a lizard would frighten an attacker by spreading a huge neck-frill or showing a brightly coloured tongue. There was a silence between them like a huge stone slowly tilting over and Pedro came over to break it.

'Someone's been on the phone. Wants specifically to see you. Wants you to do a home visit.'

'A visit? No chance. Whoever he is, he would, quite honestly, need to have no arms, no legs and no sensory experience whatsoever to warrant a home visit at the moment – if he can physically move along at all, at any speed, and exist in the same plane of material reality as me, then he can come and see me here.'

'Agoraphobic.'

'The fuck. So how did he get the credit? How did he spend the money?'

'Eric, be more sensitive. Agoraphobia is a wish to return to the womb. You have to speak to an agoraphobic very slowly and very, very softly.'

Eric imagined the womb sounds – the purr of blood, the whispering of fluids, the juicy clucks of valves opening and closing – and pictured Pedro kneeling by the man, gripping his wrist, intoning to him, imitating this internal claustrophobic orchestra. 'Pedro, you go. It's more up your street.'

'Eric, this person, he insisted on you personally.'

'Please, Pedro, I simply can't. Marjorie and I are off to Whitehaven to visit Anubis Securities. Bit of social policy work, advocacy. You know the deal.'

Pedro sighed. 'I'll try to get on to it soon.'

'And don't forget the visit procedure. We don't want you falling asleep at his house, what with all those womb sounds.'

13

Eric and Marjorie walked along Whitehaven docks towards the offices of Anubis. The tide was out and the thick dock mud was blotted with purple-brown seaweed. Everywhere dead jellyfish lay translucent and empty, like the picked-out eyes of some great animal.

They turned away from the water's edge and towards the new development. There was the jackal-headed bloke etched in gold on a small granite plaque by the door. Beside it on the wall, a brown splat of seagull shit. Anubis Securities. Eric felt a frisson of thrill to be so close to his enemies. He needed to find out how they were screwed together, how they liked to work, who made the decisions. This was important if he was to fight the order for sale in a couple of days.

Mr Coulthard indicated that they should sit, sagged into his own chair with a sigh, then began his spiel about the company. Founded in 1876, it was a one-man operation at first, later a family business with the sons helping out, then growing through the years into a little company with several branches. Always Anubis concentrated their efforts on lending to the poorer factions of society, the customers who needed their services the most, who needed money for Christmas, money for clothes, for sheets, bedding, the drab essentials of which the grey lives of the poor are woven. Small amounts borrowed over short periods and paid back weekly. And they did pay back, he was at pains to point out; these customers were the salt of the earth as far as he was concerned. Now and again, he allowed, families got into trouble; but his company was always at hand to give another loan or extend the loans they already had. He had tight weaselly features which he screwed up to emphasize certain points and his glib phrases slid out easily, worn shiny through use.

The membranes of Eric's nose prickled as he inhaled the nylon fibres of a brand new carpet. A big Mark Rothko print, purple and red stains on a black background, hung on the wall next to the window that gave a view on to the dockside. As Mr Coulthard spoke, Eric watched a solitary man walk a dog up the pier. Whitehaven docks had once been busy with men unloading chemicals from Sri Lanka for Bateson Thermometers; but now most of the dockers had been laid off and the seafront was quiet. Each of the two pier ends was, as usual, encrusted with motionless anoraked figures watching fishing rods.

'Our principles at Anubis,' Mr Coultard was saying, 'are based on simple evolutionary stable strategy theory.'

Eric looked blank.

'Credit companies are like a group of animals. Imagine us as a bunch of seals living on a rock.' He cupped his hand over the table to make a rock shape. Then he raised a finger of each hand and wiggled them in the air. 'We are competing for food, for the resources of our customers, and a strategy that works best for all of the creditors will emerge as the best strategy. That's our philosophy at Anubis. Creditors have choices of strategy. For example, you can be an attacker, always attacking the debtors with all your might, taking court action on every delinquent account. If the debtor has money, or access to more credit, or an asset they can sell, then you get paid. But the downside is it uses a lot of energy. If you were a seal and saw another seal with a big fish you would have to think carefully before you entered into a fight with him. You might lose, get killed or injured. You would waste a lot of time and strength. You would have to be sure of winning. We don't want to spend money on chasing debtors where we have no chance of a payback. So for creditors, always attacking might not be the best evolutionary stable strategy.' He screwed up his little face and his thin neck twisted in the wide socket of his shirt collar. 'Another strategy is the bully. That is the seal who goes over to the seal with the food and roars at him, threatens him.' He waggled the fingers of both hands again. Then he held one finger up. Eric and Marjorie looked at it. 'He might give up the food – you never know. The other danger is he might attack you.' He moved the finger sharply towards his other hand and dug the tip into his palm. 'In credit terms this could be a counterclaim.'

He let this second scenario hang in the air a little, while Eric looked at the desktop, and imagined the seals lying criss-crossed on the rock, all on top of each other, flapping their glossy tails, their cat's faces snarling, showing needles for teeth.

Outside the window the man with the dog was talking to a huddle of the few remaining dock-workers. Nodding cranes were unloading fish from a boat. Further out he could see the dim vertical lines of a bigger ship's masts.

Eric looked at Marjorie and then back to Mr Coulthard, who was sagging even further into his chair, his small head bobbing on his scrawny neck as he jutted his lower lip at them.

'So what sort of seal are you, Mr Coulthard?'

The manager's face tightened, his jaw shuddering with, Eric thought, suppressed hatred for himself and Marjorie. 'We probe, we investigate, we take action only in the most severe circumstances.'

'What about your policy on –' Eric hesitated '– charging orders, orders for sale on property?'

Coulthard leaned forward. 'To tell the truth, we like them. We want them. Means we can forget about the account. We become secure. I mean, be honest, Mr McFarlane; why should a debtor who owes us money sit pretty on a pile of equity while we struggle?'

The rag-rolled ceiling, the tricky paintwork on the cornicing: 32, The Loop Road.

'Do you enforce it, go for an order of sale?'

'I have to say that yes, we do. That's one area where we attack. Because experience has shown us that it works.'

There was a knock on the door. It was the coffee. They drank their coffee as Mr Coulthard told them how happy he was to be there down on the dockside development, and kept waving his arm towards the window, saying, 'Look at it, isn't it wonderful?' pointing with the fingers that had been seals a few moments ago.

Eric stopped at reception and made a point of signing himself out in the ledger. He wanted to check a name he had recognized further up the list. He was right. Mr Friday. Shopaloan. Eric looked up at the security guard. 'I see my friend Mr Friday's been here – how's he getting along?'

'He collects for the firm. Picks up his files, always brings some money back, popular with upstairs. Does a good job by all accounts.' He fumbled at the neck of his of shirt. 'Funny little bloke really.'

14

Outside the advice shop Bennett Lowe's now familiar russet teardrop was crouched like a cat ready to pounce and Eric steeled himself for another encounter with Cumbria County Council's funding tsar.

Bennett was standing between two snub-nosed plinths where saints had been replaced by leaflet spinners. From within the church he could hear that Bernard had obviously not been overly depressed by the result of his medical examination. His samba group was sending out a ragged Latin motif in wood-blocks and cowbells which curled round and round itself insistently.

Bennett was frowning at a red and black leaflet in his hand; it was called 'Administration Orders' and was the same colour as his tie, a geometric design, black and red divided vertically down the middle.

'Ah, the big man himself,' said Bennett. He put the leaflet up to Eric's face, forcing him to step back a little. '*Debts written off*, it says on the front. Can you get your council tax and council rent arrears written off using one of these?' He looked to one side, stage-puzzled, as if he'd asked himself a question. 'Because I'm wondering how that fits in with your funding.' He flicked the leaflet in time with his points. *Flick!*

'The local council gets money from local council tax payers.'

Flick!

'The local council gives *you* this money to advise local people on their *debts*.'

Flick!

'You advise local people on how to *avoid* paying their council tax.'

K'chaa!!'s Latin scumble of sound was speeding up, as if kids were running a stick along a metal fence.

'Using the law to alleviate debt problems is more complicated than you think, Mr Lowe. Getting debts written off can really turn your life around. You should come along to one of our training sessions.'

Bennett turned away from Eric. He was wearing a grey suit which at certain angles flashed like steel; his clothes seemed like an exoskeleton which might hide atrophied muscle or some quivering silver blob of slime that operated him from inside.

He shook his head. 'Detail, detail, I haven't time.' He crushed the leaflet back into the rack. 'I'd love to have time for detail, but someone's gotta do the heavy lifting, take the overview.' He turned and gazed at Eric for a time as if he wasn't finished with him, as if he were looking for closure – as Pedro might say.

'I don't have an appointment until three,' Eric said. 'Maybe you'd like to have a short meeting about money advice? I'd be happy to explain a few cases – whatever you like.'

Bennett sniffed and looked at his watch. Then something seemed to change in his face. 'Meetings,' he said, 'the not-for-profit sector's antidote to action, don't you think? The endless consultation in this sector really pisses me off.'

K'chaa!! had started on the shakers, making whispering and shushing noises like old people shuffling along on woolly slippers.

'Listen, Eric. This review. I don't want any of you to worry.' Eric noticed that Bennett had two types of voice. He had switched to his head voice now, a sort of cooing tone, different from the body voice that he projected like a short fat tenor with the syllables rolled around in the barrel of his chest to gather momentum before he mooed the sounds into the room. 'It's just a question of proving your usefulness. Why I came along today was to see if I could get a flavour of what you do by maybe sitting in on one of your interviews with a client. I'd just sit there quietly and then I'd have a real good picture. We'd all be on the same page of the script. You've got a client at, when, three o'clock did you say? How about I sit in on that one?'

Doreen.

'My three o'clock? That one's no good. You can't sit in on that one.'

Bennett looked at his watch again. 'I don't mind if it's straightforward, complicated, boring, whatever. The front line, Eric. I want to taste it, smell it, see it. In Cumbria County Council they are saying helping people isn't sexy, it's not a sexy thing at all. They don't want to fund it, they say it's just stuffing the crust. Big outdoor sculptures out of tree branches and old masonry, that's what they want to fund. They're talking about funding an artist to fill a quarry with those green chippings you use on graves, you know what I mean? Little tiny stones. A hundred thousand pounds he says he needs. I don't know what that's about, but the politicians, they love that sort of thing. Sculptures along the railway line, painting the sides of the cliffs gold, they've got all kinds of things in as bids. You see what I'm up against? All I've got is advice work, helping people . . . what? Fill in forms? Can't they fill forms in themselves? Shouldn't they just get jobs? Can't they make sculptures?

'That's not what I think, but the politicians, the councillors, they want to see something tangible, something they can touch, something they can measure. They've got this new arts development officer, you see –' he rolled his eyes heavenward '– and she's always dashing in with new ideas to spend the council's money. An early musical instruments group, a film club, a creative writing group. This community samba band, this K'chaa!!, these people next door: they're very popular, they appear at carnivals, special events; they're *visible* – do you see what I mean? Everyone knows about the community samba band. With your lot, well, there's something missing. I'm looking for texture, texture to fill the gaps, to help me fight your corner. You've got to watch out for competition. Cumbria County Council loves plans, targets, volume measurment, all that fucking crap. Minimum quality standards, answer the phone in three rings. Now if someone were to put in a funding bid based on all that heavy business-type stuff, where would that leave you? Good intentioned, I know, but targets, five-year plans, where are they? I tell you, Eric, a bid like that, with a business plan based on getting people out of the shit rather than warming it up, and a management team who would run it like a smart little company, we'd snap their fucking hands off. Apply business to the big hurting issues and you've got a winner.'

Bennett was warming to his theme. 'Do you think the poor want an extra fiver a week on the brew, a lower sub to the tally-man, a social-fund loan for a cooker? Like fuck they do. They want what you and I have got. Freedom to waste money. Freedom to spend it all on drugs, drink and fags and eat nothing but crisps. You lot, the welfare crowd, you mother them, wrap their snotty faces up in your arms, tell them everything will be all right, that they don't need to go out there in the horrible world – not if they don't want to. They've got you, they've got welfare, a big fucking blanket all around them. They don't even need money like the rest of us; rent paid straight to the council, council tax sorted, tokens for the gas, tokens for the leccy, the phone, the water, they're in a big fucking welfare prison with its own rules and its own currency.' Bennett shook his head. 'If only you lot, the middle classes, were poor. You'd be fucking good at it. Weave your own hemp shoes, knit your own computer games, grow your own Filofaxes, live off fucking fresh air and Radio 4.'

Eric had heard this sort of thing before, but he smiled and nodded at Bennett, nevertheless.

'Bennett, listen. I have lots of other clients. You can't sit in on this one. She needs really careful handling. She's liable to blow up. At any time. Look.' Eric moved close to Bennett, so close he could see the sprinkling of grey hairs in Bennett's number-two clippered temples. 'She can be violent. I don't like to have to say this, break her confidentiality, but she attacked me on the first interview. I had to hit the alarm button and it took Bernard and Pedro to hold her back. She's settled down a bit now, but anything different, such as you sitting in, might, well, it might just push her over the edge.'

Bennett looked around the room as if Doreen might be about to jump out from behind the coat stand. 'What – she hit you?'

'Tried to. Punch, scratch, the lot.'

'God,' Bennett said, 'the shit you have to put up with.' And he crinkled up his face as if he was looking into the sun. Then he placed a hand on Eric's arm and squeezed his bicep.

The door suddenly opened and Doreen walked in. Bennett took his hand from Eric's arm, looked from Doreen to Eric and put his tongue conspicuously into his cheek.

'Before I go,' Bennett said, 'I'd like you to have these.' They were tickets with BINGO written on them.

'It's for charity,' he said. 'Bingo is the new rock and roll. Come along – it's fun.'

When Bennett had gone, Eric checked his pigeonhole. There was only one item of post, a picture of a caravan, a big silver one, a travellers' caravan. On the back was pasted another word.

distress

Petrol fumes whoosh, die, then Apartfromtheobvious lets the flame lap about the tips of the feathers. The webs of tiny barbules shrivel, blacken, curl and the hollow feather shafts crinkle but don't catch. Bastard is squeezing his eyes against the smoke. Boa won't light properly, won't take.

'What about we just chuck the petrol all over him?' Magnum says.

'No point. We've got to get this candle effect going. If you just light him it kills him, sure, but it doesn't completely consume the body. There's loads left. You want those high temperatures for a big fry-up. We need to get a wick going and then he'll start melting.'

Party keeps at it, snicking the lighter at the feather, snick snick snick, then there's a knock at the door.

Party goes and it's the next-door farmer after a shot of his Nintendo. Talks with him for a bit, so as not to look suspicious, about the Nintendo games he's got, the different levels and all that, then he gets him the machine and the guy fucks off.

What's Magnum been doing all this time? Peers through the door crack. Bastard is lying back against the radiator, frazzled feather garland still round his neck. No sign of her. Where the fuck? Then the man starts wrenching at the wires again, dong-donging at the radiator.

She has put one of her tapes on. Switched his off in the middle of Slade. Slade! She hates Slade. Noddy's voice too coarse, she says. Her puréed pap is on, 'Careless Whisper' and – he can't believe it – she is dancing for him and he is going 'Mm mm mm' through his gag, jerking his head back and forth, and she does lap-dancer thrusts into his slate-eyed face, hips carving a Spirograph of loops and whorls as she swivels.

Pushes her bosom up.

'Guilty feet . . .'

Breasts into tubes.

'. . . have got no rhythm . . .'

Rubs them in the grey-eyed man's face, and Apartfromtheobvious can see his face tingeing pink as he tries to burrow away from her through the radiator.

His home, the radiator.

Watches Magnum dancing for a few moments – the first sucker-vines of desire reaching out, as they had to him – then bursts through the door. 'Magnum!'

She licks hair out of her eyes, kills George Michael with a splat of her hand.

Apartfromtheobvious goes over to Grey Eyes, rips off the mouth tape. Grey Eyes, stunned, parts his lips, spreads them wide, as wide as they go, and wails: as if his voice could propel him upwards, up, up, through the ceiling, through the roof like rocket propulsion.

15

Eric took Doreen some tea. She was hunched over stiffly with a Kwik Save bag on her knee. She always looked in a state of perpetual tension, like a drop of water clinging to a twig. She blinked at him like a startled animal. Her face looked pink, raw, the skin pulled tight over her skull.

Eric needed Doreen. At the moment he needed Doreen more than Charlotte, more than Julie, more than Marjorie. Because Doreen was essential to his plan to save his house.

Doreen spoke. 'I've been thinking, Eric – can I call you that? I don't want to make those little payments. I feel I should make an effort to pay it all back. I've had the money, after all.'

Eric noticed stains on her skirt that looked like egg. Her legs were bare and the stabbing February cold had turned them a mottled sausage colour. She was beginning to look poor; it hadn't taken long at all.

'Doreen, I've got another idea. Now it's a bit off the wall so you'll have to bear with me. Let me first tell you about another client I had and what he did. Then we'll talk about you. This other client, he had a lot of debt. A hell of a lot of debt. Just like you. But he had a good credit reference. No black marks against him, completely clean. He was thinking about going bankrupt but didn't really know what it involved. He would need help to get through that. And he got to thinking about going for advice. Then he began to think his situation through a bit more carefully. There's a Cumbrian saying: "If you're going to be hung for stealing a sheep you may as well shag it as well."'

Doreen did a high-pitched titter and her hand darted up to her mouth. Her arms were bare, and the upper part trembled as she laughed. The joke had moved things into another place. Good. Good, good. Shifting up a gear.

'This man,' he continued, 'realized that if he was going to go bankrupt he may as well use his credit facilities up to the limit. In fact, he may as well take out more credit, use it and then go bankrupt, pleading ignorance and innocent fecklessness. So he goes out and gets another twenty grand of debt: holidays, cars, the lot. Then, and only then, he goes bankrupt. All his debts written off: but not before he's slipped a few quid into a secret bank account – a bit of comfort to get through the three years of bankruptcy.' It was dark outside now and Eric could see his reflection in the black sections of the most modern of the painted glass windows, the one commemorating a life lost in the great war with its early-1970s Roger Dean album-cover stylings. He watched his hands move to emphasize a point, he watched himself smile and he watched the back of Doreen's head as she inclined it towards him as the story grew in intensity. Seeing himself telling the story inspired him to more animation and drama.

'Imagine all your debts gone, blown away.' Eric pursed his lips and puffed into the air, disturbing the motes of dust that hung low and thick in the church atmosphere. It looked exactly as if he were blowing a kiss and Doreen nodded back at him, licking the edge of her mouth to remove a crumb of food. Her lips looked greasy under the harsh spotlighting.

Eric was tipping everything into a new, dark and unknown area. And Doreen was following him every step; he could feel her behind him, her breath on his neck, her footfall mimicking his all the way. He was laying a perfect trail towards his final plan. He continued his tale: 'This man wanted all his debts gone. But he made a mistake. The official receiver asked him a lot of questions. Hard questions. *What did you borrow that money for, what did you do with it? You bought something? What did you do with what you'd bought? You sold it? What did you get for it? What did you do with that money?* And so on. You can imagine, the poor guy had no answers to a lot of these questions. His problem was, he was on his own. He needed someone with him who knew the ropes, who could go along with him to see the official receiver and add credibility to his story. He should have used me, is what I'm saying.'

With one hand still on her Kwik Save bag of papers, Doreen looked at a blank spot on the wall above his head for a long time. Then she lowered her eyes to meet his. 'I look at myself and I wonder how I got here,' she said. 'I was twenty once, I was fun, I didn't need to buy things, I didn't need things, I had myself. But I seem to have lost myself along the way – and stuff, buying stuff that I like, it's almost like having little children again. Putting things around you, things that might love you. Like making a house under the table when you were a kid: your very own place. Buying stuff is what has kept me sane. Speaking to the shop assistants, *Hello, Yes, thank you, Would you like me to wrap it? Very nice, madam*, smiling at me. I was important to them, at that moment. Sometimes, you pass over your card or your cash and the assistant's hand brushes yours and she looks at you, looks at you right in the eyes. You remember a person for longer once you've touched them, that's what they say. I always try to make a point of touching all the shop assistants I buy from. Then they give me the thing, the stuff, and it's all parcelled up in a nice bag and it has a crinkly sound. Put it on the bus next to you, you really look like somebody. Everyone stares and I know they are thinking, What's she bought? Isn't she lucky? She knows how to live life. And the smell of new things, the cellophane on them, shrink-wrapped stuff, brown paper bags, stiff plastic, nice printing on the sides, the name of the shop, the address, the phone number. I just wanted it all.'

Eric leaned nearer to her. 'I can understand that,' he said in a soft voice. 'But you deserve more, more than just a load of stuff. Now you've got to build something that will last longer. And I think I can help you.'

He sat back. He had planted the seed. In the correct depth of the soil, at the correct time of day, in the correct season. He had watered it and pressed the soil down just as the packet said. Now all he had to do was wait for the flowers, wait for the show.

Doreen took her bag of brown envelopes from her knee and placed it on the floor. She studied Eric for a short time, then said, 'You saying I should go bankrupt?'

'Yes. But not yet.'

'I should borrow more money first, like that bloke did?'

'Yes.'

'And you will help me? Why would you do that?'

'Well, to be honest Doreen, I've got problems too. I've got some money issues I need to address.'

'So how do I help?'

'Borrow more money and halve it with me. Then I help you go bankrupt, give you the cover and respectability you need.'

'But how will we explain where the money went? Won't they want to know?'

'They being the official receiver,' said Eric. 'Yes, they will, but I've thought of that. In fact you already have your story. It was the boyfriend. He took the money. For his nail-bar. You gave him cash. You never saw him again.

Took advantage of you completely. Terrible really, what men do to women.'

Doreen suddenly pinched the end of her nose, took a huge gulp of air in through her mouth, then made a high wheezing sound. Eric jumped up from his seat, thinking she was ill, but then realized she was crying. She wailed for a couple of seconds, the noises coming in waves with huge gulps between. Eric never knew whether to touch clients when they cried. There was a rule for counsellors: no touching, ever. In fact all he ever did was pass over a box of tissues, which he did now.

Doreen pulled a pink paper square through the post-box hole, another primping up ready behind it, and looked at Eric through red eyes. 'I'm sorry, it's just, it's just no one's ever been this nice to me before.'

16

After the Doreen session Eric calmed himself with Jennings and pool at the Derby Arms. He was on stripes with five balls still standing and the milkman had nearly cleared up.

There was no jukebox in the Derby Arms but the barman had an ancient Dansette behind the bar and, because he was an unreconstructed fifty-something hippy, he played 1970s rock albums: Lynyrd Skynyrd, King Crimson – at best Ziggy Stardust, at worst Meat Loaf. Today the polite gurgle of a Jethro Tull track seeped out of the speaker.

Eric felt the cold metal of his penis ring brush his thigh. It gave him a high-pitched, singing sensation at the very end of his cock and he took a slurp of his Jennings, using its dark sour taste to drown one sense with another. After the drink he immediately liked the world better.

Through the serving hatch Eric could see a group of men from Gillespie's timber yard stood at the bar. Men didn't sit down in Cumbrian pubs; they herded together in corners, where they stood like terrified beasts. Their wives or girlfriends, if they had been allowed out (which they hadn't tonight), would sit at the other end of the room, experiencing a completely separate evening.

Eric's aimless ball-scattering had sent a spot to rest on the far cushion and the milkman leaned across the table and neatly clipped its side with the white, sending it straight into the pocket.

Eric chalked his cue. He wasn't playing his best. Every time he leaned against the pool table his cock hurt. He would have a proper look at it when he got home.

The white was in an awkward place, behind the milkman's two spots. There was a stripe, however, hanging tantalizingly over the middle pocket, so Eric optimistically whacked the white against the opposite cushion, aiming for it to bounce back and hammer in the stripe. The angle was completely wrong. The white ricocheted off the cushion and shot cleanly into the bottom left corner pocket.

'Two to you,' Eric said glumly.

The milkman cocked his head on one side, reading a line from the white to the black, which was on the far end cushion in the middle. 'So that's three semi-skimmed and two full fat a week,' he said out of the side of his mouth. 'Comes to three fifteen a week. You lost last week, and the week before and the week before that by my reckoning. So that's a total of twelve quid sixty you're in for now. You still playing double-up?'

'It's cheaper in the supermarket, you robbing bastard,' Eric told him. 'A big fuck-off plastic three-litre bottle's only fifty p.'

'Fifty p? Fuck off.'

'Fifty p, I'm telling you. It's a loss-leader thing. You want to go for some training in marketing and stuff.'

'Yeh, and J S Sainsbury's going to come to the pub and play you at pool for your bill. Anyway, I've got the over-heads – personal service.'

Eric could hear the milkman breathing as he shifted his weight a couple of times, cocked his head. He pushed the white into the black, which obligingly ran a diagonal into the welcoming lips of the near right pocket by his elbow. For the milkman, it was as if the balls ran along rails, like planets on steel medieval orbits.

'Voices green and puurpuul' – from the barman's Dansette

the off-key blurtings of Strawberry Alarm Clock seeped into the pool room followed by two of Gillespie's timber yard men, the wood dust from their blue overalls spangling the air around them as they walked. They wandered across to the pool table, bumping into the milkman in an absent, affable way. Cleator Moor people seemed to discover their environment as animals do, by knocking into things. The taller man put 30p on the edge of the table and grinned at them. 'Winner stays on?'

'Not unless he pays up his fucking milk bill.'

Eric tossed his cue to the man and handed £30 to the milkman.

The milkman's lips spread into a slender grin. 'Next time try Cluedo. Or drink less milk.'

The milkman racked up the balls into the triangle again, deftly arranging them around the black.

In the toilet Eric examined his penis, the piercing. He put his finger against the piercing and pushed it. Sore. He pulled it; that was sore too. He tried to turn the ring, but it was as though the flesh had begun to settle around it, like cement around a post. His body had solidified around a piece of gold. He should turn it. He knew that much from his earring. If you don't turn it the wound will heal with the ring as part of it. It was like having a transplant. The body seemed so readily to accept clip-on extras. Why had Julie done this? It wasn't helping to get the Julie–Eric love drone switched on again.

He noticed the condom machine and bought a packet of Tia Maria flavour. If Charlotte initiated sex over the next few days, he would suggest using the flavoured condom for fun; this would disguise the piercing a little longer, until he got down to Manchester to have it removed.

DESTROY THE OBVIOUS
ACHIEVE COMPLETION

Like dozens of tiny pulses all over my face, the slugs crawled between the strategically placed blobs of Dairylea, and I lay there for what seemed like hours, before my dad shouted up the stairs that a young girl was here to see me, and I scraped the creatures into the bin and ran down the stairs in my *new-spot-free-Spangles-magnetic-face.*

The windows of the Three Tuns were blacked out, the room lit only by weak rays from a couple of red light bulbs, a dim aquarium of pink-tinged water. Teatime, a brittly cold sunny day, yet in the Three Tuns it could be three in the morning. Behind the bar I noticed the landlord had made a shrine to last year's Jubilee: a Jim Davidson Silver Jubilee tour video, a cheap plastic thermos flask with a crest on the side, and a pair of jubilee socks that said 1952–1977.

'THE DOOR TO SANITY IS IN THE ROOM OF MADNESS,' as Spangles said.

A huddle of middle-aged hairies in holey jumpers jumped up when they saw Spangles and, after many hugs and kisses, asked me and Spangles to join them and insisted on buying us a pint of Jennings each. Spangles introduced me as a text artist, which I assumed referred to the word tattooed on her arm.

'This is Rissole,' she said.

'*Entrez, mes enfants,*' Rissole said, bowing deeply from the waist.

'This is Skeeter. This is Happy Howard. This is Noddy.'

'So called because . . .' Rissole said.

I waited for the answer.

'No one knows,' Rissole said. 'So we always say –' and they sang in unison: '*So called because . . .*'

Rissole set his glass on the table. 'And the sad thing is we still think that's funny.'

A new pub. A new set of friends. A new girl. A new career. This was *the-official-start-to-my-life-as-a-bohemian*.

Skeeter, a stringy fella with greasy hair, said to no one in particular, 'Who's seen *Jaws 2* then? Anyone seen it?'

'Another existential war against the id,' Happy Howard said. 'It was all expressed perfectly in *King Kong*. No room for improvement. Ray Harryhausen is my hero.'

'You can't have heroes cos you're a fucking Buddhist and it's not allowed.'

'Buddhists can have what they fucking want. That's the point of Buddhism. I couldn't concentrate on the film anyway – it's these new pills,' said Happy Howard.

'What'd he give you?'

'Xeristar. For anxiety.'

'What about your depression?'

'*Mild* depression.'

'Anyway.'

'He says it does both.'

'As Kierkegaard said, what a load of fucking bollocks.'

'Did Kierkegaard say that?'

'He did,' said Rissole. 'Let's have a look at the bottle.'

Happy Howard passed it over. 'They make me piss all the time and I can't get a hard-on.'

Rissole looked at the only other woman in the group and she nodded confirmation of this fact.

'You should complain. I didn't get these when I went.'

'But you were paranoid as well. That's completely different.'

'As Einstein said, all doctors are lying twats.'

'Did Einstein say that?'

'He did. You need to make that useless snake-oil merchant show you what it says in the big book. There's this big fucking book about drugs. Like the secret book travel agents have about hotels. They keep it under the counter.'

'Well, as the great Bertand Russell said, he can fuck the fuck off.'

'Did Bertrand Russell say that?'

'He did.'

The Three Tuns crowd were amazing; and talented too. Among them were novelists, poets, philosophers, composers, theatre directors – all forms of creativity were there. Yet, despite these gifts, they existed purely on welfare benefits, the intricacies of which they discussed in depth, including how to claim sick benefits when you're *a-bipolar-with-alcohol-dependency*, and how to claim a single payment from the DHSS when your clothes get nicked from your washing line (this never happened, but every little helps).

Every time there was a gap in the conversation one of them said, 'Fucking Jubilee,' and they all laughed and got more drinks.

DESTROY THE OBVIOUS – ACHIEVE COMPLETION

A perfect existence.

Outside the Tuns I said, 'What now?'

She turned to me and our bodies dissolved into a surging kiss. Then we went into the park. It was freezing cold but we were well wrapped up in thick coats, hats and scarves so we lay down on our backs, looked up at the dirty grey sky and watched the day slowly thicken into night.

She told me how she'd got *sunk-into-this-deep-depression* after her dad ran away with the woman they referred to all the time as the *bitch-on-wheels*, taking Spangles' brother with him. The *bitch-on-wheels* had lizardy hands and lizardy eyes.

'So the doctor gave me these,' Spangles said. 'Look.' She held out a handful of pills. 'They are supposed to be antidepressants but they make you, like, dead floaty. Why don't you try one with me?'

'OK,' I said.

And I took a small pill and she did as well and we waited for much floatiness.

I didn't feel anything but the pills seemed to make Spangles even more talkative.

'All this stuff was doing my head in so I decided to take up transcendental meditation. I thought, right – this will be good meditation; it will be meditation to end all meditation. In the book it said I was to imagine my mind hovering in front of me, attached by a silver string. It worked, and I could actually see my mind like a clump of steam floating right about there, attached by this silvery thread sprouting out of the centre of my forehead. The thread was taut as if the steamy thing – my mind – was straining to get away, and I kept thinking, What if the thread breaks, and I raised my hand up to feel the thread but my fingers passed through it like *I* was the ghost, not it, and then I thought, surely the point of meditating is to relax and here I am with my mind out on a string straining to get away. It was taking all of my strength to hold it, so I moved on to the next part – how to pull your mind back in. *Think your mind back inside your skull; imagine the thread sliding back, pulling the mind behind it*, but it wouldn't come in, whatever I did. My mind was still out there, on the end of this silver string. So I screamed. I screamed loud and long and eventually my mother came in and she said, "Why can't you just listen to noise and take heroin like everybody else?" Then she started to cry and I knew that I wasn't helping her at all. I was making everything worse.'

'So what happened?' I said.

'The string snapped and my mind floated away. My mother had left the window open and it nudged against the walls for a bit, like a lost balloon, then, when it found the escape route, it was away. So that was it really.'

'And you've been OK since?'

'Yeh, not bad. It looks as though you can manage without your mind, like you can manage without tonsils. The mind had a purpose a long time ago, I guess, but we've evolved beyond the need for it.'

'That the *Brainbloodvolume* thing you said about?'

'Not quite. I'm saving that one.'

We were lying near a shed and, in the snowy silence, I could hear the faint burble of Father Abraham and the Smurfs' 'Dippety Day' from the park keeper's radio.

I looked up at the clouds scudding slowly across the sky. I was thrilled to be associated with this messed up girl. This was glamour. She even took *prescribed-drugs-for-depression*. She might even, I thought with a rush of excitement, be a schizo-phrenic, or a paranoid. She'd taken other drugs too, it turned out. In fact she had experimented with everything: it was a quest, she explained, for the perfect entheogenic drug, a hunt for the God within. For Spangles, life was for the taking. Suck it all in, cram yourself, gorge on experience. *Exquisitely-dangerous-gorgeously-unstable.*

I felt for her hand and gripped it. It began to snow, big flakes spinning down towards us, and it was like looking into a vortex, as if we were speeding through space past tumbling stars and planets. The snowflakes made spitting, cracking sounds as they passed, the dryness of the air causing a static explosion within each fragment.

'Can you hear it?' I said to Spangles. 'Every snowflake is bursting with love.'

'Oh, yeah,' she said. 'That's weird. I've never heard that before. That's for us. That's just for us.'

The snowflakes seemed to crackle in time with the park keeper's radio, where Sarah Brightman was falling in love with a Starship Trooper and Harry was hurrying up to get down the pub.

Spangles rolled over and enfolded me in her arms. The world dissolved; Spangles and I were as one.

'I don't want to go home, honey. I want to lie here for ever, not eat or drink and get covered in snow, and then we will rot away together and eventually dirt will blow over the snow and cover us up and plants will grow out of us, creatures will nibble at us, and we will be found by archaeologists in a thousand years, two skeletons holding hands.'

'We could do that,' I said. 'Or we could go to see *Jaws 2* at the Gaiety. I've got a fiver.'

Spangles giggled. 'That's why I like you. You're funny. But hon, I mean all I say about how I feel. I'm so – everything's so dark for me at the moment. It's not just me. My mum is down as well. The other night this bloke was at the door. Big bulbous shaved head and arms like tree trunks and very small white teeth that looked sharp. He was waving his finger at my mum, who was sat on the step, weeping into this pile of envelopes. Afterwards she told me all about it. She'd got into so much trouble with her credit cards, catalogues, electric and gas bills and rates that she took a big loan off this guy, the local money-lender. I knew about him. He's bad news. Works the door at the Slypt Dysc in Workington, deals drugs, general Mr Fix-it for the local wrongheads. I told her we'd have to pay him off. It's not like her Barclaycard, when I rang them up and some fluff-head agreed to a fiver a month and they froze the interest. This guy decorates his walls with defaulters' kneecaps. But she said she would sort it out. Since then, I keep finding her crying, weeping. The other night you know what she was doing? Washing *beans*, *baked beans*, washing them in the sink, washing all the sauce off them. Off each individual baked bean.'

I wanted to laugh at this idea but knew I shouldn't.

Tony Blackburn burst in on the muttering bass line of 'Blame it on the Boogie', his smeary, flaccid mid-Atlantic tones cooing a lost language of urgent jollity into the wind.

'Why did she want to wash the beans?'

'She didn't know. She said she put them in a sieve to drain, which I don't know why she did anyway, then as the tap water ran over them she just thought that it would be good to completely free them of all the sauce. She said she had a sudden horrible thought that they were smothering, that they couldn't breathe. That's what she said. She wanted to make each bean perfect; pure and white and shiny again like they were before it all started.'

'What all started?'

'I don't know. Because then she started to cry again.'

'Did you eat the beans? The ones she'd cleaned.'

'Honey, no, we didn't eat those beans.'

'What did she do with them?'

'Really, hon, it's just – I'm so worried about what I'll find when I get in each night. That's why I'm so fucked up. Oh, baby.' She rolled on top of me and put her mouth on mine.

We kissed. We kissed for a long time, and while we kissed the park keeper's radio leaked ABBA's 'Dancing Queen' and its swooning chord changes – delirious, yearning, flooding – seemed to suck me down to some deep cavern where my delicate desire was tended to by ABBA's Swedish lovelies like it was a precious orchid on Jupiter.

Then a voice behind our head said, 'Oi, you two. Shouldn't you be at home filling in your exercise books or summat? This park's for families and little kids.'

Spangles got up and brushed herself down.

'Listen to the jackboot of oppression,' she said to the man. 'In your uniform, the uniform of the, the damned. They make you wear it so you'll follow orders, so you won't think like an individual. Plastic people from plastic suburbs with plastic minds. This park is for everyone. And I'm an artist so I report to a higher court.'

We got a bus back to Cleator Moor and I walked down my road with a new bounce in my heels. I was in love. I had found my perfect partner, life was *a-shiny-cartoon-road-unrolling-in-front-of-me*, and I would be skipping along it with Spangles, right into the sunset.

I fingered my new earring and wondered how long it would take my father to notice. Spangles had pierced it using a needle and an ice-cube. I had to look a bit, well, cooler, for Crass and the Poison Girls at Maryport Civic Hall next week. What I had to learn, Spangles kept telling me, was how to MISS THE POINT.

17

At home, he called out for Charlotte, but she didn't answer. She was definitely in because the house was filled with sounds; she always went from room to room turning things on and leaving them.

It was then he noticed the strange smell. And the dark stains all over the floor. He bent low, stuck his finger in a patch. Wet. Sticky. He sniffed it. It was musky, warm.

It was, apparently, blood.

His eyes raked the floor, walls, stairs. Blood patches everywhere. He panicked. Where was Charlotte? In the kitchen the kettle top was rattling; beads of water rolled down the sides, hissing against the gas flame. He flipped off the burner. The television was belching its early evening bland chat in the front room and he fished the remote from behind a cushion and killed it with a press of his thumb. He raced into the back. There was the Mac, the fish eating their specks of food, but no Charlotte. The CD was playing: Cocteau Twins. Eric hated their ethereal rambling but Charlotte, now that she had tired of the spit, clatter and boom of her punk singles, now drooled over the Cocteau Twins' sweet dissonant ramblings, a sound that only reminded Eric of that gorgeous pang of loneliness and pointlessness he had felt in his teens and had never been able to recapture. He let the Twins drone on.

Where was she? Where was Charlotte? He went into

the hall again. More sounds from upstairs. Another radio. A trail of dark red splatters up the stairs. In the centre of some of the splats, a swirl of yellow, like cream piped on to tomato soup. He thumped up the stairs, following the sounds. Jazz FM. *Dinner Jazz*. Vibes humming smugly, thucked double bass, brushed snare. Coming from the bedroom. Charlotte face down on the bed. With a speed that suggested anger he leapt on her, pulled her to him. She whimpered. Been crying, used it all up. Her face was pale like putty, as if someone had squeezed all the colour out of it, and there were dark patches under her eyes. The tears had dried in crusty lines on her cheeks and pink threads around her mouth showed where she had used the bedspread to dry her face. Her upper lip was glossy with phlegm. She raised herself on one arm. Maroon splotches all over her stomach. Eric's eyes strafed her all over for wounds, punctures, he didn't know what.

She spoke through sobs. 'Eric, it's Scooter.'

Eric leaned over the bed and put his arms around her.

'Are *you* all right?'

Snot bubbled from her nose. 'Yes. I am fine. It's Scooter.'

'What's up with him? Is he worse?'

'I can't look at him. I rang your dad and explained what had happened and he said bring him as soon as we can.'

'Where's the cat?'

'In the spare room. On the floor. I carried him there. That's why I'm such a mess.'

Eric pressed Charlotte back down on to the bed and went to the spare room. The door was half open and he immediately got a cat-food smell, cat food gone rotten. He put his head round the door and breathed the word, 'God.'

The cat had exploded. That was the only way he could think of it. It was lying on its back and its insides seemed to be on the outside. Red, orange, yellow, all the colours you aren't supposed to see. Everything was slimy and seemed to be hot, there were ribbons of steam coming off it. Eric's first thought was, could he put it back in? He closed the door behind him and it looked like a biology diagram, a bisection from the how-it-works chapter, everything on top of everything else, and muddled up, heaving and sucking: the tubes, the sacs, jellies, syrups.

The cat was alive and making a thin whining sound, as if it were singing a song to itself. Next to it on the floor were puddles of brown and red goo.

He shuddered, and walked out into the hall to breathe. Charlotte was standing there. 'What's happened to him, Eric?'

'Wouldn't Dad come here?'

'No. "Not for cute and furry, remember." And I thought I'd wait so we could take him together. How can everything –' Charlotte brought her hands up to her stomach, made scrabbling motions with her fingers '– come out like that?'

Eric felt as if he were floating. Broken, ill things sent him spinning, looking for weight, solidity. The cat was a part of him, his family, and it felt as if it were his flesh, his offal, hanging out in the cold air.

'I think it's called a prolapse.' Hearing the name of it in the air gave him back some control, chased some fear.

Downstairs he could hear the Cocteau Twins still, Liz Fraser's voice winding around itself, backwards and forwards, underneath and on top, and a phased guitar phut-phutted dampened strings. The wrong music for a dying cat, a creature that now resembled nothing more than shovel-scraped roadkill.

Charlotte's face knotted up. 'Let's get him to your dad.'

Eric's father's surgery was in the seaside village of St Bees, and the road was deserted at that time of night but for a few speeding cars. The road was built of curves and dangerous twisting sections, and the overtakers always appeared just before a blind bend, several young boys' heads bobbing about inside. Each year in West Cumbria there was a melancholy harvest of teenage drivers who died mid-whoop around these switchback curves.

On the straight road into the village the big Georgian hotels – names like Seaview and Fellside – swung up in front, their faded wooden signs in watery blues and yellows looking dry and withered under harsh halogen lights. Ever since Sellafield advised against 'unnecessary use of the sea', the hotels had been empty and the caravan park, once full of families, buckets, spades and beach balls, was now used by Copeland District Council as temporary accommodation for the homeless.

Eric's dad, dressed as usual in his baggy corduroys, V-neck jumper and knitted tie and smelling of damp sheep and dung, led them through to the surgery and placed Scooter on the table.

Had Eric heard about the problems at Hale Farm? Eric hadn't heard.

'I was called out. Rustlers. They don't even bother to take the whole animal now. Just lopped off its legs where it stood, left it to bleed to death. Animals,' he added bitterly, without noticing the irony. 'Probably up from Manchester or Liverpool. Get here and back in a couple of hours now, with the motorway and the new bypass.' He looked off into the distance. 'Your mother was upset.'

Eric nodded. He imagined the legless sheep standing propped up on bricks, like a wheelless car on a housing estate.

Eric's dad wrapped both hands around Scooter's head and tilted the cat's face upwards, his thumbs under its chin, looking into its eyes. 'This little fella,' he said, 'is not very well at all.' Scooter's doleful face and sticky eyes gazed back at him. He patted the cat and turned to Charlotte.

'We can't do anything, I'm afraid. I suppose you guessed as much.'

'We can't understand what caused it,' said Charlotte.

'It's difficult to say. I may, if it's OK with you two, run a few tests later.'

Charlotte held Scooter as the needle was inserted. *Put down.* Like take him down, or go down to hell. Why not send him up? The injection, Eric's dad explained, stopped the heart then collapsed the lungs. There was a slight shudder, a ghostly rush of air as the lungs folded in on themselves and Scooter sagged on to the table.

Outside the surgery they were teary-eyed and couldn't face driving so they went along the village road and down to the seafront. Charlotte said that she had sensed Scooter's last breath on her hand and it had felt hot and damp.

The tide was in, the wind was knifing-cold and there wasn't a soul about. St Bees Head stood solid in the dark, massed against the sky. Cumbrian dark inked in everything; all you could see in the weak moonlight were a few white flecks on the tops of the waves as they crashed on to the pebbles, sucking the stones back towards the sea with the sound of videotape rewinding; crash, suck, crash, suck, crash, suck, the pebbles grinding each other down to smooth ovals, smaller, smaller still, then grit, then sand, then nothing.

They sat down on a bench and Charlotte put her arm through Eric's. 'I've been thinking,' she said. 'This cat thing, do you think – I know it sounds stupid, but since we had those pictures through the door, I can't help feeling under attack in some way. Could someone have done something to Scooter?'

Eric shivered. It was cold but it was more than just that. 'You heard from Greg lately?'

'Gregory? Gregory wouldn't do this.'

I'm gonna rip your fucking liver out and eat it.

'Gregory loves animals,' she continued.

'So he'd poison me but not the cat?'

'It was years ago. Gregory's got someone else now, he's forgotten all about you.'

The voice on the BBC phone-in: *You are getting worse and worse.*

He remembered Charlotte lying face down on the bed. He had thought the blood was hers. He flashed back to thumping up the stairs, the longest set of stairs he had ever climbed; he had seemed to be climbing for ever.

'I'm going down to the beach,' he said.

Eric jumped down off the walkway, feet crunching on the wet stones. He picked up a handful of pebbles and sent them spinning into the Irish Sea. He couldn't see or hear them hit the water over the suffocating noise of the waves and spray. He turned to Charlotte and stretched his arm up to her on the path above. She helped him up and they stood for a moment in the wind and spray. He put his arms around her and pulled her head to him. They hugged. She pulled away after a short time and looked him in the eyes.

'I hate to think of Scooter on some slab.' Her face was blurry with tears again. 'With him gone, it's part of us gone.'

Eric thought of 32, The Loop Road, and how Charlotte would react if the house were lost. They would fly apart like atoms. But why was that so impossible to think about? What did the present Eric and Charlotte have in common? Where had she buried the Charlotte he had loved? The druggie Charlotte, the punk Charlotte, the thrilling Charlotte? Could they dig that old Charlotte up one day and breathe life into her again? Otherwise, they were just particles in a random collision, changing with the encounter, but ultimately having separate and private trajectories. Some sad old battery couple who saw no one and did nothing, surviving on memories of Sonic Youth gigs and wraps of speed tipped into lager dregs.

In the car Eric noticed a bulge in his back pocket. The Bingo tickets. He handed the crumpled card to Charlotte as they glided through the unlit car park. 'A bloke at work gave me these. He thought you and I might be able to use them.'

She clicked on the courtesy light and held the cardboard shape up. 'What's the matter with you?' she said, and flung it back at Eric.

'What? They're free, so –'

He looked down at his knees and saw a crushed carton of Tia Maria condoms.

Charlotte reacted badly, in no time knitting all the components into a paranoid plot. When they got home she went straight to bed after a promise that they would need to go over all of these things again the morning.

In the bathroom, multiple jets flew from Eric's dick like yellow sparks from a roman candle, the droplets bouncing off the floor, walls and sink. He quickly sat down and sitting there, spouting, pointing it down towards the water, he felt like a child on a potty. He began to wonder if he should take the hoop out to piss. Would the urine damage the ring, or cause infection? With this in mind, he stood up and carefully dried all around the tip with toilet paper, leaving tiny shreds of pink paper stuck around the bulb, like crêpe-paper flowers.

Afterwards, he crept into the bedroom, insinuated himself under the bedclothes and lay rigid, one hand cupped between his legs, the other hand lying between him and Charlotte to detect any breaches of his security in the night. Sleep came quickly. His dreams were of entrails, case law, orders for sale, and money, money, money spurting out from three holes in a huge fountain.

18

Eric would lose the house today, he knew it. 32, The Loop Road. Despite gorging himself on legal textbooks the previous night, his arguments against the order of sale seemed now, in the light of day, utterly puny. If he lost the house then everything, it seemed to him, went with it: Charlotte, his job, the lot. So he had no option but to cough up, pay them it all back. There were two hours before the court hearing, two tinchy hours in which to raise £5,000 of arrears.

The incandescent faces of Poundstretcher, PayLess, and Scoop N Save glared mockingly from between the plywooded eyes of a dozen defunct businesses. Whitehaven town centre had changed since Eric was a kid. A big shop called the X-Change claimed to buy or sell anything, and had a fluorescent sign outside telling the world that they did not accept stolen goods. Might as well have read *Fence Your Hot Property Here*. It also offered a cheque-cashing service, adding DSS WELCOME in proud bold italics. In the window were a video camera, an electric organ, some hairdryers, a couple of hi-fi speakers and some liquidizer kitchen-type things. Next door, amongst sun-curled photographs of semis and terraces, an estate agent's discreet notice told you that there were houses for sale at auction: repossessed properties, bargains to be had.

He turned into the shopping precinct. Everything was different. The camera shop was missing. And what was once a music store – pianos, guitars, trumpets – now sold washing machines and fridges. The specialist hi-fi shop was now a Help the Aged junkshop whose scrawled sign hollered that house clearances were their speciality.

The full-length mirror next to Shoe Express tossed back a picture of jeans, check shirt and leather jacket and Eric, realizing he was far too casual for court, decided to scour the junkshop for a bib and tucker.

Inside there was a wet-carpet, sweaty-sofa smell. He ran his fingers through a rack of shirts, garments to end up drooping from the shoulders of the elderly, the offspring of income support claimants and the mentally ill. He spotted a black jacket and trousers, tried it on and bought it, along with a narrow woollen tie with a square tip.

He was meeting Doreen in the LunchBunch, and he could see her sitting in the window, waving. She had dressed up for the occasion. Her mouth was redder than usual and he could see a line under her chin where a thick crust of foundation petered out too quickly into the pale pink of her skin. It didn't feel right meeting this blonde woman in secret like this. He felt that he should be attracted to her, but for some reason he wasn't. He sat down opposite her on the fixed plastic seat.

'Eric, I'm excited,' she said. 'I had to have half a Valium before I came out.'

She had told him about her Valium before. She kept her supply of the small pale tablets loose in her handbag, where they drifted around amongst letters, hairbrushes and make-up apparatus. She snapped the pills into jagged pizza-slice-shaped crumbs so that she could numb her mind in tiny increments and take the shallow steps down to oblivion at her own pace.

'I had another quarter when I got here. You want tea?'

'Thanks for coming, Doreen,' Eric said. 'But can we get on with it?'

Doreen slid her teacup to one side, sending the teaspoon clattering on the floor, and slammed her handbag on to the table. From it she plucked out a ratty red wallet that said *Mallorca* on the side in fat yellow script, and extricated a stack of plastic cards.

'*Dah-dah.*' She smacked them on to the table as if enjoying a peculiarly energized form of snap.

Eric nodded in approval. Doreen extended them into a curved fan shape like the broad steps descended by dancers in Busby Berkeley musicals. Green, blue, red: Lombard, Visa, Access.

'Are all these in your name?' Eric asked her.

She nodded and he picked up the top card and turned it over slowly to look at the signature.

'So let's go to work.'

The first stop was white goods: a fridge-freezer, a microwave, a cooker and a dishwasher. The saleswoman didn't bat her stubby eyelashes. And then it was brown stuff, white stuff, black stuff, every colour of stuff, all over town. The man from the X-Change shop was happy to pick up all the purchases in his van and give Eric half what they'd paid. Everything went smoothly and Doreen disappeared for a hairdo and a new outfit as Eric wandered over to the court, a wad of notes putting an obscene lump in his trouser pocket.

Finally the scream stops, and he goes to the kitchen for more ideas: electrical appliances with the power to kill.

Magnum is at the kitchen table, sorting out the aerosol cans, filling the milk cartons with petrol, unscrewing the video player to isolate the timer, as instructed.

Apartfromtheobvious thwucks off the tape in the middle of the electric piano intro to Sparks' 'Never Turn Your Back on Mother Earth' and continues to look around the kitchen for deadly weapons. Goes up close to the dark glass of the microwave, looks in. Own face thrown back, murky double image. Could they force a man's head inside and switch it on?

Opens the washing machine and looks in. Feather boa crumpled up inside.

Puts his hand in one of the toaster slots.

'Mags. Why did parents tell you not to shove knives in toasters?'

'Dunno. Maybe you'd get a shock.'

'You think?'

'Well a knife's metal, isn't it? Metal conducts.'

'What about we put him in the bath and drop the toaster in? That's a definite. I've seen that done so many times, in films. That one where they're in a jacuzzi outdoors and someone throws in a big light.' He picks up the toaster, makes as if to throw it, jerks it back up and makes a pssst sound, shaking his head with his eyebrows raised and his mouth wide open.

He turns the toaster upside down, peers into the base, feels around for some sort of switch, fingers find a purchase, and burnt crumbs scatter.

'Jesus!' He slams the toaster on to the floor. A section of trim flies off and spins on the concrete, a shaved curl of silver, glinting.

Someone in a factory sat and made that trim. Someone like him. Thinking about the toaster trim, the people making it, designing it, caring for it, gives him the nice feeling again, like someone running fingers through cellophane shreds in his head. Picks up the toaster and places it gently on top of the fridge. Appliances. Finding switches, finding out how they work. The grey-eyed man is an appliance that won't switch off. Find the switch, find the way, that's all. Don't think of him as human, think of him as a machine.

Woolly rubbing noise, high-pitched grunts of exertion from the hall. Grey Eyes has broken free from the radiator! He is hauling himself out of the living room on his elbows, hands still tied together, dragging his body towards the front door. Apartfromtheobvious looks at the man's squirming back. How easy it is to detest, as if he has carried this hate around with him like a virus and only now have the symptoms become apparent.

19

Eric passed through the security arch in the entrance to the county court, the alarm whoop-whooped and the security man ran his baton up and down Eric's body. He patted his pockets, found nothing and then sent him through again. It rang again.

'You got a pacemaker, steel plate in your head, any other metal on your body?'

Eric realized what it was and a chilly hand gripped his balls. 'It's a piercing. Down there,' he said.

The security man raised his eyebrows and beckoned to a colleague. He pointed lazily at Eric. 'Says he's got a piercing. Do we need to see that?' Eric saw him wink at the man.

'I don't know. I'd have to look in the manual. Should I buzz Ian?' He pulled out a radio and said some codewords into it. Eric pointed towards the courtroom but the man indicated him to wait. He covered the radio with one hand. 'We might have to check this out. It's a high security day. They have different levels, they never tell us why.'

In the toilet, the security men stopped him as he began to slide down his zip. They had just been kidding around. Eric didn't join in their laughter.

The receptionist told him crisply to sit down. Disdain percolated through the voices of the court staff and was made official in the brusque signs on the walls:

THERE IS NOTHING OF VALUE HERE!

JUDICIARY HAVE PRIORITY IN THE LIFTS

**WE ARE NOTHING TO DO WITH
THE COFFEE MACHINE**

He sat down under a poster:

**DIVORCE IS EASY – DO IT YOURSELF
GET FORMS D8 AND D440**

Scouring the noticeboard was a man in his twenties in a crumpled beige double-breasted suit that flapped around his slim frame and pale grey slip-on shoes, stained with mud. He looked like a bus conductor after a gruelling night shift.

The man turned. 'Mr McFarlane?'

The agent for Anubis. Some bottom feeder who lived off the dregs of the financial market, the scraps that fell to the floor from the mouths of the bigger fish. The man gripped Eric's stiff palm, giving it more of a stroke than a shake.

'May we sit down and talk through the case? I am here to help, you must realize, but at the end of the day my instructions are to seek an enforcement of the charge, an order of sale.'

The bottom feeder positioned himself next to Eric and flicked through a wad of papers. Eric felt a physical pain whenever the man mentioned his house. It was as if Anubis had nipped a thread about one of his teeth and they were yanking at it, threatening with each tug a hard pull that would wrench the tooth from its warm pink socket.

Eric focused on the bottom feeder's tie – Bugs Bunny in red, silver and lime shimmering against a black background.

'An order of sale, you must realize, is very serious,' the bottom feeder was saying. His voice was thin, like the cheapest of radios, and his face emitted an odour of dental rot and stale mucus. 'Very serious indeed.' He engaged Eric's eyes and nodded wisely. 'It means losing your house if you can't pay off the debt in full . . .'

His sentences trailed off, his voice braking softly, as if he were afraid of making his meaning clear. A lecture on the law from a backstreet lender's gimp boy. The bottom feeder was hopelessly disorganized, fumbling through the same papers over and over again, in between running his fingers through his thick dusty hair. Eric felt like telling the guy to fuck off, let's see what the judge has to say. But he needed to win this, the bottom feeder was right: it was serious; he could lose the house.

'Can I say something?' Eric asked meekly. 'I don't know much about the law, but if I had some money to pay to-wards the debt, would I be able to suspend this hearing?'

'Mr McFarlane,' the bottom feeder said, shaking his head sadly, 'you've made offers before.' He flicked through the papers. 'In 1993 you offered fifty pounds a month. Only one instalment was ever made. Later that year you said you would find a lump sum of five hundred pounds. That didn't happen. A few months ago you said that a rich relative was about to die and that you would be able to make a serious offer in full and final settlement. It didn't appear. Frankly, the bank have lost patience. They need payment in full.'

Need payment in full. As if it were a statement of fact, a naturally occurring phenomenon. Eric was silent. He con-sidered playing the man along until the last minute and then producing the money. Then he beamed at the man and said, 'How would payment of all the arrears do, now, in a lump sum?'

The bottom feeder sat back in his seat. Gold-rimmed round spectacles sat crooked on his face. The plastic oval nose-pads were stained waxy yellow with evaporated body fat and where the metal screws entered the plastic of the pads, green flecks the texture of moss had appeared and this oily mould seemed to glow, giving the spectacles a green tinge all over. The bottom feeder removed his glasses, tugged out a fistful of shirt from the front of his trousers and polished the lenses. His pale eyes gazed without focus at Eric, seeming to sink back into his soggy-looking skin. 'Five thousand pounds is a lot of money, Mr McFarlane, a lot of money to pay in one go. You realize the court won't accept cheques or credit cards.'

'Cash.'

'Cash?' He shook his head. He didn't believe Eric had the money, thought it was some last chance saloon proposal. He replaced his glasses which, newly polished, flashed as he turned his head. 'But where is the cash, Mr McFarlane? Do you have it with you?'

'Here,' Eric said, and he pulled out his wad and dropped it on to the floor next to the grey slip-ons. The bottom feeder winced when he saw the money. He was silent for a short time. When he spoke again he couldn't suppress a slight yodel of anger in his tinny voice. 'Mr McFarlane, I can't – I can't do anything with that. I'm an agent; I can't take money from you. I just – I mean, where does the money come from, just like that?'

'What's it matter where it comes from? Your job is to recover money – but you don't want to touch it?'

It was as if the average beefburger eater had been shown the insides of an abattoir. The reality of his job was in front of his eyes, a great steaming turd on the freshly hoovered carpet. Eric thought of all the work performed to earn the money. The sinews of a shoulder picking up a weight, the tendon of a leg climbing a stair, the muscles of a finger assembling a part. In this money lived all this effort, all this energy.

'Let's put this to the judge,' the bottom feeder said. 'It's up to the judge in the end.'

Eric picked up the money slowly and stood up so that he could shove it into his trouser pocket.

The judge didn't look up when Eric and the bottom feeder entered the chambers. The room was small, with two large tables placed in a capital T shape in the middle. The judge sat on the top of the T, and Eric and the bottom feeder sat on either side of the T's long descender, near the top, in its armpits.

Behind the judge the door to a little anteroom was open and Eric could see a sink, a dressing table, a rail on which hung a row of black gowns, and a full-length mirror. The judge's dressing room. It made the whole thing feel like part of the entertainment business.

A picture of the queen hung on the wall.

Nobody spoke. The judge had his head down, reading.

Now the cotton was screaking against the enamel of Eric's back molar as Anubis pulled at the thread.

The only noises were the sounds of Eric and the bottom feeder shuffling papers and of the judge tapping a finger lightly on a glass.

After long minutes of this the judge pulled his head up from the papers and said, looking at the bottom feeder, 'Yes?'

'An application for an order for sale, sir.'

'And are you fully prepared?'

'Yes, sir.'

The judge smiled without parting his lips. 'Then go ahead.'

'Well, sir, it's a repeat application. At the last hearing the decision made was –'

'Wait a minute, wait a minute. Haven't you forgotten something?'

'Sir?'

'Who are you?'

The bottom feeder was speechless, he had no idea what was happening to him. All he knew about the world and how people behaved, how they related to each other had suddenly been changed, without any consultation. People were supposed to be polite. He struggled to explain himself. 'Oh, my firm, you mean. I see. Well, I'm from Farrer McNally representing Anubis Securities.'

'OK. Let's hear it.'

The bottom feeder went on to describe the case in some detail and passed several pieces of paper over to the judge. The judge scrutinized each item without expression before handing it back to the bottom feeder.

Eric began to worry that he too might get a verbal roughing up and felt he should interject: 'Excuse me, sir,' he ventured timidly, but the judge merely held up his hand in his direction as if he were stopping traffic.

'And finally, sir, I am pleased to tell you that after a discussion outside with Mr McFarlane, I think that we can come to some agreement.'

The judge, whose lips had been pursed into a tight pockmark, uncoiled a fat smirk in the direction of Eric, holding it for a time. Eric grinned at him. The judge just as quickly recoiled his lips into a puckered hole and turned back to the bottom feeder.

'I'll be the judge of that,' he said, unaware of his inadvertent joke. He sat back in his chair, staring at the bottom feeder. There was a long pause and then the judge spoke to the bottom feeder again: 'Well, you needn't have bothered coming. You may as well have not bothered, because nothing you have provided, nothing you have said and nothing you have done has illuminated this case one bit for me.' The bottom feeder looked as though he might cry, but the judge went on: 'Don't you ever come in front of me: A, wearing a frivolous tie; B, without having evidence of proper searches; C, without an up-to-date legal charge; D, without a full account history; and E, without having investigated your client's wishes in all events.'

The bottom feeder said nothing. A sigh escaped from his lips.

The judge turned to Eric. 'That's a nice jacket you're wearing.'

Eric looked down at his jacket. He had no idea where this was leading.

'Did you get that with the money from the bank?'

It was his Help the Aged suit. But he had in fact bought many clothes with the money from Anubis Securities. He was worried. Would the judge ask him to remove the jacket and give it to the agent to sell?

A crooked smile spread across the judge's face. 'Only joking,' he said, and threw himself back into his huge chair, looking down at Eric with an amused look on his pink well-fed face. 'Now, young man, what have you got to say about this? Do you understand why you are here?'

'Yes. And I've got the money,' Eric said.

'And you are going to pay it, when?'

'Today.'

'And how much?'

'All of the arrears.'

'All of . . .' he looked down at his papers '. . . five thousand, six hundred and seventy-eight pounds including costs?'

'All of five thousand, six hundred and seventy-eight pounds including costs, sir.'

The judge leaned forward again and looked into Eric's face. 'Well. I might ask where you got it; I might ask why you didn't pay it earlier; but I don't think that our friend over there deserves me to do his job for him.' He began to scribble very quickly the way a doctor fills out a prescription. 'So, I'm ordering the case struck out. That means, Mr McFarlane, that our friends at . . .' he looked down at the papers again '. . . Anubis Securities will have to begin all over again – a new application. However, as they most certainly will start again and, all things being equal, there is every chance that they will get it right next time, I would suggest you paid them their money anyway. How does that sound, Mr McFarlane?'

'Yes, sir.'

'OK, then.'

The bottom feeder shot Eric a yellow-toothed grimace before disappearing out of the door, out of the court building and back to his undoubtedly shabby office, and the judge closed the file, tossed it to one side, picked up another and adopted again the inscrutable reading position to which they had been introduced earlier.

It was straight to the bank for Eric, where he paid over the £5,678 including costs and then it was just a step across the road to the Three Tuns for Jennings and an Irish whiskey chaser. The whiskey jolt coaxed his cheeks into a broad smile and he turned to the barman (there was no one else in) and said, 'What more can a sinner want at three-thirty in the afternoon than no work to be done, no one anywhere waiting for him and a pocket full of money for drink?'

'You might want this,' the barman said, and handed Eric a note.

'Do I know you?' Eric said.

'No. But I was told to give you this envelope.'

'By who?'

'I don't know. I got it in the post and then there was a phone call.'

Eric took the envelope to a corner and opened it, expecting yet another caravan picture.

But it was an Ordnance Survey map with typed instructions for a mountain walk. A place was marked on the map and the notes said that a message for Eric was buried there.

Eric had never been up a mountain. West Cumbrians didn't do that kind of thing. He mocked the tourists in their knee-length britches and cagoules. But there was something about this message, something thrilling, magical. Something that said *Julie*.

20

In the office the next day, Bernard and Marjorie were looking at the office diary, serious expressions on their faces.

'Eric, Eric – have you seen Ped?'

'Pedro? No. Not since he went off to make womb
noises to the agoraphobe.'

'That's the problem. He didn't check back in. He's gone
off radar.'

'Who was he checking back with?'

Bernard did the thing with his mouth. 'Me. Here, or at
home.'

'And no call?'

Marjorie was nodding her head up and down. 'We're
getting worried, Eric.'

'Who was this client? Have you checked the handle
with care database? Pedro should have checked the list
himself before he left.'

'No sign of the client's name anywhere. The address is
listed in the phone book, but under a different person. The
house is deserted, a boarded up council shack.'

Marjorie grasped Bernard's elbow, shook it. 'Tell him
about what you saw when you went in there to look for
him.'

'That's not important, it doesn't mean a thing.'

'One chair, in the middle of the room. One plastic chair,
and that was it.'

'Kids would have been using the house – for glue, smack, anything. Means nothing.'

'Why was Pedro asked to go there?'

But it wasn't Pedro asked to go there. It was Eric. The person had specified Eric. They had wanted Eric.

They stood silently looking at the diary as if Pedro's ponytailed head might suddenly pop out of it.

Eric told them he needed the afternoon off. 'Personal issues,' he said. 'I'll explain later.'

Charlotte had packed every inch of the car with walking detritus; boots, maps, water bottles and complicated-look-ing jackets. There was a large silver foil sheet rolled up on the parcel rack. With its sinister side-zips it made Eric think of body bags.

'This is the first time you've ever agreed to go walking with me, West Cumbria. I can't think what's gone wrong with you.'

Eric squeezed into the passenger seat with difficulty as he was wearing a large black overcoat and he was much too tall for the tiny space. He looked down at his legs, long and stringy, ending in clumpy large feet. He had to crumple them up, forcing his knees into his chin.

'Is that what you are wearing?'

'What?' He looked down at his black Chelsea boots, assuming they were unsuitable for the mountains.

'The coat.'

'Well, it can get cold up there, you said that yourself, so I thought I'd better wrap up.'

Charlotte set off driving at a furious pace. Close masses of pine trees flickered past making strobe lights in the car. Fields and the odd congregation of farm buildings went by and soon nothing but mountains filled the view on all sides.

'See that peak?' Charlotte pointed up towards the top of a large hill where the grass stopped and the sky started.

'That's the one you said you wanted to do. Last time I climbed Haystacks it was so windy we had to crawl. And then the mist came down and we couldn't see further than the hand in front of our face. It was lucky we had the cairns.'

'Have you brought them today?'

'You don't bring cairns. They are the piles of stones left by other walkers to help keep you on the path.'

Charlotte stopped the car by a closed gate and looked at Eric.

'Is this it then?' he said, starting to climb out of the car.

'No, I need you to open that gate so I can drive through. Then you can get back in.'

Eric opened the gate, which was weighted by a lump of rock on a chain. He noticed the house on the fellside, miles away from anywhere, that had fascinated him as a child. It was light purple, lilac, and it was its colour that Eric and his friends had found so exciting: a peculiar cube of energy amidst the sickly green-brown fells. To live out in the fells was perverse enough. To paint your house lilac was incredible. Eric would have hated to live in the fells. He looked at all the green slopes then up at the brown sides of the mountains, at the yellow brushy bits of gorse and, higher up, the grey stony bits, the rocks, the terrifying ridges. He didn't want to go up a mountain. A sheep with lurid red and orange slashes painted on to its dirty matted wool stood in front of the car, clownish, like a London punk. Eric shivered. He felt the mountains pressing in all around him.

The sheep moved and Charlotte drove through the entrance. Eric got back into the car. He noticed a washing line strung up outside the lilac house and smoke coming from the chimney. He pointed. 'Who do you think lives there?'

'I heard it was a businessman.'

'Out here? I wouldn't have thought business people would want to be so cut off.'

'You can work anywhere now, West Cumbria. Even here.

Someone, an ex-Cleator Moor resident, told me that the success of a Cleator Moor person is measured by how far away from the town they now live.'

'I'm three miles away in Whitehaven – what's that make me?'

'A failure,' she said, with a firm nod of the head.

'Well what about incomers like you? You would have to be an even bigger failure to actually choose to live in West Cumbria.'

'We are measured from the place we left.'

Once she'd parked, Charlotte opened the boot and began to put herself into her walking gear. Eric watched her as she laced heavy brown boots over thick red socks and then shoved a cagoule into a rucksack. She also packed a bottle of water, a whistle, a first aid kit and the silver foil blanket. Then she turned to Eric, who stood in his black coat pondering the absurdity of his position. He had never been up a mountain and he realized he was not equipped and that he didn't know what to do. He wondered whether there was a special way to walk or a special thing to do before you set off. And once up on the fells, would he break an ankle or get lost on the tops and have to be rescued? He had often heard the wop wop wop of helicopters hovering over the mountains and seen raggy bundles on stretchers hoisted up and then rushed towards West Cumberland Hospital.

As they walked, Eric grew tired very quickly. His legs hurt around the calf area and his breathing got heavier and heavier. The coat weighed a ton. He would have liked to stop and sit down but Charlotte seemed insatiable in her search for higher and higher ground.

After about an hour of climbing, she turned and said, 'We'll stop for a drink in a minute and then we'll strike out for the summit.'

When they did finally stop to rest, after another half an hour of painful staggering, Eric tore off his coat with relief.

Despite the cold, he was soaked with sweat and his feet were killing him where they had rubbed against the ridge of his Chelsea boots. He glugged greedily from Charlotte's water bottle, then took his shoes off and lay down in the bracken. 'Come and lie down with me,' he said, leering at her, his head upside down.

'Eric, remember when we first met – after the Hoover-cock gig. You said that you loved the countryside and the fells. You said that the fells were your heritage, that you were a West Cumbrian and the mountains were your bones and the lakes your blood. That's exactly what you said in the back of Gregory's van.'

'Is that what I said? Really? Aye, well, that's quite good, isn't it? Mountains, bones and blood and all that.'

'But Eric, it was bollocks. I have no idea why you've asked me to bring you up here.'

A deafening grunt of thunder accompanied by a muffled rushing noise startled them. They scanned the skies only to find that the plane was passing below them, the pilot's face an orangey blur, his autoguidance bobbing him up and down as the jet hugged the contours of the valley a house-height off the ground.

At the top of Haystacks, looking at the still tarn, the marsh, the treeless emptiness, Eric felt suddenly intensely unloved, lonely. That was the effect countryside had on him. He wandered over towards the tarn and, once he was out of sight of Charlotte, pulled out the map the barman had given him. A series of dots marked a path round the tarn, and he followed it. He stopped at a pile of rocks, but there was no sign of anything near by. He pushed at a few stones, but there didn't seem to be anything underneath. Then he noticed some sticks laid on the ground in a kind of trail – trodden in, old, but definitely there – and followed their direction to a bush. He looked at the map. Yes. A bush was marked with a cross, near a small stream that ran into the tarn. He pushed his way into the bush and deep inside found a transparent plastic bag hanging on a branch, glinting a little in a shaft of sunlight. The bag looked very old and had hung there a long time. Inside was a scrunched-up piece of material. He felt the package. A hard cornered oblong shape. He untied the bag from the branch, tore it open. Whatever he had been sent to find had been wrapped up in an old T-shirt, and Eric felt a twinge of recognition when he saw the shirt's logo: the silhouette of a hawk above the words *The Poison Girls*. He held the shirt against his cheek for a moment and allowed the memories to unravel and retangle in his head.

Then he unfolded the shirt to reveal a small dark purple box of the sort that might hold a wristwatch. He unclasped it. A crushed-velvet interior of scooped out hollows in which rested a strange silvery tool, a little like a corkscrew or a drill, with a mother-of-pearl handle that reminded Eric of the casing of a piano accordion. A handle on one end and a sharp point on the other with a circle of sharp saw teeth around it which turned when you moved the handle. He recognized it and felt a thrill so abrupt and surging, he forgot where he was for an instant and things swirled about him.

Julie.

He fastened the implement back into its case and slipped it into his pocket.

Charlotte was sitting looking at the tarn. 'It's called inno-minate tarn,' she told him, 'because it doesn't have a name.'

'But then it does have a name; its name is Innominate Tarn.'

Eric and Charlotte set off down the hill, Eric patting his pocket every now and again to check his treasure was safe, Charlotte pointing out the names of the mountains, valleys and lakes to him as they went, Eric nodding and smiling, his mind in another place entirely.

WHEN ALL IS DARK
EVERYONE WILL SEE

I was round at Spangles' house, watching *Screen Test*, when
I heard it. A snapping sound, a whack, against the window.
I turned down the TV. A few seconds later, there it was again,
something pinging. I looked at Spangles and she frowned.
'Sounds like someone chucking stuff,' she said, and then there
was a loud crack and something punctured the window,
squealed through the air and slapped into the wall with a soft
thump.

There was a tiny round hole in the glass and an air-gun
pellet embedded in the wallpaper.

They were over the road. Hoods ups, crouched on BMXs,
one of them waving a .22 air rifle around. *Heavily-denimed-
youth-bent-on-surly-trouble-as-seen-on*-Border-News-*and*-
Lookaround-*associated-with-white-Transit-vans-and-crime*.
I recognized one from school. I opened the door and risked
putting my head out.

'McFarlane? Is that you?' The lad signalled the others to
stop. 'Eric McFarlane,' he said. 'Weird round 'ere, innit?'

I crossed the road and walked slowly over towards them,
my heart pumping and my skin growing cold. 'Why you
shooting fucking pellets through her window?'

'I know,' the lad said sadly. 'It's what it is. My dad asked me
to do it. No offence, like, but her mum will have to sort her
shit out. She owes him money, like. Know how we do things.'

I grabbed him by the throat and he let me, looking me
in the eyes all the while. Then, before I realized what was
happening, his mates rushed behind and I was grabbed and
wrestled to the ground. The leader stood over me. 'Listen,
McFarlane, you're having problems knowing what things are.
Things are this: you're from Cleator Moor, you're one of us.

Cleator Moor's in you. But you . . .' I looked at his face: ghost-white skin the texture of Formica, a constellation of scarlet spots round his chin, head shaved to a number one, a small butterfly tattooed on his neck. 'You don't seem to have any team spirit. Where's your sense of community? Your sense of fucking place?'

I struggled against the three lads lumped on my back. 'Do you want us to fuck him up?' one said.

'No,' said the leader. 'You're funny, Eric, a funny boy. And so is that Spangles one. But you shouldn't push us. We do the pushing. You seem to have forgotten who can do the pushing.' He sighed. 'If this all gets any more difficult I'll come and see you as well. Then you and I will run away together.'

The other lads guffawed at this.

Then Spangles appeared and they all turned to look. 'Lads,' she said. 'Take this and read it,' and she handed each of them a slip of paper.

The lead lad read it aloud.

WHEN ALL IS DARK EVERYONE WILL SEE.

He crumpled it up. 'What the fuck does that mean?'

'Read that twice a day,' she said, 'and you'll get better.'

They jumped on their bikes, spitting on the ground, laughing, and rode off, and I stood there, my arms about Spangles, my eyes moist, staring up at a dimming moon climbing up a grey sky.

21

With the extra money supplied by Doreen, Eric show-ered Charlotte with gifts: punk CDs to replace her lost 45s, expensive art books she stacked on the coffee table for visitors to admire, more computer games. He explained the money by saying he'd been having a good period at work. He also bought himself one of the many things he'd coveted over the years; a semi-acoustic cherry-red Epi-phone guitar which he cradled in his lap while watching television. He loved the switches and toggles. If you turned the amp up loud and shoved in the jack plug it made a delicious electric clunk followed by humming strings. As well as the guitar, he bought a nice camera, some expen-sive shirts and a huge black Issey Miyake coat. He enjoyed having a bit of money, but there was something he missed: the morose delectation he had felt when he was unfortunate, poor and struggling. He realized, with an even deeper mo-rose delectation, that possibly he was one of those people who couldn't be happy as a happy person.

A worrying letter had arrived from Julie, though: silver ink on corn-coloured hemp paper. Julie had had a visit from her landlord, the overspill mayor. He wanted his money, all of it right now, with an increased tribute, as he called it, on the top. He wondered where Damon-out-of-Blur-indie-cunt was; he wasn't a dog with two dicks any more, he was something else. She wanted Eric to go down and sort it out. Eric thought of the jolly-faced hard man, his big round baby features, pink. He didn't want to face him.

He'd never risked it before but now was the time. He picked up the phone and dialled Julie's number. It rang for a long time and when a voice answered, his stomach froze.

'I, I wanted Julie. Is this the tattooist's?'

But the man recognized Eric's voice. 'Wotcha, my little indie-cunt, my little Damon-out-of-Blur boy. Fancy speaking to you. You're just the man.'

'Where's Julie? Put her on.'

'I don't know where she is, little fella. She ain't here. She's not working today. But it's you I need. I hope I'll be seeing you soon, little matey. Very soon. I'll give you three days. That's a standard term. We are not animals. If I don't get it by then, I don't know. Maybe that Julie can help me out, give me a clue, so to speak.' And he hung up.

He was now demanding £3,000, and only Doreen could get him such a large amount quickly, so he immediately rang her and arranged to meet her that night down at the local river, Hen Beck, where no honest person ever went after dark.

He was on his way out to the car when he noticed a wheelie bin had been left in front of his door, with a note pinned to it.

The note said, *Wish you were here.*

He circled the bin a couple of times, rested his palm on the lid. It wasn't hot. Why *would* it be hot? He tilted it on to its wheels and felt that it was very heavy. That's when the shuffling noises began. He hopped back, stood there in the dark, looking all around him. The street was black, silent; how could sinister items get left on this prim street of smug semis, with their burglar alarms and dazzle lights that flashed on in a sequence as you walked down the street, a leg kick rippling down a row of dancing girls? He fingered the edge of the bin's lid. It was sealed; the plastic had been melted. From inside he could hear scuffling, scraping, muffled grunts and squeaks. And he thought, It's rats – I'll open it and the rats will spring out. But it didn't sound like rats; it sounded human. He examined the bin for other clues. Sometimes people painted on their house number. All he found were a couple of holes where the plastic had been pierced.

Charlotte came out of the house behind him. She had been up late, sorting through more of her old stuff to throw out.

'What's in the bin?' she said.

'I . . . I think it's another caravan-type thing.'

Eric was thinking of the lemon man. The lemon man was inside the bin, ready to leap out, flailing a glinting machete.

'I've been looking at old photos,' said Charlotte. 'My mum and dad. They were so glamorous. And look at me now. Stood here in the freezing cold, looking at a bin.'

'There's something in it, something inside, moving about.'

'You know, Eric, at this time of night when my mother and father were our age, they would have been out some-where, at some function, playing bridge or poker or at an art opening or a post-theatre party.' She sighed. 'And here we are. It's not even late, not really. Their evening would have been just starting. And I have –' she looked down '– slippers on my feet.'

'I'll take it to the police.'

Charlotte sighed deep and long. 'West Cumbria. Do you know what my mother used to do, West Cumbria?' Eric knew that if she was calling him *West Cumbria* again then all was not well. 'She used to have her cocktail cigar-ettes dyed the same colour as her dresses. Can you imagine that? And we live like this.'

Then Charlotte swung her hand up to her mouth and staggered backwards. The thing inside had begun to ham-mer at the bin walls, rocking it from side to side.

They stood frozen, staring. Something alive, something sentient, something with motion and consciousness was pummelling the plastic walls. Charlotte's hand was locked on to Eric's arm. The knocking stopped.

'Eric, I'm frightened,' she said, 'frightened of all this, these caravan pictures. Scooter dying. And now this bin. Things are going wrong.'

'Let's put it in the car and drop it outside the police station.'

It wouldn't go into the boot so he tied it to the trailer hook and pulled it along. He hadn't got far when blue light strafed through the car and a red stop sign expanded in the mirror.

Two police officers, a short man and a tall willowy woman, got out.

'Would you get out of the car please, sir?' the willowy woman said, her long face angling in at him through the window.

They all stood at the back of Eric's car, looking at the bin.

'What's inside it?' the short officer asked.

Eric didn't know. The officers gave each other impatient smiles and shook their heads in unison.

'Domestic refuse?'

'Yes. Refuse. That's why I don't know what's in it, exactly. My wife deals with that sort of thing.'

'Taking the rubbish out? I would have thought that was a man's job – if you were going to divide these things up traditionally,' he added quickly for the benefit of the tall woman officer, who was eyeing him closely, 'because of course you can divide up your household jobs however you wish, sir.'

'That's what we do, officer. We divide them up how we wish.'

The tall woman officer was smiling at the short officer, waiting. The short policeman sighed, strode across to the bin and gave it a forceful kick.

It kicked back.

He looked at the woman, then asked Eric if it was some sort of animal he was disposing of, a dangerous wild beast perhaps. Because he didn't want any of that round here.

Eric thought of crocodiles, baboons, leopards.

'I really don't know, officer.'

The short cop said to the tall one that they could take it to the lab and open it there.

'What do you think it might be – an alien?'

'Well, with diseases, HIV, who knows.'

'You think a gay man might jump out,' the lanky police-woman said, a cruel smirk on her mouth, 'and ram his tongue down your throat?' She went to the police car and returned with a sharp-toothed saw, which she used to rasp away at the top of the bin.

Pedro's head appeared slowly over the rim, his face bruised, his hair wild. He sucked and gulped in air like a landed fish, blinked and looked about him, his eyes eventually stopping on Eric.

'They thought I was you.'

22

A sour smell of wet vegetation rose up from the edge of the beck. It was pitch black, the beck was whooshing and Eric's skin tingled with pin-ends of brackish water. The tick of cooling metal drew him squelching over the boggy picnic area to where Doreen was sat in the back seat of her Allegro, alone, as if delivered by some ghostly driver.

She beckoned him inside.

'You're late.'

'I had to rescue Pedro from inside a dustbin.'

'Well, waiting for Eric McFarlane, debt counsellor, has given me plenty of time to think. I've decided it's time to do it.'

Eric raised his brows.

'The bankruptcy thing. I think we've gone far enough.'

She wiped a hole in the condensation on the side window, making a squeaking noise, and peered out into the blackness. Then she leaned into the front and twiddled the radio knob. Radio 1 swelled up – M People.

Doreen had been enjoying the extra money. She was wearing a well-cut designer coat and giant silver earrings like shovels and she smelt of something expensive, complex and beguiling.

M People blurred into REM and Eric squirmed in the back seat.

'Doreen, I need another dig-out. This will be the last, I promise. Every debt paid in full.'

'How much?'

'Five.'

'Who?'

'Firm in Manchester.'

'Firm?'

'Company.'

'Called?'

'Doreen, I don't think you need to know all that.'

'You did, when you first helped me out.'

'Yes, but this isn't the same at all.'

She turned to him; her top was low and her skirt was short – as usual. 'We are different now. With each other. Aren't we?'

Doreen occupied some strange crossing point of desire and memory, drawing him close without him quite understanding why.

She looked down at her cleavage, then laughed and turned away. 'Eric McFarlane. This money. When do you have to pay it?'

'Tuesday. And it has to be cash, has to be paid in person, has to be paid in Manchester.'

She pulled her coat around her and shivered. 'It's cold.'

'Can you get it, Doreen?'

'I don't know whether I can, to be honest.'

Eric clicked on the courtesy light and pulled a sheet of paper from his pocket. Figures and names of creditors. 'You can use the Northern Trust, by my reckoning, and have another bit yourself while you're at it. When that's used up we'll go into Universal Credit, which has got a lot of room in it, and then use the Executive Finance revolving account to pay them off. Then we can start again if we need to. Unless, as you say, you've had enough and want to do the bankrupt thing.'

Doreen was silent. Then she said, 'Well then, I'll have to come to Manchester with you.'

'Doreen, no; can't I borrow your cards? We don't even have to buy stuff and sell it on now that we've cleared the arrears. We can get cash from the hole in the wall – using a few different machines we can get ten grand.'

'No. I need to come. Remember our deal. This isn't just for you, you know.' She turned to face him and moved in close. He was rigid. She whispered: 'Pick me up at nine on Tuesday.'

'I might not have the car. Charlotte might need it.'

'Pick me up at nine,' she repeated.

'Doreen, I have other people to see in Manchester.'

'That's no problem. I'll wait for you. I'll enjoy the shops. I've never been to Manchester. We could get tickets for something.'

The headlights from a passing car picked out a couple huddled on a bench near the riverside and their kissing heads divided in the glare.

'One other thing, Doreen,' Eric said. 'Can you come into the advice shop on Monday? I need to put on the pretence for the others that I'm working on your case.'

'You're asking an awful lot of me, Eric McFarlane.'

Eric opened the door of the car. She said something else, but the beck whooshed it out.

Apartfromtheobvious and Magnum watch him lying on his belly by the front door. Slides the bottom bolt out of its metal sheath with his tongue, tugs weakly with his mouth. Locked: a Yale and two mortices above. The keys that work the locks hang from Apartfromtheobvious's belt loop and he jangles them meaningfully. Small grey eyes move from the door bolt to the man and woman standing over him.

'Come on. Up,' says Apartfromtheobvious.

His legs are tied with fencing wire. Can't stand. They grab an ear each and lift his upper body towards them. Mouth a mess of blood where the tape tore his lips.

'Give me something to drink.' The man enunciates each word carefully to avoid moving his cut lips. 'Get me something to drink and I'll just lie here. I promise. But don't move me again. Don't like being moved.'

Magnum turns to Apartfromtheobvious. 'He can have a drink, can't he, Party?'

Apartfromtheobvious wrinkles his brow, pulls his lower lip into his mouth and sucks in air, thinking. Then he says, 'Can you die of dehydration?'

'Yes,' she says. 'People in deserts die, don't they?'

Ponders this. 'They live a long time, though, is my recollection. It isn't all over in just a few days. First of all you go mad. Start seeing things. Mirages. That's what you see.' He pushes the man with his boot. 'Are you seeing mirages?'

'I wish you were a fucking mirage.'

She gives Apartfromtheobvious a thump on the shoulder and jerks her head down at Grey Eyes. 'You should hit him for that. Swearing at you. You should hit him more, generally. You should be hitting him all the time. Every now and again you should slap him. This is why he's not scared of us; you're not violent enough.'

Apartfromtheobvious flexes his fingers and stretches out

an arm. Then he whacks her across the face. 'Don't tell me what to do. Concentrate on the job in hand. Now. A drink. That's what he says he wants. What do you think?'

She rubs her face. Where he slapped looks pulsing and scorched.

'He's not afraid of you one bit,' says Magnum. 'It's your eyes. Your eyes should be colder, deader.'

'Shut up. What do you bloody think about this bloody drink idea?'

'What about giving him something on a sponge. A sponge on the end of a stick like they gave Our Lord Jesus on the cross.'

'Wasn't it vinegar they gave Christ?'

'Well, vinegar's liquid, so it'll quench his thirst, but he won't enjoy it. We don't want him enjoying the drink, do we?'

'Go and see what's in the cupboard, then.'

She goes to the kitchen and after a few moments calls back, 'Soy sauce. That's all we've got. Can we give him that?'

The man splutters. 'Soy fucking sauce. Are you two fucking mad?'

'Oi,' Apartfromtheobvious says, poking the man with his toe. 'Less use of language, please.' Swivels his head towards the kitchen. 'Get a sponge from the bathroom, fill a saucer with the soy stuff and soak it up. That's what he's having and he'll bloody well like it.'

'There is some limeade,' she says, softer-toned.

'We need the limeade. We might be here for a bit longer. Or we might need it on the journey. Go and get the sponge.'

Magnum passes him on her way upstairs and he pinches her waist with his thumb and forefinger, causing her first to wince, then to smile.

The sponge is in the shape of a turtle and the grey-eyed man sucks on it, seeming to enjoy it. They stand over him, Apartfromtheobvious's arm encircling Magnum's waist, as if looking down on a baby in its cot. His eyes go all over the man hope-fully, looking for signs of stress, signs of deterioration. Col-oured marks on the man's face and neck. Takes his arm away from Magnum's waist, bends down and pushes a fore-finger stiffly across the grey-eyed man's cheek. Looks at the fingertip and then back at the man's face. Grey track through pink dust. He wipes the pink stuff off his fingertip on to Mag-num's cheek, pushing her head back into the wall. 'You've covered him in what's-her-name! You've covered him in make-up! What did you put make-up on him for?'

'I didn't, I didn't.'

Stares at her. Tears spring to her eyes.

'Why did you put make-up on him?'

'I don't know why I did it. It was just something to do. It's not my fault. Banged up here, miles from anywhere, nothing to do, stuck in with him all the time.' Then she throws the hooks right into him. 'You have to stay here because you have no friends. You have nothing to do. I've got lots of people I could be with, lots of things I could be doing.'

The man's grey eyes are decorated with green eye shadow, lashes heavy with black mascara, cheeks daubed amateur-ishly with hectic spots of rouge.

Apartfromtheobvious takes Magnum's shoulders and shakes her. 'Don't put make-up on him. It's weird. Makes us look like pervs.' He lets go her shoulders and walks towards the kitchen. Then he turns back. 'When the papers get hold of it, that's what they'll pick up on; *Killers Put Make-up on Body*. It's sick. I don't want it reported that way. Wash it off.'

'No one would have noticed, Party.'

There is a pause, then he sighs and his face droops. 'No. I suppose you're right. No one would notice it at all, not at all. NOT UNLESS THEY HAD *EYES*, YOU FUCKING IDIOT.' He grabs her head and jams a forefinger hard up her nostril. Blood gushes, she boo-hoos, he feels a grin slide along his lips. Party likes to make her bleed. Gives him that nice feeling in his head like his skull is full of glitter and someone – maybe God – is sifting through it.

On the floor the grey-eyed man uses his nose to push away the sponge, stained with blood from his cut mouth. Speaks in a crackly voice, like a distant radio. 'I don't care about the make-up. Let me go. I won't say anything.'

Apartfromtheobvious draws in a big breath and says in a tight voice, his head directed towards his chest, 'But you will say something. They'll make you. The loft. We can loosen the wire around your legs a bit. Send you up the ladder. There's a bolt on the hatch. That OK, my friend?' The man lies folded like an unborn animal, eyes closed tight, face screwed up into a snarl. 'Your own room?'

He bends down to the grey-eyed man and pulls him up towards him. Fingers intertwine like lovers.

23

Pedro smelt of cooked chicken, like a cheap shopping arcade. His hair was up in a baseball cap, his skin looked stippled and dry and you could see the bones of his face, the orbital ones, standing out. Also he was smoking, which he didn't use to do. He held the cigarette like a dart he was about to throw; it looked uncomfortable and he kept emphasizing his points with the fag, as if each point were a screw he was fitting in.

'At first I thought they were kids, that they were going to rub heroin into the roots of my hair, something like that.' He pointed with his cigarette, searching the air for the precise minute hole. 'But then I could tell by their voices they were every inch adults, adults with a . . .' he hauled a big draw out of the fag '. . . serious grudge against someone.' Pedro was sitting on the edge of Bernard's desk. At his feet, stripy paperclips had rained all over the office floor – Bennett and Marjorie at it again; the thought gave Eric a sharp thrill along with a sense of annoyance. Marjorie and Bernard were listening to Pedro intently, with worried looks on their faces. They had tried to persuade him to go home, take some time off, but Pedro wouldn't have it. His counsellor, who he'd first seen that morning, had told him to keep things normal, to try to keep his mind off it. Pedro was enjoying having a counsellor; the attention added to the other pleasures he was enjoying as a result of the kidnapping:

the reduction in workload, the gifts, the letters, the love. The whole thing appealed to something remote and outcast in him.

'I went into this house,' he continued, 'and there was just this one chair in the middle of the room. Plastic red stacking chair, if I recall.'

Marjorie stretched her eyes at Eric.

'Then a voice came from the floor, from a –' he waggled his fag madly about '– a thing, a – what do you call it? – a baby alarm, intercom. And it says I am to sit down. Then the voice says it's got the agoraphobia bad today and it can't come out of the bedroom. Even the living room, the voice says, is too big; *it seems like Antarctica* was how he put it; he felt all the time, he told me, like the only creature on a huge continent and he could see the earth curving away into space. Well, I think, I can see why you wouldn't come out if you felt like that. So he starts telling me about his debts. And that's when they grab me.'

He allowed this chilling note to reverberate in the silence of the room for a little while, then he turned the cigarette around so that the lit tip faced him and creased his brow at it as if he hadn't realized he was smoking. 'Now I know,' he said, 'how hostages feel. Your freedom taken away. Indescribable doesn't describe it. How human beings treat each other. I saw this bloke today tending his pigeons. That man worries more about the needs of those birds than any of us does about each other.' Pedro let out a long, low impossible moan and said in an awed half-whisper, 'Eric, you need to watch your back.'

24

Doreen was in the waiting area after her mock meeting with Eric. Disturbingly, she was chatting earnestly with Mr Friday from Shopaloan. That debt was to be written off completely in her bankruptcy. Eric hoped Mr Friday wouldn't make too much fuss over his lost revenue – sometimes the smallest creditors squealed the loudest.

Mr Friday called a shrill goodbye to Doreen, then walked, cowboy boots chink-chinking, under Eric's arm into the interview room, his oily curly hair brushing Eric's jacket sleeve. Seated, he dragged a rectangular section of cardboard box from his pocket and placed it on the table.

'It's all here.'

Eric sat down opposite. 'If I were going to act for you, Mr Friday, I would need to see a full set of accounts from your last year of trading.'

'This,' Mr Friday said, indicating the cardboard list, 'is everything I owe, everything I have to pay out. She's gone now by the way.' He jerked his thumb over his shoulder. 'My wife. She left.'

'I'm sorry.'

'See, it's the tax and VAT giving me a problem.' He turned the piece of card so that Eric could see the writing. 'All the card debts, catalogues and the like, they're all gone with her.'

Eric looked out of the window. Doreen's Allegro was

crawling out of the car park. He turned to Mr Friday. 'How hard are they coming at you?'

'They're coming at me hard.'

'When did you stop trading, exactly?'

Mr Friday leaned into the table. 'Listen. I'm fifty. I consider myself retired. But they –' he waved his arm towards the external wall '– say fifty is no age. They say I'm to look for a job. I've got to be available for work twenty hours a day and I've got to be actively seeking. At fifty years old! What age is your old geezer?'

'My father? He's about sixty. But he's not what we're here to talk about, Mr Friday.'

Eric's father would at this time be daubing foul-smelling chemicals on to some beast's abscess. Eric wondered whether his own need to tend to the poor was a twisted, corrupted version of the gene that compelled his father to treat sick animals.

'If he lost his job,' Mr Friday went on, 'he'd be on the shitheap like the rest of us. And who's going to offer a fifty-year-old a job? They told me to go to B&Q, said that they specifically wanted older men cos us older men know how to fix things. You know how I fix things?'

Eric was looking out of the window. Through the plain glass of the lower part of the Annunciation stained-glass window, just below the pink-haloed Mary and the hovering blue-winged angel, Eric could make out a russet car creeping jerkily into the car park. It stopped awkwardly, blocking the entrance. It was a Saab, like Bennett's, but different, and he wasn't due for the finance meeting till later.

'Eric, do you know how I mend things about the house?'

Eric didn't know.

'Sellotape. Everything's fixed with Sellotape. I don't think that is the sort of fixing they are after.'

Eric took the fragment of box from Mr Friday. 'Let's have a look at your list. Tax, VAT, business rates, bank overdraft, business loan. Mr Friday.' Eric looked at him. 'You should go bankrupt. That's the easiest and most sensible thing to do. You don't own any property, do you?'

'Not now, no.'

'Well, then. Petition your own bankruptcy. I'll give you the forms.'

'No, no it's not right. I want to pay them back. Even if it's just a small amount each week. My brother-in-law's brother is a solicitor. He says to me bankruptcy ruins you for life.'

'Listen, Mr Friday: VAT, the Inland Revenue, they'll bankrupt you anyway, they're bastards when it comes to the crunch. They'll bankrupt you for fun, make you an example. Like how farmers kill crows and hang them from the fence.'

'No. This is what we do, Eric. You write to them and tell them what happened. On headed paper, like, so it looks official. Tell them I will give them each five pounds a week.'

'You can't afford five pounds a week to all of these people while you're on welfare benefits.'

'I'm the best judge of what I can afford, I'd have thought.'

Eric returned the cardboard list to him. 'Did you read the self-help pack? It tells you how to write to the creditors yourself. Gives you sample letters.'

Mr Friday pushed out his lips and creased his brow. 'You are not listening.' The coloured light from the stained glass gave Mr Friday's face a bruised look and made the tips of his curly hair glow brightly like fibre optics. 'Listen to me,' he said, 'I want you to write to all of the companies. That's what you are here for.'

'Only if I think it's the right approach.'

'It's because I've been a creditor myself, isn't it?'

'No, Mr Friday. I give you the same advice as I give any sole trader who comes in here with a failed business and debts to pay.'

'I've bloody worked. Not like those lot on benefits, the ones you help wriggle out of debt. I've paid taxes. I'm entitled to help. You are running a two-tier system here, one service for Mr Idle-sponge' – Mr Friday's right leg began to shake violently, 'Mrs Milk-system' – the shaking got faster and faster, 'and Mr Lead-swinger.' The shaking made the spurry buckles on his boots tinkle. 'It's a different system for respectable working types like me.'

'Mr Friday, none of that is true. We have policies. I can show them to you. They set out exactly who we should advise and how we should advise them and they state clearly that we can't discriminate.'

Friday looked up at the vaulted ceiling. 'The thing that gets me is this place being in a church. The Lord God didn't turn anybody away. If He knew what was happening in His house, the house of God, He would strike you down.' He extended his arm towards Eric in a lightning bolt. Then he pointed at the Good Samaritan window. 'See that window, that picture? You should learn from that.'

Eric opened a drawer in the small desk and pulled out a slim blue leaflet with *How to Complain* printed at the top.

'Mr Friday. I can't agree with you and I can't help you. If you have a genuine complaint then please make it in writing.'

Mr Friday expelled air in a loud and exasperated sigh. 'Writing. Put it in writing. Put it in fucking writing.'

He picked up his cardboard list, stood up and shoved it into his back pocket.

25

Outside the advice shop was the Saab Eric had seen pull up earlier. Russet. But not old, not out of the sixties: new, brand shining new. Eric walked over and squinted in. No sign of an owner, no bags, nothing. He noticed a piece of paper under the windscreen wiper. Doreen's writing: *I hope you like this – I knew you admired that council bloke's car and Trucker Finance was clear for a few grand. This is a new one – not like his old heap. Now we can go to Manchester in style. Love Doreen.*

He pushed the seat back to allow his long legs into the driver's compartment, the last driver having been Doreen. The car smelt of shoe shops and marker pens, not a clean smell like just been cleaned but the never-been-dirty smell of warm plastic and unmatted fibres. He moulded himself into the vinyl and nylon of the cockpit, tapped at the pedals with his feet, clicked the indicator and windscreen-wiper stems up and down, took the wheel in his hands and loosely clenched the gear knob, waggled it, testing its clicky mechanisms. He sat for a time breathing in the newness, the brightness.

He set off for St Bees, to steal some thinking time while watching the waves pound the concrete apron, and took the car screaming along the narrow, snaky switchback road, the tall hedges dipping and tilting in the rain-speckled windscreen.

He clicked on the radio (Radio 2, Doreen's favourite) and was bellowing along to the Carpenters, 'Close To You', when the car appeared in the rear view. It was approaching fast, its grille and headlamps resolving like a face coming into focus. A Volvo. He edged in to the side, expecting the Volvo to overtake, but it didn't; it came close, right into his slipstream, and almost kissed the back of his bumper. Eric accelerated and the bared teeth of the car's grille backed away in a metallic grin. The driver couldn't have seen him properly or had misjudged Eric's speed. But the driver accelerated towards him again, right up his arse, nearly clipping his backside with a dipping motion as his front brakes snatched at the wheels. Kids, Eric decided. There was a bad bend approaching so he slowed down. But the car loomed up again and filled the rear view, so Eric stood on the throttle, leaning his body like a motor-cyclist, riding the bend at a head-spinning speed, the car bucking from side to side, the steering wheel slipping in his sweaty palms. He hurtled back on to the straight on a trajectory that would have led him into the field on the other side of the road if he hadn't managed to put on the brakes and twist it back on course. Out of the bend he saw that the car had fallen back a little and he slowed down, craning in the mirror to make out its occupants. A driver, no one else. He couldn't make out the driver's face: the features looked dark, obscured. The Volvo accelerated towards him again. That was when he saw that the driver was wearing a black ski-mask with yellow piping.

Eric considered pulling over but was worried he might be rammed from behind. He was approaching the double hairpin bend, a bend difficult to negotiate even slowly. The driver pushed up against him again, this time flashing his lights and sounding his horn. Eric decided to touch the brakes and show a bit of red to see what happened – and the driver did fall back slightly but immediately surged forward again. Then, Eric slammed them fully on and the car was forced to swing out beside him. The driver made a crooked finger at him and nodded *pull over* just as Eric's wheel became locked into the ditch and his car tilted and he seemed caught on a fast-moving track. He couldn't steer and the car ran along the ditch until it hit a mound of earth near a field. Eric flew towards the windscreen and hit the inertia seat-belt. His head flicked back and forwards on his neck as he watched the Volvo speed into the distance.

The Volvo was black, splattered with dirt, mud spread over the number plates. As it rose higher on the road towards Cleator Moor, he saw the driver slide off the ski-mask and toss it over his shoulder. The caravan man. The phone-call man. The cat man. The man who sealed people into wheelie bins. It had to be.

The front nearside wheel was bent and the carburettor must have burst because water had spread all over the road. He sat on the car bonnet looking out over a hedge that had been brutally clipped like a £1.50 barber's flat-top. Beyond were fields. Molehills and thistles, cows, sheep. Around the edges of the fields, daffodils were beginning to show. The wind vibrated the car's aerial, making a lonely sound. Eric listened to that sound for some time before he stood up and began the long walk home to Whitehaven.

FOOL THE REVOLUTION

Spangles turned up at the railway station in a bin liner held together with safety pins, fishnets with rips all over them and black and white make-up topped off with crimson lips. Her hair was stuck up all over the place in fat wodges with sugar and water. She was anti-establishment. That's what I loved, *dancing-naked-in-front-of-authority*. Embracing danger, laughing at power.
PLAY NEAR POWER LINES.

She looked me up and down. Blue jeans, black T-shirt, denim jacket. She wasn't impressed. But nevertheless her face split into a huge grin and she kissed me on the mouth.

'Hiya, gorgeous – look, here's the train. Come on. I'm excited.'

All eyes on the train jumped to her, and a middle-aged woman wrinkled her nose. 'Fancy dress is it, love?'

'Yeh, what you going as?' Spangles said back. 'Mrs Slocombe? Where's your pussy then?'

The woman shook her head and pursed her lips. I was thrilled to be with *someone-so-rude-and-horrible*.

We looked out of the window. Foaming waves crashed over sandstone rocks. Cormorants dived in and out. It was a luminous evening with orange in the air.

It was then that Spangles began to tell me about her ghosts.

'At the moment,' she explained, 'I am seeing three different ghosts. There's this young girl about my age and I see her at the top of the stairs. She beckons to me, then when I get close she is crying. I think something must have happened in our house. I am going to find out.'

'Does your mum see it as well?'

'I don't think so. When you are going through immense stress like I am and you're my age, like, an adolescent, you become sensitive to messages from the other side. I was reading about it. Stress is a door to other planes. One of the good things about it. I sometimes think how dull it would be to be happy. You know what, Eric? I hate happy people. You're not happy, are you?'

I considered this for a moment. 'Only sometimes. When I'm, like, really *out* of it.'

'That's cool,' she said.

'What about the other two ghosts?'

'One I don't actually see. I just feel a weight sitting on the end of my bed and when I put the light on I can't see anything. But I can see where he has sat.'

'It's a he?'

'Yes. It's a man, a man who has done terrible things, and I think he comes to me to apologize. I think he hurt me when I was in another life. That's what I sense. And he has come to say sorry.'

'What about the other one?'

'That's an old man and I see him everywhere. I see him always a long way away and he walks towards me but when I speed up I never reach him even though he is coming towards me. I saw him the other night outside your house.'

'What were you doing outside my house?'

'I've been spying on you. It's interesting. I could see your shadow moving about in your room.'

I worried whether she had seen me squinting at my puny muscles in the mirror, or using my chest expander. Or worse, miming to T Rex with Dad's mandolin.

'Maybe he's just an old man.'

'He's not. He's dead, I know he is.'

'Is this that *Brainbloodvolume* thing?'

'No. You're not ready for that yet. Maybe later.'

'You know, I haven't told Mum and Dad where I'm going.'

'Me neither,' Spangles said. 'But did Johnny Thunders tell his parents where he was going? It's not wrong. It's kind of, uh, unright. Unright is different from wrong.'

I nodded assent.

UNRIGHT

Maryport Civic Hall was spilling over with kids from all across West Cumbria – a lot of locals who, by their unpunked-up appearance, had come along to see a show, any show, whatever it was, and a few hardcore local punks with Crass, Poison Girls, or massive letter As scribbled in white on the back of their biker jackets. These kids eyed me and Spangles up and down, before eventually coming up.

'Who are the children of the revolution?' one said, menacingly.

I looked at Spangles.

'Those people are,' she said, pointing outside.

'And can you fool them?' he said.

'Of course,' she said, 'with the right equipment. And you should, it's your duty.'

'Ha ha ha,' he said. 'That's right. FOOL THE REVOLUTION!'

We had made friends. They bought us beer and, with Spangles' help (she seemed to know exactly how to behave at a punk gig), we elbowed our way to the front. The DJ played dub, a music from another planet, all echoey thuds and scrapes, shush-shushing cymbals, melodica squawks and immensely long silences. Spangles got a wrap of speed from one of the Maryport punks and showed me how to rub it along my gums and teeth to better ingest it and get-the-full-effect.

Now I was on a speeding motorbike tearing round a bend, leaning over, nearly touching the floor. Spangles and I were Bonnie and Clyde.

Crass appeared with the revving of a thousand guitars and everyone went mental. The snare cracked, the cymbals fizzed, bass lines shuddered with stomach-sucking rage and the guitars knifed through it all with staccato metal clangs.

Outside in the street Spangles ran up and down in front of a parade of shops, shouting and leaping into the air, spouting non-stop garbage at an intergalactic rate, shrieking out lines from the Crass tunes still ringing in our ears. Our clothes were soaking with sweat and it was freezing. The cold was *hyper-real-*

pulsing-predatory and I couldn't stop shaking. Spangles seemed immune to it – and all she was wearing was a vest with a bin liner on the top. We wandered out of Maryport on to the main road and, after putting our thumbs out a few times at passing cars, Spangles said, 'Forget getting home, let's stay out all night.'

'Well,' I started. 'My mum and dad will go wild. And what about yours?'

'My mother's sunk into one of her low ones. She probably had a couple of Valiums. She won't even know I'm out. Let's go back and find those punks. Wait. Stop. Look.'

There was snow everywhere, the road was frozen up badly and it was misty too. It was like *snow-as-metaphor-for-lostness.*

'Can you see him?'

'I can't see anything.'

'It's that old man I was telling you about. The ghost. There he is coming towards us.'

I could feel Spangles trembling.

'I'm frightened, Eric. I don't like it. He's getting closer and he never comes that close. I think it means something. Make him go away.'

I put my arm about her and stared at the spot where her eyes were fixed. I could see nothing but a few leaves swirling, a vague gap in the mist, but nothing else. I tried to see the ghost man, wanted to see him more than anything – so we could fear him together and have it in common. But no matter how hard I tried to see the ghost, nothing appeared for me.

She insisted on closing her eyes and I had to pilot her down the main street like that till she felt that the ghost man would have gone. Soon we spotted the Maryport punks.

'Hey guys,' Spangles called over. 'FOOL THE REVOLUTION.'

The punks took us to someone's house whose parents were away. 'We're going to be playing drink-along-a-*Dallas*. When they have a drink you have a drink. It's the oil barons' ball episode.'

It was a long night.

*

The plink of glass bottles and the nasal whine of a milk float creeping up the street woke me. I opened my eyes to see a brown rectangular shape full of purple gunge spotted with white lumps. Thick and liquidy. It was a drawer, a half-open drawer. It wasn't my chest of drawers, in my bedroom, in my home. I didn't know where it was. Where was I? My head was inside a grinder, iron fists pounded behind my eyes. I looked closer. It seemed as though someone had opened the drawer and vomited into it. But whose drawer? Whose room? Whose house? I shut my eyes and watched white lines of static fork across a dark green background.

I racked my mind to remember what had happened the night before. I remembered drink. I remembered pills. I remembered powder. I remembered little bits of paper with stuff on it. But I couldn't remember what Spangles and I had done in this bed.

I wandered downstairs, stepping over a carpet of grunting shapes swaddled in sleeping bags and duvets, giving off the sour reek of alcohol.

Spangles was in the kitchen holding court with the Maryport punks, telling them about the time she saw the Fall at Newcastle, when they had used an ironing board to stand their electric piano on. They were watching her, utterly rapt.

I looked out of the window. Snow had fallen again and everything was white. There were no footprints to be seen anywhere and no sign of cars. My parents would be going insane. I was fourteen. They would definitely have rung the police. Why had I been so stupid? They would ban me from seeing Spangles ever again.

I grabbed Spangles' arm. 'Listen, we had better go.'

'In this?' She indicated the white scene outside.

'We can walk, let's set off walking. Everyone will be wondering where we are.'

'Anyone got tennis rackets we can strap to our feet?'

We walked and walked, then the snow began to swirl again and the cold began to bite, and eventually we ran for cover in a barn, where we lay on bales of hay and laughed our heads off. We sat in that barn for hours, talking, talking. Like *time-was-amber-and-we-were-puny-fossils-in-it.*

It was there she told me all about Brainbloodvolume, the thing she wanted me to help her with. She took out a crumpled, smudged booklet from her bag, with a picture of a head on the front, the sort of head you see used for phrenology, with areas divided off and given names. Moons and stars all over.

'Have you heard of trepanning?' she said.

'No.'

'It's to help you find yourself, find true happiness.' She stroked the booklet with her knuckles. 'Trepanning frees the mind, gives it space, gives it air.'

She put the booklet on to a hay bale and motioned me down on to the same level. I crouched next to her, feeling warm and close.

She fanned the pages until she came to a picture of a man with a hole in his forehead. Emitting from the hole were wavy lines, like the way a cartoonist indicates sound spurting out of a radio.

'That's what you end up with,' she said, pointing at the head-hole. 'The hole allows the brain to breathe and really *feel* reality – the constriction of the head around the brain is what's to blame for all the uptightness of the world. Things like my dad. My mum.'

I straightened the booklet against the line of the hay bale. 'A hole in the head. And how . . . ?'

'I'll show you,' she said, and flipped to a linocut of a head with a drill sticking out of it. 'Like that. That's what I want. And I want you to do it.'

I looked at her, mouth ajar.

'It's about how we think.' She lay back on the hay and I lay next to her, listening. It was cold but together we seemed immune to it. She went on. 'Our consciousness is related to the volume of blood in the brain. Brainbloodvolume. Have you ever noticed how weird and nice it feels to stand on your head, or to jump from a hot bath into a cold shower? Liberated, everything's clearer? That's because it sends more blood into the brain.' She closed her eyes tighter, as if she were squeezing images from her eyelids. 'When we came down from the trees we walked on all fours; that was OK. But when mankind began to walk upright, gravity reduced the flow of blood through the head. This reduced the range of human consciousness. Walking upright meant that some parts of the brain stopped working altogether; some parts carried on working but didn't work so well, while other bits, the bits that do speech and logic and reasoning got bigger, more dominant. They took over the brain. That's when consciousness became corrupt and that's why we're as we are today – violent, cold, rational, unfeeling. Those parts were overemphasized to compensate for the loss of the more spiritual side.'

I leaned over her as she spoke and gazed into her face. She seemed to be speaking a prayer, she was lost in it, as if she were passing on a legend, the sentences falling and rising in cadences which seemed to have no relation to the meanings of the phrases. The more I listened, the more each word, each sound, each breath seemed enormously intricate, fractal music. I was caught up in its dreamy undertow. It was like an *every-word-had-a-universe-inside-it* thing.

Then she handed me a small dark purple case, the kind that might hold a musical instrument; its crushed-velvet interior had scooped-out hollows in which rested something like a drill, with a mother-of-pearl handle that reminded me of the casing of a piano accordion.

'This it?'

'Yes.'

I lifted the trepan. A metal spike you forced into the bone to keep it steady surrounded by a ring of sharp saw-teeth, which were turned by a handle. I felt the saw teeth. Sharp. I pushed it against my forehead. I imagined the heat, the pain of the saw cutting through bone.

'Where did you find it?'

'There was a load of old medical stuff up for auction at the Cockermouth Saleroom. I didn't find it. It found me. I'd never even been into the saleroom before but something that day seemed to drag me in, magnetically. I didn't know what it was, but it seemed to throb with promise and when I looked up what it did, everything clicked.'

'Spangles, I won't help you do this. You can't crack open your head with some rusty iron prong.' I thought of my father's instruments – glinting, tapering, pointy, the grabbing pincers, the tubes with needles inside like alien extra mouths, the valves, the levers for doing unspeakable things to horses, cows and sheep.

'It's the most stupid thing I've ever heard you suggest. There is no way I'm doing that now. Here in this crappy barn!'

'Not now, you idiot. When we've prepared everything, sterilized everything, then we'd do it.'

'Christ, Spangles. Look. It's four o'clock. We've been gone from home like nearly a day and a half. Let's go to the police station. They'll be looking for us anyway. We're not far from Cockermouth. I know the way.'

The police had indeed been notified of our disappearance and they rang both parents right away and gave me and Spangles a cup of tea in a little interview room.

The policeman said that kids like us should know better.

By the time Spangles' mum arrived it was dark and snow was falling again.

She said a curt hello to me and gave Spangles a hug. 'I'm not angry,' she said. 'Just glad you're safe. You. Young man.' She looked at me with empty black eyes. 'Your mum and dad are out of their minds.'

Spangles' mum looked distant, like she was not really there. As she drove she seemed to drift away into some unreachable place full of deep unfixable problems. I held Spangles' hand in the back of the car. Like I was *in-the-moment-but-the-moment-was-actually-in-me.* As we approached Spangles' house, I wondered why Mrs Coan hadn't dropped me off first. Then the car stopped.

We were right next to the frozen pond. I shuddered.

Spangles' mum turned round to us.

'Can you both get out? It's a bit slippy getting up our drive. I might need a push.'

We opened the door, clambered out and set off up the greasy narrow lane to Spangles' house. Then we heard a tyre squeal and turned to see that Spangles' mum had driven the car on to the frozen pond.

Spangles' hand flew to her mouth. 'Oh.'

I ran towards the car. The ice cracked a little, but the car stayed on the surface. We could see that Spangles' mother was sitting very still, her head thrown back, her eyes squeezed shut, her hands tight on the steering wheel in textbook ten past two position.

'Mum, no!' Spangles tried to run out on to the ice, but I grabbed her. 'Listen, you run and ring 999. I'll stay here. Go now!'

I watched Spangles disappear off towards the house and kept my eye on the car, which was tilting slowly forward. I remembered what she had said the night she rescued our car off the ice, about how it would feel to drown in freezing water, the enveloping, the nothingness and the cold grey cloud.

'Mrs Coan,' I called out, 'Mrs Coan, Mrs Coan, don't move. We'll get you, don't worry.'

The car tilted forward, the ice groaned, then all was still.

26

The train pulled out of Whitehaven past a churning grey sea fluffed at the edges with nitrate-nourished orange. It veered east towards Carlisle where Doreen and Eric had to change for Manchester.

Doreen whisked out a leaflet – 'Days Out In Manchester' – and explained to Eric what she was going to do.

'Granada Museum – see where *Corry* is made, then it's the opera house for the *Les Misérables* matinée, then I want to go to Kendals.' She took in a deep breath. 'I think I might have something to eat, possibly in that Simply Heathcotes place. You will pay those people, won't you?'

'They'll be paid.'

He dragged his eyes from the melancholy farmland, punctuated by stacks of black bin-linered cylinders, down to the pink mesh tights that held Doreen's thighs, to her feet in strappy black heels. She was all wrapped up in a feline perfume that seemed to tug him down. Her painted nails, long and tapering, sawn off square at the end, rattled against the sides of the coffee carton.

'It's made such a difference to me, this extra money. My friends at Bruno's, that's the hairdresser's, say that it's taken years off me. I had my face *ironed* the other day.' She slapped at her cheeks. 'Can you tell?'

'Yes, it looks . . . fresher.'

'I'm to have it done once a month, they said. Then I'm

having this fluid injected – so that you can't frown any more. Botox, from botulism. It takes years off you and I have to say it works. Then I'm having collagen injected into the top of my lip.' She pushed her lips into a pink rosebud. Then she showed him her fingernails: French manicured. 'Very square. It's trendy – not round. He goes, I hate it, I go, I don't care.'

Eric watched her mouth move as she talked; she worked her lips carefully so as not to disturb her make-up. Eric wondered who the *he* was.

'Last week I had seaweed treatment. I take everything off – everything – and it's very *fishy*. Green stuff over every bit of me, even under the soles of my feet. Bruno says I've been under the shadow of Saturn for eight years and I'm only now beginning to see a way out.'

Eric looked out of the window and thought of his new Saab. It had been towed to a garage in Whitehaven. He had told Charlotte that it was a present from a client – a rich businessman he had advised on debts. She had no idea all his clients were poverty stricken. She imagined, and he had never contradicted her, that he advised struggling financial wizards on how to maximize tax breaks by buying forests.

He thought back to the car that had run him off the road. A Volvo. Big enough to pull a caravan. So there might be some link there. Greg? It didn't seem likely. But Greg was violent, that they knew. He pictured Greg on stage with Hoovercock, all those years ago, stripped to the waist, his 14-hole Cherry Doc Martens up on the monitor, blood streaming down his face from where he'd slashed his scalp with his light bulb, fisting the air, bellowing into the mic, which was almost down his throat, his angry eyes burning into the audience. But could Greg have kidnapped Pedro? And why? Just to put the fear of god into Eric?

I'm gonna rip your fucking liver out and eat it.

At the cashpoint Doreen held the roll of notes away from him for an irritating moment. He was to make sure he paid this – she laughed bitterly – 'company'. Her square-ended talons scraped the air in inverted commas.

27

The overspill was brightly lit. Low-rise blocks made bridges for the eye between each high tower. It was eerily quiet. A man was talking into an intercom and a crackly voice spat back at him: 'She's not in, fuck off!' The word *off* echoed off the buildings all around. The man shook his head and walked away, swinging a milk crate. Eric pushed the button for the flat number he had been given and got nothing. He waited in the silence. Car tyres fluttered on the nearby dual carriageway, a generator hummed and from somewhere the mewling of a baby swooped in and out, low in the mix.

He pushed the button again. Nothing.

He was about to try the flat next door when from the dark passageway a narrow-shouldered young man appeared and glided up. He was short, wore a hooded top and had a bumfluffy goatee beard. His eyes were pink and watery and his skin looked spongy with a greyish glow to it. He was carrying a large grey mobile phone like the overspill mayor himself always did.

The man looked up at Eric dolefully. 'You here for Fokse?' It was a voice that knew many things, a voice that had dealt in conflict and become bored with it, a soft voice that carried violence in its contours. Eric had forgotten the overspill mayor had a real name. FOKSE. Pronounced foxy but you had to spell it f-o-k-s-e. He was very specific about that.

Up close the man's breath smelt of warm milk.

'Are you fucking with us?' he asked cheerfully. Eric said that he wasn't fucking with him and that he had the money along with the – and he paused before he said it – *tribute*.

'Because,' the man went on as if Eric hadn't spoken, 'my friend Fokse is a sparkling man, fucking sparkling, but he don't take crap from fuckers.'

'I've got it all,' Eric said, suddenly wishing he hadn't told this man anything. The man might not be a friend of Fokse's at all; he might be from a rival gang, or just a chancer.

The man raised his mobile and tip-tapped a few numbers. Something glinted in the dusty brown glass lozenge.

'McFarlane. That you?' The pink eyes searched Eric's face.

Eric nodded.

'How you going to pay? No credit card shit.'

Eric pulled a triangular plastic sandwich carton from his bag.

The man rolled his watery eyes and folded his arms. He glanced over his shoulder, mumbling, 'C'mon c'mon.'

Eric beckoned the man closer and handed him the sandwiches. The man let the corner of his lip rise up into a sneer, took the package but kept his arm outstretched. 'Whoa whoa whoa what are you doing, cuntface?'

'It's in there.'

The man peered through the grey corrugated plastic at the ham and salad sandwiches.

Eric had removed the ham and salad and stuffed the twenties inside. The man squinted harder, held the box towards the porch light from the flats, then gave a couple of giggly laughs, his face crinkling around the eyes. 'You are,' he said to Eric through an amazed expression, 'a fucking head-the-ball. Will you look at that. Money in a sandwich. Who's going to steal a fucking sandwich? I'll tell Fokse about this and he'll think it's a fuck of a laugh.' He said this to Eric as if he thought Eric would be proud at the anticipation of causing, even indirectly, merriment in Fokse. Then he stopped. 'Wait a minute. What the fuck's this five p for?'

'That's your change,' Eric said, 'from the forty-nine ninety-five charge.'

'What fucking charge?'

'My delivery charge. You know? Like Fokse's collection charge? Well, that's my delivery charge. Funny, it's the same amount, isn't it?'

'Fokse won't be happy,' the man said, shaking his head with an air of sad finality, before gliding away into the dark passageway.

28

Corbieres was the only bar in Manchester to stock Jennings and the only bar in Manchester with the Fall's version of 'White Lightning' on the jukebox, which Eric selected along with a few of their other favourites.

Julie took a careful sip of her beer, avoiding getting her Modigliani nose involved in the foam at the top of the glass, and shuffled up close. Eric smelt surgical spirit, sharp chemical notes reminding him she spent her days forcing sharpened steel through bodies in her current job at the tattooist's. Back at her flat she had showed him how to remove the Prince Albert, his cock piercing, and offered him literature on how to take care of it, but he had assured her he wouldn't be keeping it in.

There was no one else in the bar and they sat in silence looking at the jukebox, waiting for their songs to begin. But there must have been some sort of problem with the machine, because all it did was dribble out static and burp white noise.

'The guy came round,' said Julie after a time, 'the over-spill mayor, and he starts talking to me like I'm shit, you know.' She swilled the beer around the top of her glass so that it nearly leapt out. 'He tells me I'm in trouble if this debt doesn't get paid and then, wait till you hear this, he starts coming on to me, saying he knows my type, all that, saying maybe there's another way he and I can sort the problem. It was like he thought I was some Jilly's Rock-world indie night chick or something.' She took a long drink. Eric found something heroic in Julie's tales of the city: the ducking, the diving, the drug deals, the raves, the muggings, beatings, the overspill estates. Each day a tangle of unmeasured hopes, threats and possibilities.

Julie continued: 'Anyway, I told him I didn't know where you were and he told me to make sure I let him know as soon as I found out and that he'd be back in a week to check I was OK. What with mixing with people that borrow money and don't pay it back, I wanted to be careful and all that. Can you fucking believe the cheek? Then you rang. Weird or what?'

'Don't worry. I've paid him. Just now, over at the estate.'

They sat in silence again. Eric went over to the jukebox and fed it a second time, adding a kick to its side just to make sure.

Nothing.

'Have you brought those weird photos you were telling me about?' said Julie.

He tipped the caravan photographs on to the table. Several had been ripped up then taped back together. Eric had thought carefully before asking anyone else's opinion; Julie's fascination was certain: she was obsessed with all conspiracy theories.

Julie picked up one of the caravan photographs and looked at it for a long time.

'We must discover what caravans mean,' she said, 'in dreams and in symbolic language.' She went on to talk about the significance of the caravan in Romany culture, as a symbol of escape and of freedom, but Eric couldn't concentrate. Julie had a new piercing – a silver ring in the middle of her lower lip. It had a little ball on it and, as she spoke, the ball jumped up the hoop, now and again landing in her mouth to be tongued out again the way a cat laps milk.

'So we can assume several things from the pictures,' she was saying. 'There is a clear sequence.' She laid the caravans out in a row. There were fourteen. They had been coming regularly for three weeks, at unpredictable times on unpredictable days. She had found a pattern and it wasn't the sequence in which they had arrived. She ordered them as to age. The most modern, a large static caravan on a big site, was first, and last was a tiny caravan with big rusted wheels which seemed to be in some sort of farmyard and had chickens standing on its roof.

'We can also sequence them by speed, I think.' And she moved a few around as if she were doing a tarot reading. The fastest (well, the one Julie thought would be fastest) was the streamlined American one Eric had received from the Lemon Man. The last, the chicken's mobile home. 'Does that tell you anything?'

'But why would someone send me these? What do they say to *me*? That's what I want to know. Is it just a nutter or is it serious?'

'Everything is serious, everything has a meaning, you know that, I've told you so often.' The silver ball shot into her mouth and she flicked it out again, saying, 'OK. Let's see. You live in a house. That's the opposite of a caravan for a start. A house is grounded, static, doesn't go anywhere. So that's you. You don't go anywhere.'

'But I do. I go here.' He indicated the pub around him.

'Caravans are freedom, but they jam up the roads, they are socially unacceptable.' Julie took a long drink of her Jennings, leaving a foam moustache on her top lip. 'Caravans are freedom for people who pretend to be free, those who think freedom can be a . . . a prison . . . a prison on wheels.' She had trapped the silver ball on the top of her lip and was rolling it backwards and forwards with her tongue, thinking. 'Who do you know like that, who thinks like that?'

She went on to order them by shade – the lightest to the darkest – by size, by number of wheels, by the setting (countryside, town, sea) but none of the sequences told a story to Eric, or said anything to him about himself or about his vague and intangible enemy.

They drank more Jennings and went through every possible meaning of the word *caravan* and got nowhere. And all that night the jukebox never coughed out a single tune.

Finally, Eric snatched up one of the photos and scrutinized the back. 'What about the words? Can you help me with those?' And it was then, as he sat gazing at the dull, even text, wearing its seriffed grey font like a formal suit, that he saw it, a magic eye picture shooting out at him:

coerce – harass – demands – manner – occasion –
threat – publicity – accompanied – calculated –
family – household – alarm – distress – humiliation

These were the words of the Administration of Justice Act 1970 Section 40 Harassment of a Debtor. 'A person commits an offence if, with the object of *coercing* another person to pay money claimed from the other as a debt due under a contract he *harasses* the other with *demands* for payment which, in respect of their frequency or the *manner* or *occasion* of making any such demand, or of any *threat* of *publicity* by which any demand is *accompanied*, are *calculated* to subject him or members of his *family* or *household* to *alarm, distress* or *humiliation*.'

Julie's voice came through a mist. 'Forget all that now. There's something I want you to help me with back at the flat. Remember Brainbloodvolume? You promised.'

Julie's room was gloomy, dimly lit. The main source of lighting was a car-mechanic's inspection torch set on the floor, its lead running to a car battery. Julie's other appliances were plugged into four-gang sockets which in turn were plugged into another four-gang socket whose white tail snaked along the floor and out of the window. She followed his eyes. 'It goes into the neighbour's. I give her a fiver a week and run everything off that. The car battery's great for the lights and the telly. I got cut off for fiddling the meter.'

A weak pink glow came from the bulb behind the fake-coal front of the two-bar electric fire. The disc that simulated flickering flames had long stopped spinning. Julie slotted a CD into the player: Loop Guru – a soft bass muttering like the beating of wings overlaid with clinky primal percussion, ethnic chants and fluty warblings.

She took Eric's hand. 'Remember in the barn? I told you all about it. You said no. I was hoping you'd change your mind.'

'I know. I remembered. I have it with me,' Eric said, and from his pocket took out the dark purple box he'd dug up on the top of the mountain.

'Thanks for hunting it down. It means a lot to me. Look, in here. It's all ready.'

A sterilizer hissed, boiling water rumbled.

Julie washed the trepan carefully then placed it in the sterilizer. Silver implements clinked together and there was a smell, a sterile smell, reminding Eric of the smell of farms and disinfectant in the barn in Maryport when she'd told him all about this, and it brought back the smell of her hair back then and the feel of her breath on his face, and then he remembered the little song she used to hum to him all the time, a Monty Python song called 'Eric the Half a Bee', and she'd hum it under her breath when they were together and he knew when he heard her humming 'Eric the Half a Bee' that she had been thinking of his name and his name had triggered the song and it had never left her head, and she was humming it now and Eric didn't know what to do. He stood there listening to the sterilizer hissing, considering his task. He imagined the whole thing from start to finish as a scratchy loop of speeded up film; the first cut, neat, the way you'd trim wallpaper round a light switch; blisters of blood oozing, a splash of white gleaming through. A dull screak, like a needle into chalk. Saw teeth rasping like fingernails on brick. A churning sound, like a distant washing machine. An enormous slurp, then dark liquid rising and falling in a pulsating rhythm. Julie's limp, bleached face, smiling up at him, happy, happy, happy, singing his song, the 'Half a Bee' song.

He watched her in the kitchen as she lifted the instruments from the water with tongs and laid them in a glittering row on a towel.

Then she came towards him, bobbed out her tongue and placed on it a tiny picture of Ren and Stimpy. She swallowed, giggling, then handed him a syringe of anaesthetic, its needle fine, slender, a trembling drop of fluid clinging to its tip.

'I can't,' he said to her. 'I can't hurt you.'

Julie took his hand and squeezed it. 'Remember how my mother was? Back then?'

Eric thought of the icy pond – the cold grey cloud her mother had wanted to embrace.

'Those feelings,' Julie went on, 'that darkness. It drips down through the generations. This will be my release.'

He looked into Julie's face. The light from the car inspection torch put wispy bars of shadow on her skin.

Apartfromtheobvious picks the last few pieces of toaster trim off the floor and drops the silvery shards into a freezer bag. Puts them on the sideboard in front of the photographs that go from his first day at school to his wedding. A pink round face growing thin and wary over the years. His wedding picture: flares and wide ties.

Thump. He looks to the ceiling, waits for another. None comes. Grey-eyed man went meekly into the loft, said he would be glad of the privacy.

He picks up the wedding photo. Behind the happy couple is a red van with the words *Waste Disposal* in white. Everything a waste.

Groaning sound from above, then a creak. Prisoner moving about. His prisoner. Apartfromtheobvious has started to feel proud of his captive; it is as if he has made him, as if he owns him. The hatred is starting to go away; he's beginning to feel affectionate towards him. It's the way you might feel if you had to look after a friend's dog and even though you actually hated dogs, hated even that particular dog, having it in the house and looking after it made you come to like it. He doesn't want his revenge any longer. Lost the appetite. But he *has* to have it. Has to taste revenge, taste it then spit it out if needs be. He's made a deal with himself. How many times has he made deals with himself in the past and not kept to them? That's his problem. He will do everything he promises himself from now on. He isn't going to mess this up the way he messed up the marriage.

He sets the photograph back on the sideboard, goes to the kitchen and switches on the tape. 'How Does it Feel?' wows and flutters into shape, wobbly. A crinkly length of tape he Sellotaped back together after his car cassette chewed it.

Clunk of the first mortice lock on the back door, then the second, then the Yale key goes in and he hears the door being pushed. He has kept the bolt shot across. For a moment he considers whether to keep her out. But she knows too much. She is too involved. He opens the door.

'What's all the water?' Magnum says, looking down at his feet.

A river of water an inch deep is running down the hall. He hadn't noticed.

'Christ!' He runs to the bottom of the stairs. It's pouring down from above, the ceiling is sagging under the weight, water streaming through the light fittings, bulbs sparking blue and yellow lines.

'Shut the leccy off!' He calls out and runs up the stairs. A torrent is coming down in the back bedroom. The water tank in the loft. He runs back down the stairs. 'Shut the water off. At the mains!'

'Where's the mains?'

'Under the sink, you idiot. Oh Christ!' he says, 'I'll do it.'

He turns off the main but water continues to gush. Runs through the house twirling taps. In the hall he sees the grey-eyed man's leg come through the landing ceiling and kick in the air. Apartfromtheobvious watches the detached leg move against the ceiling like some undersea plant waving around for food. Then the man falls through the ceiling, hits the banister and lands on the stairs. Water cascades down, plaster and dirty clumps of grit everywhere. Fluffy orange loft insulation hangs sodden from the ceiling hole, like swathes of thick skin flayed from an animal. Grey Eyes man lies groaning, tries to lift himself up. Lights fizz out.

29

Doreen came dancing slowly and dreamily through the bar of the Midland Hotel as if to the sound of a wah-wahing trombone. Eric was too exhausted to even speak. He sat there, smiling wanly, and allowed Doreen to buy him drink after drink after drink while she told him about *Les Misérables*, the shops, the restaurants and cafés, and the peculiar Mancunian characters she'd encountered.

Eric felt gluey all over, his body throbbing with the sticky secretions of stress.

He didn't even remember getting in the lift, then all of a sudden they were in a hotel room and, on a bed that lurched and swayed before him, Doreen lay in her pink mesh stockings suspended by a complicated maroon basque, strappy high heels still on her feet, hooking a finger at him with one hand while pouring champagne with the other. All that was lacking were the words *Serving suggestion* written on the headboard.

He was woken in the early hours by Doreen snoring. On his way to the bathroom he caught sight of himself in the mirror, Doreen's maroon basque bulging at the front where Eric was developing a little paunch, the pink mesh stockings drooping down below his knees. *Before we evolved into land mammals*, he heard himself saying to Doreen, *there would have been no contact during sex – the egg and sperm would have fertilized in the water. All this internal bit is new.*

He looked to where Doreen lay, comfortable in Eric's jeans and T-shirt, and fell into a soft chair by the window. He watched the sun coming up over the city, a glass of flat champagne in one hand, the other absently stroking Doreen's foot. He felt in his pocket to check that the small hard disc of bone was safe.

Three

30

The maximum punishment for bankruptcy fraud is seven years' imprisonment, so Eric felt a little nervous as he parked the car outside Whitehaven County Court. He noticed Doreen further up the street, climbing out of the passenger seat of her old Allegro. The man dropping her off was short and squabby, and he spoke to Doreen for a few moments. He had curly hair and cowboy boots. It was Mr Friday. Eric hoped he wasn't there to object to the bankruptcy order. But Mr Friday had driven Doreen to the appointment. Eric watched as they spoke, her nodding, him spreading his hands every now and again, now pointing to the building, now to himself, now to her. Then Mr Friday looked all around him and gave her a push (or was it another kind of touch?) towards the court and drove off.

Doreen handed the completed bankruptcy petition forms over in triplicate, signed and dated correctly, and the pinch-faced clerk blinked to show surprise.

'Are you representing yourself, Mrs Jackson?'

She smiled. 'My adviser has come along to help me out,' she said and indicated Eric, who was pretending to read a leaflet. The man nodded.

Eric hadn't spent any time with Doreen since the night in the Midland Hotel. She'd rung him a few times, and he'd spotted her Allegro belching white clouds of exhaust fumes outside the advice shop while she sat peering at the doorway, waiting for him to come out, but his message to her was clear: no more hotels. No more of that. She'd been a little upset about the non-contact sex concept and the swapping of clothes; she'd thought Eric was making fun. He'd assured her it was his preferred method. But now she'd thought about it, she was beginning to like the idea. In fact, she felt she had discovered a secret underground river within herself, a racing stream of berserk desires. Eric made it clear they would not be exploring this underground stream together.

Today, she made a straight stiff smile at him, as neat as a tuck stitched into a fat cushion, and dealt with him with brisk, cool efficiency.

The clerk flicked through the application, now and again sucking in through his teeth – once, on the page detailing amounts owed, noticeably shaking his head in disapproval. He sent them in then to see the judge, who read through the papers and looked for a long time at Doreen.

'So, Mrs Jackson, you know what you're doing, do you?'

'Yes,' she said, 'I do.' He continued to look at her. 'I really have tried to pay but –'

He cut her off. 'I'm sure your adviser has explained that the official receiver will go through the details. I'm making a bankruptcy order today, at fourteen minutes past twelve precisely.' He scribbled casually with a fountain pen and looked admiringly for a moment at the well-proportioned scrawl.

The official receiver was impossibly young, a pink face with crimson cheeks, hair falling in curls over white-bread good looks that had walked off a knitting pattern. He looked as though he'd just been running and laughing at the same time.

Two chairs had been placed opposite him ready for Eric and Doreen.

'Good morning,' he said grimly, shaking first Doreen's then Eric's hand. 'Let's find out what's been going wrong.'

Doreen seated herself without being asked and crossed her legs cockily. 'Well, I've been having a little financial difficulty, as you can see. Frankly, I've been stupid. And I will use the term –' she pushed her tongue into her cheek making a big lump '– *deceived* throughout. You will hear that word from me often, I am afraid.' She threw a quick look at Eric.

'I understand,' said the official receiver. 'So what we're going to do is this. We're going to go through some paper-work and then we will see where we are. Once I know where we are, I can see where the whole thing is going to go. OK?'

He spoke only to Doreen. Other than when Eric offered useful information, he ignored him altogether. He had a slim blue wad of paper like a school exercise book which was lined and had a space for a signature on every page. He began to write on it and didn't stop writing until the interview was over, two hours later.

Eric fumbled in his pocket. The disc of bone, five p-sized, wrapped in a tissue. He had kept it close since he got home – a difficult object to explain to Charlotte. Julie had left a strange message on his voicemail at work after he left her: *It hadn't gone through, it hadn't gone through, call me.* He didn't know what she meant. Here was the bone, here was the proof. He'd been ringing her day after day. He'd tried the shop, the flat, local pubs – nothing. It had been nearly a week.

The official receiver moved on to life history – where and how did Doreen live? He went right back, every job, every relationship, every address, even to when she left school and her qualifications. He had a sharp voice that came in little snapping stabs and his knitting-pattern lips formed a prim O-shape after every response. He asked several questions about her early marriage and her son, and although Doreen kept referring to the nail-bar man, he didn't seem interested in him at all.

'What I'm looking for,' he explained at one point, 'are offences committed under the Insolvency Act. Things like loans gained illegally, fraudulent dealings with goods bought on credit, transactions under the value – that means things you've sold at lower than their worth to keep money from your creditors – and concealed goods, money or assets.'

But when he reached the part about assets he seemed uninterested in the video players, TVs, tables, chairs, washing machines, tumble dryers, CD players, microwaves. He shrugged them off with a 'Well, we all have to live, don't we?' He did seem interested in vehicles, however, and in particular the Saab 900 on the conditional sale with Trucker Finance. 'We might have to take a look at that later,' he said ominously, adding, 'Any jewellery worth much? Just dress jewellery is it?' She smirked at him and he smiled back as if to say 'I understand.' He was like a cunning second-hand dealer at a house clearance, squinting cynically at her possessions, mocking her foolish ambitions, her immature values, her tacky taste.

Eric grew uncomfortable when the official receiver began to move down the list of credit agreements. When was the agreement taken out? What was the money used for? Where were the goods she had bought? And if these goods had been sold, how much did she receive? And where did that money go? He was particularly interested in whether she was making regular payments to Mr Friday and about the nature of her relationship with Shopaloan. The official receiver was following a thread and Eric was holding one end; if he took the right turning he and Eric would be cheek to cheek.

At the end of the interview the official receiver asked Doreen to sign every page. This took another twenty minutes. Then he began asking about the mysterious nail-bar man. His last address. And he took all that money? And all those goods? Did he? Did he really? Had she told the police? Eric shifted in his seat. She hadn't told the police. They hadn't thought of that.

She pointed at a box of tissues on the official receiver's desk, he handed her one, and she blew her nose into it loudly. When she removed it from her face there were traces of tears.

'No,' she said, 'I haven't. There didn't seem any point.'

'I understand it's upsetting,' the official receiver said. 'But this nail-bar gentleman, it could be a case of undue influence. No doubt,' he said, looking up at Eric who was twisting a paperclip into a distressed shape, 'Mr McFarlane has investigated that aspect of the law thoroughly.'

At what submerged secret was he tugging, what loose threads had he found?

Eric placed the paperclip on the desk. 'Yes. Of course. Undue influence was something we initially explored. But the legal cost seemed prohibitive and, as Mrs Jackson had no money, she agreed that bankruptcy was the best option.'

The knitting pattern looked at Eric blankly. 'Best?'

'Well, not a good option, but best in the circumstances.'

'Let's hope that turns out to be the case, Mr McFarlane.'

31

'Now, Bernard,' Marjorie instructed, 're-enter the room as if you were walking into the Incapacity Benefit Appeal Tribunal.'

Bernard flicked open the door, trotted lightly across the floor and lowered himself smoothly into the chair. He swung his upper body round with a healthy whipping motion and said good morning with a cheery sing-song lilt.

Marjorie, the mock-chair of this mock-appeal tribunal, shook her head. 'Bernard: you cannot enter an incapacity appeal tribunal in that way. Remember the appeal tribunal are expecting to see somebody who is so ill that he is unable to work. Now, *I* know you are too ill to work, we all know it. But the appeal tribunal have never seen you before; this is the only time they will see you in action. It's no good skipping in like a gazelle. Try it again. This time, slowly; try to remember what it was like when you first had the pain; let the pain register in your posture and in your face. Watch me.' She went outside the door and came back in. 'Close the door slowly. As you push the door, it's hurting, it's hurting to close it. When you finally click the door shut, you sigh like this – aaah – and then you turn to take on the next task – crossing the room. Remember, for you everything is an epic journey, an enormous task. You pause frequently, you take your time, you cover only small distances with each step and after each step, you survey how much you have left to do.' Marjorie baby-stepped across the room to the table at which the 'tribunal' (Pedro and Eric) sat. 'So you've crossed the room. Fine. But the journey isn't over. You have to sit down. Pull the chair a long way out like this, and sit down slowly. Once you've sat down, don't relax. Raise your head to face them, but not quickly; imagine your head is on a rusty ball socket – it grates when you tilt it, your neck is a poisoned ball of nerves, you are in constant, constant pain.'

Bernard re-entered in the manner she had suggested. Eric had to admit, this time he was good. The appeal tribunal was tomorrow so everything had to be perfect.

He found Marjorie sitting on the church wall that ran around the St Cuthbert's Centre, smoking. She was worried about Bernard's case. She had absolutely no confidence in her ability to represent him at the tribunal. Would Eric help her? Go through the main points, read through her written submission? He would, but he insisted they should do it in the pub. She agreed, if he promised not to let her get drunk, because once she started, well – and the appeal hearing was at ten-thirty sharp.

At her feet were a number of shopping bags from local clothes shops and he helped her to gather them up.

In the pub they looked at Bernard's papers for five minutes and agreed that his demeanour would speak for itself – he would win the appeal tribunal no problem at all. As long as the tribunal knew nothing about him leading K'chaa!!, working as volunteer treasurer for the advice shop and all his other community work, he'd be fine. They should get more beer and talk about other things. It was relaxation she needed.

Marjorie got in more Jennings. Eric liked it that she went to the bar – West Cumbrian women normally didn't.

The clock in the Derby went from 3.00 to 4.30.

'More beer?'

'Sure.'

The clock went from 4.30 to 5.30.

'More beer?'

They had now had five pints, Marjorie keeping up swallow for swallow. The hippy barman was playing *Sabbath Bloody Sabbath*. 'Trapped inside my embryonic cell,' shrieked Ozzy. The album cover propped against the lager pump showed red winged devils hovering over a bed. The barman piled up albums to fall down one by one and play in a pancake stack with no regard to the deterioration of the vinyl surfaces. Eric saw from the other airbrushed covers scattered over the bar that the discs waiting to grind around on top of Sabbath were no improvement.

But the music didn't matter. He was with Marjorie. They were in a pub. They were talking and laughing. He was with a woman who had the word *thrill* tattooed on the back of her wrist. What more could he want?

6.30.

Marjorie lifted her chin and looked down at him through sleepy eyes.

'More beer?'

A sixth pint of Jennings stood before them. They looked at the two white-hatted brown cylinders, not moving to take a drink. The beer had given Marjorie a blotchy red face, she had begun to slur and her sentences staggered in circles around the same theme, over and over again, about Pedro and how they should find out what happened to him. 'Aren't you worried that it is you these sickos are looking for, Eric? I mean, what exactly are the police doing? They don't seem to be getting anywhere.'

Eric had an idea. They should go and see the house where Pedro was abducted to see if there were any clues.

'Thing is Eric,' she said. 'I still don't know what to wear to the tribunal tomorrow.' She explained how her intention had been to spend the rest of the evening trying on clothes. When she did this, she lowered her eyelids and squinted at him, as if she wasn't quite sure who he was. She would come with him to the house, she said, as long as he would look at some of the clothes she had bought – she indicated the large collection of shopping bags – and help her choose the right thing. After all, he had represented at many appeal tribunals, he knew what would be best.

'I'll have a look,' said Eric, 'but I'm not a fashion consultant.'

She knew that.

They bought a four-pint carry out and left the pub.

Outside was a vicious rain, a numbing rain, blinding sheets of it, drops rolling off the walls, bouncing off the pavement, ankle-deep puddles on the road. They stood for a time blinking, thickly drunk, wobbly. Then they held hands and ran all the way, taking a short cut over the White Stuff, grey beneath the stinging curtain of rain.

The abduction house was on the Leconfield Estate, a collection of flat-roofed grey boxes thrown up some time in the 1970s, now a graveyard for stolen and burnt out cars, where clutches of teenagers sat with their snouts in bags of Plastic Wood, waiting to go into the army. Behind the estate, on Cleator Moor's biscuit-tin-lid backdrop, you could see creamy waterfalls barging down the scrubby sheep-chewed fells.

They hesitated in the garden, and Eric peered through the broken panes of glass, the shredded curtains. In the gloom he could see that the police had taken away the plastic chair, but there was no crime scene tickertape. Eric banged on the near collapsed door. Nothing came back. He motioned to Marjorie and they went inside.

The dust on the floor had coagulated into the sort of soft grey wool a hamster would sleep in, and was studded with bottles and cans, syringes too. By the door was a mound of junk mail and free newspapers. They looked at the addresses – mostly *The Occupier*, a couple of names they didn't recognize.

There was no electric and the only light was from the lamp outside, which gave everything a soft peachy tinge.

'Pedro got as far as the living room. He would have sat about here.' Eric stood in the centre of the room looking about. He glanced down and peeled a sliver of brown parcel tape off the floor. He held it up for Marjorie and she gave a large sigh.

Then she dropped her shopping bags and pointed to a pile of sofa cushions.

'Sit down, Eric. First things first. Before it gets too dark I want you to have a look at these clothes.'

Eric sat down cautiously on the filthy cushions, pulled his long legs up to his chin and waited as she disappeared into the back room of the house to try on the first tribunal outfit. He was to wait there and she would come out as if she was entering the tribunal room. He should tell her exactly what she looked like – exactly, mind you; she didn't mind the truth.

A tall mirror leaned against the back-room wall and in it he watched her remove her skirt and fold it. Without it she appeared taller for the length of nylon-clad leg. He thought of her own mirror at home and the memories it would hold in the mercury behind its glass, a thousand naked Marjories.

She bent to place the skirt on top of the shopping bags, momentarily suspended in an arabesque. Then she disappeared from the mirror, reappearing with her legs encased in a different colour, a thin brown, a coating of pale chocolate, almost not there. She tugged her blouse over her head and let it sail to the floor. Her bra was white, childish, nipping her small breasts into uptilted scoops. She disappeared again then appeared in the mirror wearing a dark brown suit in which she shuffled out, in stockinged feet, over the fag ends and bottle caps, and asked him to imagine she was wearing black court shoes with a kitten heel. She pushed herself up on tiptoes to help him imagine the shoes. Her feet looked dainty, pointed, arched. Eric shook his head firmly; the suit wasn't right. Too assistant-shoe-shop-manager.

Three outfits later they agreed on a blue jacket, blue trousers, cherry-red Doc Martens. She changed back into her short skirt so she wouldn't mess up the tribunal gear, then found some mugs in the kitchen and rinsed them with beer. Eric watched her bumping into the kitchen units, dropping the plastic beer carton, laughing.

She sat next to Eric on the floor, handed him his mug and he balanced it on his knee. Some kids across the street were trying to hook a bicycle tyre over a lamp post and it made a swooping and spinning shadow on the wall as it sailed up and up with each failed attempt.

Eric sipped at the beer. The mug was sticky around the rim with old coffee granules. The ribbed sofa cushion kept catching at the undersides of Marjorie's thighs as she crossed and uncrossed her legs, making a hissing sound.

Marjorie rolled on to her front with a crunch and a snap of bottle fragments and lay with one leg in the air, balancing her shoe precariously on her foot. 'So why do you do this job, Eric?'

'I thought it would help people. My dad wanted me to be a vet like him.' A myth had been fostered in the family that Eric was 'political' and couldn't be expected to go into the veterinary business.

Her shoe fell off her foot and she rolled on to her back. 'You think Pedro quite enjoyed being captured and tied up?'

'He likes the attention now, I think. But at the time – you know, don't tell him I told you this – but he pissed himself.'

The shadow of the bicycle tyre, a dark blurry ellipse, soared across the wall and then its lip caught the top of the lamppost and it hula-hooped down the length of the post. There was a loud cheer from the kids.

'I don't think that's unusual.'

Then, quite unheralded, Eric knelt down beside Marjorie and put his hand on her pale-chocolate-coated inner thigh. Marjorie looked at him sternly, crinkle-lipped, and wagged her finger in his face like a metronome; those lanes were coned off. He followed the diversion and removed his hand. They looked at each other for a time, he smiling, she schoolmarm reproachful.

A hard rapping on the door burst the moment. They waited. The knock came again. It was now completely dark. The kids with the bicycle tyre had gone.

The door opened and a small figure in a heavy coat swished a torch beam over the pile of mail, kicked at it, then bent and extricated a letter.

Eric and Marjorie watched in silence and the figure disappeared. They ran to the window and saw the person ducking off around the corner. A car started up followed by a squeal of tyres.

'Some mail drop?' said Eric. 'Empty property fraud? That sort of thing? Maybe that's why they got Pedro – he'd disturbed their scam.'

But as they left, Eric noticed something in the mail mountain. *Caravanning Today*, three cellophaned virgin copies.

32

At home Eric watched television, sitting up close, his hand on the remote. He drank two glasses of icy water. He felt dry, his insides sucked out. The effects of coming up out of a hangover while awake were unpleasant; he was used to falling asleep drunk, leaving his body to fight without him the dehydration and depletion of vitamins and minerals. He was tired. Charlotte was out at some meeting with tedious internet spods.

He shunted through the channels, eventually finding an Open University programme about sea squirts. The presenter wore a low-cut top and had brightly painted lips. She explained that the sea squirt spends its larval life swimming freely, capturing its own food, living its own life, making its own decisions. But in its adult state, it fixes itself to a rock and stays there. Food is no longer hunted out and nourishment is gained by filtering passing plankton. And because its new life is less demanding, the first thing it does is eat its own brain. The woman seemed to enjoy telling this part, like the favourite piece of food a child leaves on its plate for last.

Near midnight he got a call from Doreen. He imagined her looking out of her council-house window as she spoke, down into a dark yard. He was to come and meet her right away. It was urgent. He was to go to Number One Hollow where she would be waiting.

A blurry path threaded its way down the side of the old pit shaft that was Number One Hollow. The deep green water was still, the moonlight giving it a solid look that made Eric think of lime jelly. This deep brooding lagoon was a relic of the iron-ore mines and had a gloomy tragic quality, enhanced by the fact that it had claimed several children's lives – tangled up in its weeds, sucked through its ice, plunged into its deep centre from rafts of lashed-together doors.

In the beam of Doreen's headlights you could see toads mating in the water, motionless, stuck together, spawn streaming out behind them.

Doreen was sat on a rock looking at the toads. He sat alongside her. 'You think the official receiver interview went all right?' he asked.

'I hate it every single time.'

'You've done it before?'

'Over and over, it feels like. Interviews. Telling people stuff about me, about my insides, my debts, my spending. People, people like him, people like you. What's the difference? It's like I'm a car; they jack me up, crawl under me, see how I work.' She had her faraway look, the Valium curtains drawn over her face. As she spoke, she turned a small crucifix which hung from a chain around her neck.

'So what you want to see me for?'

'I thought you might want to swap clothes again?'

'I don't think . . .'

'I'm joking, McFarlane. You know, it's strange, it's all ended now. We've done it.'

'Almost.'

'All that juicy cash; good to have, good to hold, good to spend. Now this old purse is empty. I spent the lot. There must be something else we can do, something to get some more.'

A toad had crawled away from its amphibian orgy and

hop-jumped past them into the grass, its grey and brown back lumpy in the car headlights.

'I was thinking. You enjoyed it, Eric, didn't you? You liked the free cash. But it wasn't just the money, was it? It was getting it for nothing, stealing it. Well, now I need some more. There's things I need. Bruno's booked me in on this expensive programme at the salon. Injections into the face.' She turned from the toads and looked at him. Her pretty features looked stretched, taut as drum skin. 'Can you get any money out of the St Cuthbert's Centre?'

'What do you mean?'

She patted him on the shoulder, as a kitten bats a ball of paper. 'The funding from the council. Can you write cheques from their account? You could write me a cheque. Tell them I'm a supplier, I sold you a photocopier or something.'

Eric was silent. He thought hard, then said, 'I've got a better idea. What about a new centre? A skills and resource centre. Something to get people off benefits, out of debt and into work. Something to give them confidence, training – qualifications even. A bid to set up a new centre run along modern, measurable objectives with modern management – no hippies – and we can do what that fucker Bennett Lowe really wants to do – close down Cleator Moor Money Advice Shop.'

'Could you make an application like that? Is it so easy?'

'Doreen, it's a cinch. All we need to do is persuade the council that we already have part of the money from another funder – the lottery say, or a European fund, or Northern Rock – and then –' he was speaking to himself now, thinking aloud '– ask them to fund the difference.' Doreen was nodding and umming and yessing to every point he made, her eyes on the midges that made fuzzy swirling stalks out of the car headlamp beams.

Eric went on: 'I've got all the papers at work. I can forge a letter from the lottery offering us the money. I'll work out some figures and some paperwork. Next time I see you I will have an application form for you to sign. It's near the end of the financial year and I know that if the council can't find the right projects they'll have to send this money back.' He put his hand on hers. 'You are the chair of the management committee of the all new Cleator Moor Skills and Resource Centre.' Ideas streamed through his head, dragging more ideas behind them at a rate too fast to register. He knew he was on to something that would work.

Bubbles of spawn covered the green surface of Number One Hollow and, as Eric walked away, he could hear the toads making noises like cars pulling on handbrakes and the water slurping as they rose and fell between copulation.

33

He spent the next morning in Cleator Moor Library preparing the bid. He knew it would need to be European Regional Development Funds, knew West Cumbria was a priority area, knew Copeland District Council and Cumbria County Council had access to this money. And, most importantly of all, he knew that if the council hadn't allocated the funds to suitable projects by the end of the following week the money would have to be returned. He couldn't believe his luck with the timing. He filled in all the forms, disguising his handwriting, and made them ready for Doreen to sign. He hesitated, before writing the name Bernard Roberts down as treasurer, and then mocked up some offer letters from the National Lottery and Northern Rock, using the training materials picked up from Bennett Lowe's funding session.

THE CLEATOR MOOR SKILLS
AND RESOURCE CENTRE
ITS MISSION?
GETTING YOU OFF BENEFIT,
OUT OF DEBT, AND INTO WORK

He looked at the first page of the application.

Total cost of project (Capital + Revenue) £1,000,000.

Total income agreed: £400,000 (National Lottery Good Causes funds.)

Balance required from Cumbria County Council: £600,000.

It was looking good. At the library computer he invented bank account numbers (they never check these things) and fabricated a set of projected accounts for the next five years. He used a scanned-in bank letterhead to mock up a bank statement. After putting in the last few names and addresses of the various committee members, he sat back and stared across the library. A couple of men, wispy, under-fed, with apology in their posture, were reading the jobs pages of the local paper, slowly transcribing recruitment details on to what looked like pages torn from kids' exercise books. In these men, Eric saw himself, each of them a walking X-ray of Eric's insides, a template for all Cleator Moor men. These were the very men that might benefit from this fictional skills and resource centre. Maybe it was a shame it would never exist. Yet the more Eric thought about it, the less it appealed; there was something swashbuckling about digging people out of trouble; he wasn't as interested in being a mere preventer.

His opportunity to get the crucial signature on the application came later that day, when Bernard and Marjorie stormed into the office.

'That tribunal chairman, Bernard,' Marjorie was saying as they entered, 'is a bastard.' Bernard collapsed into a chair, threw his head into his hands.

'You have to know, Bernard, that this wasn't your fault. We have clear grounds for an appeal to the commissioners.' Marjorie was wearing the blue suit she and Eric had chosen together. It hadn't worked. She turned to Pedro and Eric. 'They asked him what TV programmes he liked to watch.'

Bernard looked up at her. His face was as red as if it had been boiled, his brow slimy with sweat.

'And Bernard says, innocently, "History, wildlife that sort of thing."'

Bernard moved his lips along with the re-enacted replies. He looked like he could sleep the sleep of every tired animal on the planet.

'"Mr Roberts," Professor Jones says, "you state on your form that you can sit for only fifteen minutes at a time, yet you regularly watch hours of documentary programmes on the *television*" – television pronounced as if it was some exotic technology introduced yesterday. I try to jump in at this point but he waves me down; can he take direct evidence from the claimant, please? Even the dozy gonzo from the Social is looking surprised. But what clinched it for their side was the anonymous donor who sent this.' Marjorie was brandishing a video-cassette. 'This is a tape recording – taken by hidden camera – of Bernard coming in and out of the St Cuthbert's Centre carrying large drums and percussion instruments and also – God knows who had access to the St Cuthbert's Centre to film this – lengthy footage of him leading K'chaa!! in a set of particularly vigorous samba sessions. As you can imagine, the tribunal didn't need to hear any more from me or Bernard.' Marjorie planted her hand on Bernard's shoulder. 'Don't worry, Bernard. We'll take it further. We have a very strong case. You were,' she gritted her teeth and beads of water blistered at the edges of her eyes, 'doing what anyone would do. Think about how it would have been had you not had a professional representative with you.'

Bernard peeled himself off the table surface like a man pulling himself off a Velcro wall. 'It's not the money, it's . . .' he tented his fingers and gazed through the triangle '. . . the feeling that I have to prove I'm not well, prove to others I'm not putting it on.'

It was much later, after they'd rerun the case a dozen times, deconstructed every legal concept, analysed every gesture, unpicked the definition of every word, that Eric finally found an opportunity to speak with Bernard.

'Bernard,' Eric said, 'I'm sorry, mate, but there's something I need your help with. I know it's a bad time, but it has to be done now. Something that needs your signature.'

And Bernard Roberts, volunteer treasurer, without even glancing at it, signed Doreen's funding application for the brand new million-pound skills and resource centre, before leaving for what he said was going to be his very last samba session for K'chaa!!

Bernard gone, they watched the video evidence. After the images of Bernard's extraordinarily athletic drumming had fizzed away, scenes from an old TV programme, the last thing taped, appeared on screen: a documentary about caravanning in the 1960s. Tiny little caravans tugged along by Ford Anglias, footage of breathlessly happy families playing ball games on caravan sites. Despite the circumstances, nobody could help laughing at this. No one apart from Eric. Because the caravan pictures hadn't stopped coming. More were appearing all the time, in all kinds of different places. The last one had been under his pillow. And to make matters worse, Charlotte had been talking to his dad about why Scooter died. And it turned out that Eric's dad had kept the real reason from them. It looked to him as though the poor cat might have been poisoned.

Eric didn't go home. He sat alone in the advice centre, watching the caravan tape over and over, and thinking about poor Scooter. Images of potential poisoners crowded his mind, darting figures in thick coats, laying down their deadly meat. He tried to fit all the people he knew into this template, faces flashing up like mugshots in a slide show, but to each one he said no, not him, no, not her, no, never, no, that's not the one. Not even the overspill mayor fitted, even though he was exactly the type. Eric kept getting snagged up on one name: Gregory Torkington, lead singer of Hoovercock, Greg the ex.

I'm going to rip your fucking liver out and eat it.

He picked up his keys and bag. He would have to see Greg and confront him.

34

Greg lived in Hillcrest, the posher part of Whitehaven, and it was easy to spy on him tonight because Greg was distracted. Incredibly, that evening was, Eric gathered from the notice on the garden gate, Hoovercock's annual reunion barbecue and Greg had booked a punkeoke band, so his garden teemed with balding, overweight, middle-aged punks, their biker jackets and ripped T-shirts buried deep under thick anoraks, gloves and woolly hats as they huddled around a huge bonfire, waiting for the fun to begin.

Eric wiped his hand, sticky from the buds, and parted the rhododendron leaves for a better view. The green-mohawked lead singer of the punkeoke outfit passed around a list of songs that the band were able to subject to the punkeoke treatment, then, after a few thrashed chords by his safety-pinned, bondage-trousered punkeoke backing band, he leapt up on stage.

'Hey, hey, hey, Greg! Ten years of Hoovercock, wow!'

Whoops, whistles, then Greg made a deep bow, took the microphone and went straight into 'Death to the Dead', everyone singing along. When it came to the bit when the younger Gregory used to remove his shirt and slash himself with a light bulb, the shirt came off, but the cutting – well, even Greg was too dignified for that sort of thing. Greg had the same menacing stage presence he'd had all those years ago in Whitehaven Civic Hall; the way he leaned in to the audience and glared was chilling. Eric pictured Greg creeping up the path with poisoned meat or slipping pictures of caravans through doors.

Caravans. Next to the house was a garage. It would be worth checking – that would clinch it. There was a side door into the garage and, leading to this, a path which skirted the edge of the gravel drive. Eric got down on his belly and began to slither alongside the hedge. If he could reach the garage before Greg finished the song . . . He pushed himself along with his elbows, keeping his head down low, nose brushing the earth. What were the five rules of concealment? *Shape, shine, shadow, silhouette –* what was the other one? He had learned it on the one day he spent in the army cadets. Something beginning with S for movement.

Clapping, cheering, the green-mohawked punkeoke man saying, 'Yes, yes, that was brilliant. Now Greg's wife Sandra is going to do "Sugar Sugar", the Archies, yeh!' and Sandra Melon, the Ennerdale farm girl Charlotte said could carry a sheep under each arm, lolloped up on stage and took the mic.

Then the garage door opened and a little boy in *Lion King* pyjamas asked Eric what he was doing.

Eric smiled at him. 'Hello. What's your name?'

'Mikey.'

'Mikey. You not asleep yet?'

'No. Didn't wanna to go to bed. Wannaed to stay up for punkeoke. What you doing. Is it hide and seek?'

'Yes. Yes.' Eric said, seizing on it, 'that's what it is. Hide and seek. Listen, don't make a sound.' Eric put his finger to his lips. 'Can I come in there and hide?'

'OK,' the boy said, and opened the door wider.

The garage smelt of paint, oil. A big Citroën BX took up nearly all the space; there was no room for a caravan. Ladders and a lawnmower hung from struts running along the ceiling. A Marshall stack stood in a corner. A shotgun was bolted to the wall inside a locked glass case near the door; Sandra Melon was off a farm, so a gun wasn't unusual – but still.

The boy tugged at the hem of Eric's jacket. 'Where you gonna hide, mister?'

'Listen.' Eric knelt so that he could look into the boy's face. 'You go back to your room.' Eric searched in his pockets, found a packet of Fisherman's Friends and handed the kid one of the dusty brown tablets. 'Have this.' The boy took the sweet without smiling. 'And I'll hide here and they'll never find me.' Eric raised his hand and fluttered his dangling fingers towards the door the way kings in films dismiss servants.

He walked round to the back of the car. A hook on which a caravan could be attached and one of those electrical plugs that make the indicators work. But did that mean anything?

From outside he could hear Sandra Melon's punkeoke version of 'Sugar Sugar' – Sandra singing 'sugar', the others responding 'ah, honey, honey', the fuzz guitars ramming through the chord changes to much guffawing and whooping.

How could this happy family be his persecutors? The embittered, the malcontent, the vengeful, the dispossessed, they lived in tiny bedsits with candlewick bedspreads; they shared bathrooms, they cut up newspapers and stuck them all over their walls, they wrote copiously in exercises books, they ate cold spaghetti out of the tin, they carried the evidence of their ruined lives around with them in plastic bags, handles stretched thin under the weight of information. Eric had met them. Some of them were his clients. They always wore hats and badges. When they wrote letters to the money advice shop, they filled every available space on the page, scribbling up the sides of the margins and scrawling pictures.

With his healthy farm-girl wife, his *Lion King*-pyjamaed little boy, his hundred friends, his posh house in Hillcrest, his punkeoke, Greg wasn't like those people. He was happy.

Eric opened the door a crack and peered out. The party people were standing round the punkeoke band with their backs to the house, so he was able to crawl back along the hedge and to the rhododendron bush. He stood in the bush for a time, watching and listening. Greg was on stage again, doing a punked-up hyper-fast version of ABBA's 'Dancing Queen', and despite the clanging, rasping block chords and snarled lyrics, the song still possessed the yearning, sultry quality of loss Eric remembered as a teen-ager – dissonant high octaves tumbling downwards, out of tune and haunted, desperate chords that seemed to tear his heart out with their hunger – and all so incongruous with the shirtless Gregory Torkington whirling and jerking and bawling out the words over screaming guitars.

It was a solid sort of click, a worrying click. He turned and Sandra Melon was in the bush next to him, pointing the shotgun at Eric's chest. Then another sound came from the gun, this time a serious clunk like the shutting of the door on an expensive car, as if pins and rods, pieces of metal that did important things were lining up, setting themselves ready to work, oily steel casings, precision lathed, slipping silkily into firing positions, and Eric stared at her, imagined her picking him up like she would one of her sheep.

Then everything Eric had learned on his one day with the army cadets snicked into place as smoothly as the gun's parts.

He ran away.

Eric lay in the darkness feeling the warmth of Charlotte spreading through his limbs. Sometimes, she seemed extra solid, a mineral thing, and next to her he felt ghostly and insubstantial. The day had left him shredded, eviscerated.

'Bennett Lowe has been on the phone,' Charlotte said.

'What did he want?'

'I don't know. He sounded worried, serious. It wasn't a breezy, "Is Eric in?" it was, "I need to speak to Eric." Just like that. He said he needed to give you a chance to get in front of something.'

'In front of something?'

'That's what he said.' Charlotte turned to face him. 'Are we still special, West Cumbria?'

'You are special to me.'

'You feeling OK?'

'Yes,' he said. 'We didn't get any caravans today.'

'That's good. Maybe they've stopped.'

'I think they might have.'

The house made its usual ticking and shuffling sounds as it cooled down and every purchase settled against the other for its night of motionless contemplation. He could hear a lorry powering down the hill into Whitehaven, the reverse thrust of its low gears as it hit the surprise blind bend just before the town hall. He went into a wakeful sleep, alert to every snuffle, squeak, scratch and shuffle: it was a sleep of fear, a sleep not of endings, but of beginning, the beginning of a long descent into something vile, and its ragged edges reached out to him as he floated towards it.

'The lights! Get the lights!' he shouts. 'Get the fucking lights. He's out, he's on the stairs. And get that knife!'

'I can't get anything. I can't see a bloody thing!'

Apartfromtheobvious tries to see through the darkness. Listens; he can hear breathing close to him. Where is the torch? Under the stairs. Bastard won't try to escape in the dark. Bastard won't know the way out. And bastard hasn't eaten for a couple of days so he'll have no strength. Strength enough to pull the pipe out of the fucking water tank though. The man could have improvised some sort of weapon while he was up there. Sharpened pipe, something. Apartfromtheobvious rests his hand on the wall, wet and sticky where the paper has peeled away. Water seeps from the loft, trickles down his arm. Fishy stink of dissolving wallpaper paste, darkness, damp air, plop plop of water into the puddles. He moves towards the top of the stairs and listens again. He can make out the rubbing sound of a body squirming, a squeaking noise on the wet carpet.

Shouts down into the blackness: 'You can't get away, you bloody idiot. The house is all locked up. Listen.' He jangles the keys. 'It's a fortress.'

Silence. Then, the sounds of movement along the stairs.

'You've messed things up now, haven't you? I'm going to have to get a plumber in.'

Should he jump on him from here? No, not in the dark. He may well have some sort of weapon, maybe a sharp wood splinter of floorboard. Putting him in the loft was stupid.

'We're not going to hurt you, you know. Just keep you here. We just need time to get away. Out of the country. Don't worry. Relax. I tell you what we'll do. We'll lock you in one of the bedrooms and give you some food and drink if you promise you'll stay there. Otherwise, I'm going to have to do something drastic.'

Voice sounds odd in the dark, in the wet air. 'Can you hear me, dickhead? Can you hear what I'm saying?' That rubbing sound again, like clothes being pulled on over a wet swimming costume. 'The farmer next door has got a shotgun. A big, big shotgun. I borrow it for rabbiting. How would you like that? Blow your bloody head off, dress you up in my clothes, I disappear, they'll think the body is mine. Write some notes that look like someone's been threatening me. That's my fallback plan, see. I'm letting you in on it now, to show you what you'll get if you don't conform. What do you think?'

Nothing. Silence.

'You downstairs?'

Magnum: 'What is it?'

'Plug in the table lamp – wait, listen –' Metal scraping metal: the door bolt again. 'You bloody cretin. You've already tried that; you know we've got the keys. Christ, we are dealing with an imbecile.' Door rattles again. Light comes on. Bastard is stood up, pulling at the door. Eyes a darker grey, almost black. Without the make-up his skin looks pale and damp, there's no light, no light behind it, it's a dead face, a doll's face. Bastard's hands are shaking as he tries to get a purchase on the edge of the door as if he could slip through the crack – elastic-man.

'Here, Party.' Magnum hands a carving knife up to him.

He points the shiny blade at the man, who continues to scrabble at the cracks around the door. 'Get in that cupboard under the stairs. Or you'll get some of this,' and he twists the blade in the air, dappling murky spots on the wall, like the view seen through a sick person's eyes.

35

Light spilled through the crimson border of the donkey man window (a figure lifting a naked man on to a grey mule's back), streaking the office walls in an oily pattern. A Post-it said *Ring Bennett* in Bernard's fat round letters. Eric looked at the message for a long time. Next to it was a smart clean white envelope, the kind you didn't have to lick to seal. Advice shop letters usually wore brown envelopes with a glue that tasted of sweet chip fat. A notch of anxiety began in his stomach. He didn't want to open the envelope. How was it you checked for bombs? The smell of almonds. He sniffed. Nothing. He looked from the Post-it to the letter and back again and wondered whether they were connected. A feeling of dread crept into him; his head prickled and his neck and hands felt swollen. Fraudulent funding applications. Obtaining money by deception. Theft. Illegal use of credit. What could they do to him? He had never been in trouble before. Never even shoplifting. That time his friend had stolen a leather belt and stashed it in his armpit: scared shitless. Would they send him to prison? For fraud? How had they found out?

He tore the top off the envelope and yanked out the contents.

. . . irregularities in expenses claims. Pending investigation, it will be necessary to suspend you from normal

work. Please leave the building immediately. Do not
clear your desk. While under suspension do not contact
any members of staff of the advice shop or of the council.
Staff will be under instruction to not correspond with
you. This is to enable the investigating officer to explore
the matter thoroughly. The precise details of the discip-
linary proceedings can be had from the County Council
representative on the management board.
    Yours sincerely,
    Bennett Lowe.

He relaxed a little. It didn't seem to have anything to do
with Doreen, the money scam. Nothing to do with the funding application for the fictional Cleator Moor Skills and
Resource Centre. It was to do with – he flicked his eyes
back up the letter – to do with expenses. Nothing about
bankruptcy scams, nothing about Doreen, nothing about
his personal abuse of credit and the English and Welsh
court system. An expenses fraud. Sacked for a triviality.
He had never lost a job before. In fact, he hadn't had any
other jobs; just education, the dole, a bit more education,
a bit more dole, a bit of volunteer work and then this: debt
counsellor, money adviser, credit therapist. So dole wouldn't
be new to him. But it would be new to him as an adult; he
had been young on the dole and it had always seemed OK.
Now it wouldn't seem grown-up to be signing on, queuing
up in the post office for a giro. And the new tests: are you
available for work, are you actively seeking a job, will your
appearance deter potential employers?
    Footsteps ticked down the stone passage and Marjorie
strode in, tossed her coat on to the coat stand and fitted a
cigarette into her mouth.
    'You're early, McFarlane.'
    'That fag your breakfast?'
    'Aye.'

'You do know that a cigarette does not contain all the main food groups.'

'Aye. You need amphetamine, beer and a Pot Noodle to balance it out. You got the kettle on?'

'Maybe I'm not allowed *your* tea and coffee.'

She squinted at him and spread her hands as if the answer to his riddle would be slapped into them like a fish.

'Bennett fucking Lowe,' said Eric.

'Oh, not this again. Bennett's a cool guy.'

'Bennett's a cool guy,' he mimicked in a mincing voice.

'Talk sense, Eric.'

'He's got it in for us all. You as well.'

He handed her the letter and stared at her polished smoked-glass nails while she read, moving her lips and shaking her head slowly. Then she kissed him on his forehead and said, 'Eric, you're a fucking idiot.'

He looked at her face: her shaved round head tilted to the side, her plump lips set in a quizzical pout, her big eyes expanding at him.

'What?' said Eric, as Marjorie turned and left to see Bernard about his appeal to the social security commissioners.

Eric spent the rest of the morning trawling through his stuff, nabbing everything incriminating he could find. He deleted hundreds of computer files, shoved a load of papers into his car for disposal at home and shredded the last four years' worth of diaries to prevent the day-by-day records of his movements throwing up contradictions to his expenses claims. He was hiding his tracks; and what could they do? With no manager, nothing.

There was a clear blue bowl of sky above as Eric left the Cleator Moor Money Advice Shop for the last time. It was March and it was cold. The usual grey shroud had lifted from Cleator Moor and everything looked hard edged. He glanced back at the Georgian church building, its short bell tower, a comedy cathedral. It was two-thirty. A drink? Too early. He walked up the alley to Cleator Moor Square. The town was quiet. Most people at work or school. He felt odd. His perceptions had altered; sounds seemed suddenly over loud or too close. A sniffing noise which he thought was right next to his ear turned out to be the sound of a man brushing the pavement on the other side of the street.

At least now he knew that Bennett's message had nothing to do with the funding application he and Doreen had cooked up. The idea for a new skills and resource centre for Cleator Moor would sail through every council assessment and would land just before the end of the financial year, before the investigation into Eric's adventures in expenses-land. All it needed was Doreen to say the right thing to Bennett Lowe in her meeting with him that afternoon. He rang Doreen from a call box and arranged to meet her at Ennerdale Lake.

36

They sat in Doreen's car as Doreen flipped through the fat application form. The sun sent a milky light over the water and a light wind nudged ridges of water against the stones, making a soft clacking sound.

'There's a lot of pages, Eric. I hope he won't ask me many questions.'

'Just remember the main objective of the centre. It's about prevention, not sticking plasters. Keep saying that phrase. Bennett Lowe loves that sort of thing. You got someone to pretend to be Bernard, like I said?'

Doreen tensed up, the square ends of her fingernails digging into the wodge of papers.

'Yes, I've got someone with a background in finance as it happens. A friend.'

'This friend thinks it's all above board?'

'He wants to do something for the community, something to help.'

'And it's Bennett Lowe you'll be meeting?'

'Mr Lowe, yes.'

'Just play it calm. You're not supposed to be a whizz-kid entrepreneur, just an ordinary member of the community with a good idea and common sense.' He moved in close and searched her eyes. 'How are you feeling, in yourself?'

'I haven't had anything at all yet today. I'm staying sharp.'

'That's best. You don't want to be drowsy.'

'Do I sometimes seem drowsy?'

'No, no. Just when you're tired.' He wanted her to act before the swamp of Valium sucked her under. He had to admit she looked the part, in her crisp business suit, with pink high heels; an ordinary woman dressed to impress her bank manager. Bennett would be taken in completely.

He left Doreen by the lakeside reading through the papers, drove to Steve's Wines and bought a bottle of Bell's. He sat in his car, sipping whisky, watching through the pixilating twilight as the school run thickened the traffic.

When he got home, two men in suits the colour of cheap chocolate were stood at his gate, smoking. Big moustaches, big bellies; big grins when they saw Eric coming towards them.

'The householder arrives,' said one.

'To allow entry,' said the other, 'to the premises of the debtor.'

'You've not forgotten,' the first one added, 'about Vlad zee Impaler and ees children of zee night, have you?'

Eric stood between them and the gate.

They had come to take away . . . one of the men uncrumpled a ball of paper from his side pocket and read aloud: 'An Apple Macintosh computer and a collection of valuable pottery.'

'We'd like to come in,' the other brown man said, 'if we may.'

'Well, I'm not actually the householder,' Eric said. 'I'm the gardener – did I not explain that last time we had the pleasure? I don't know when Mr McFarlane will be back.'

Eric walked off down the side path and into the back garden where he began to move some leaves around with a rake. He continued to move garden debris around for a long time after he'd heard the bailiffs' van leaving.

He looked to the bottom of the garden, where a large bush had overgrown; its shade had created a dead spot where nothing else would grow – no grass, no moss, no nothing. It looked cool, comfortable under the bush.

Sitting there under the bush he could see his house and no one could see him. He felt the safest he had felt for years. Safe, safe, safe. As safe as tucked up with a hot-water bottle and a *Narnia* book, the sounds of the rest of the house rumbling below. The light was fading and he felt as if he might fade away with it. In fact, he wished he would. Another man would have smashed up the house, broken the windows, driven the car into a wall, anything. He had seen that happen in films. But he just sat in the deepening gloom. He thought about his job, about Charlotte, about the Doreen scam, about his piercing, about the strange caravan pictures, about the phone calls, about Julie and the trepanning, and about how it all might be linked. And where was Julie? Why did she not return his calls? It was all some strange constellation moving against him, an accretion of bad deeds that had become too heavy to carry.

He saw lights go on in the hall. He saw Charlotte walk down the hall with some letters. She went into the back room, sat down to read them. He watched her reading. He could see her plainly. She had the light on and hadn't drawn the curtains. He watched her get up, leave the room, then saw her enter the kitchen. The house had become a stage. He watched her boil a kettle and make a drink. Then he saw her look at the calendar and at the clock, and then she disappeared down the hall. He imagined she was using the phone. She returned to the living room, but didn't sit; she paced up and down, moving things about, aimlessly tidying up, but he could tell she wasn't doing anything with a purpose – something was worrying her. If she was relaxed she'd have switched on the Mac by now, played a game, something.

It was dark in the garden, completely dark. A cat was sitting a few feet away, watching him, its eyes shining like hot little coals.

He stood up and walked from the garden down the path to the street. The street lamp burned orange. Everything was fucked up. Bennett, it was all Bennett's fault.

He had to see Bennett.

He left the Saab at home and walked quickly down the hill towards the town, swigging from his Bell's as he went. He spotted a phone box. As he waited for the phone to be answered, he tried to picture Bennett and what he would be doing, imagining him at his slippered ease. A woman's voice told him that Bennett had gone to the Bingo.

'Bingo?' Eric said, not disguising the note of ridicule in his voice. Was this a new brand of council hexology?

The woman said the word again, flatly, followed by a silence that she didn't feel it necessary to break. 'Where you cross numbers off a sheet of paper. It's for charity.'

Eric remembered his earlier invite.

37

Mirehouse Working Men's club was full of smoke. Ranks of long tables, old men, old couples. Clipboards for the serious players, marking ten cards at a time.

Two little ducks!

Eric marched across to where Bennett was marking off his numbers with a bingo-dabber, a spongy-tipped cigar of a pen you patted on to the number to leave a smudge.

Bennett was with three others: a woman who Eric knew to be chair of the grants committee, a local building contractor and the chip-shop owner. They were all on pints.

Clickety click!

Eric sat down next to Bennett. Bennett nodded hello, but put his finger to his lips. Eric pointed to Bennett's half-empty glass and flared his brows. Bennett waggled his hand *no* and by way of explanation scribbled a circle in the air around himself and his friends.

Legs! (whistles)

Eric tore a piece off a beermat wrote *Why?* on it.

Major's den!

Bennett read the word and looked at Eric, shook his head and held both hands out to show Eric the whole room and the people it.

Heinz varieties!

Bennett blobbed a number and held out his book for Eric to see. He needed one for a line.

Top of the shop!

Bennett whispered into Eric's ear that he relax, just relax and have a pint.

All the threes!

Eric grabbed Bennett's nose and twisted it. Bennett sat back, shaking his head.

Two fat ladies!

Bennett stayed silent, pretending he hadn't been touched. The friends stared at Eric. Bingo's a laugh. Like the dogs in Manchester. Playing at working-class culture.

On its own!

Bennett showed the others his near win. Eric wandered away, bought a drink. The long bar was empty. No problem getting served when the bingo's on.

Unlucky for some!

He returned to Bennett and his gang and sat down with them. Bennett stared at him and flicked the bingo book in the air, making a snapping sound. Eric picked up Bennett's pint and held it over the ashtray. He poured. Beer quickly filled the ashtray and began to dribble out through the cigarette-butt grooves. He repeated this with the other glasses on the table. Soon the beer flowed over the top of the ashtray and on to the table, running in a sheet across the veneer and first dripping, then gushing on to the shoes of Bennett and his friends. They picked up their feet, lazy kids while Mum hoovers, and continued to mark their cards. Eric watched calmly as the beer flowed over the edges of the table. Nobody protested.

Blind!

Eric continued pouring the last beer until the glass was empty.

Anyway up!

The rest of the evening saw Eric in a corner, working his way mechanically through as much Jennings as he could stomach and then a large amount more that he couldn't.

The resident trio (Bob on drums, Mick on organ, and Jackie B on vocals) had launched into their dance set by the time Eric pulled himself up from the vinyl seat, which his trousers were stuck to with dribbled beer, and staggered straight into a toothless dancing man. He curled an arm around the old man's neck, pretended to dance a waltz, then collapsed into a chair and watched the old man pull a younger woman on to the floor. The pair of them twitched maniacally to the revolving Leslie speakers and the cardboard thud of the bass drum, the dancing man's gummy smile glistening with spittle as he mimed the words, pointing his finger at his young dancing partner and squinting with his head on one side.

What do you want to make those eyes at me for
If they don't mean what they say.

Eric took several pulls of Bell's as he wandered back home. He couldn't remember ever feeling as pissed. The pavement buckled up in front of him as if there were an earthquake and he walked as though he were climbing up the sides of a steel tower in magnetic boots.

The bedroom light was on. He could see Charlotte looking out of the window. It was no good pretending to be sober. He was pissed. He had been sacked. That was all there was to it. There was nothing to be said, nothing to be done. That was it. That's what he would tell her. Nothing to discuss, nothing to get worked up about. Anyway, soon it would all be over. Greg's wife, Sandra Melon, was armed. She had a gun. She was probably looking for him now.

After a long period of working the key into the slot he staggered into the hall.

There was a red gleam of gum from under Charlotte's lips as she snarled the word *debts*.

'What about debts?' he slurred.

'How can we have debts, Eric?' She was holding a piece of paper. 'We don't have debts. We have money, cars, holidays. Not debts.'

He tried to see the text on the letter, work out which company had sent it, work out what she was talking about, but he couldn't.

'Charley, I can't talk now. I've got bad news. Sus . . . sus . . . I've been suspended!' He coughed, gulped in a ball of air that tasted thick and dusty, and then a long brown stream of vomit shot from his mouth, hitting the wall.

Charlotte ran up the stairs screaming, 'Fuck, fuck, fuck!'

Eric woke from his drunken stupor with the sharp smell of vomit in his nose. He was on the sofa. Charlotte was standing over him. She touched his head.

'How are you feeling?'

'Not good.'

She snorted: 'What do you expect?'

Eric sat up. She was gripping a letter, the letter she was brandishing last night. 'We have to talk about this, Eric.'

'Let me have a look.' He took the letter. It was a bailiff's notice. Inventory of goods removed. The brown suits had returned and Charlotte had let them in. And they had uplifted the Mac and the pottery.

'We can get them back. I know how. The process for getting the goods back is called replevin. I'll make an application at the court later.'

'Yes, but why were they ever taken? You said you didn't have debts. And last night you said you'd been suspended.'

He told her about the debts and about the expenses fiddling. He said nothing about Doreen or about the grant scam. Nothing about Greg and his gun-toting wife, Sandra Melon. Charlotte listened but refused to understand. They talked around the same topic for a long time, for hours. The whole morning. She asking why; he explaining the situation and how he would get out of it; and she asking why again, and he explaining again the position he was in and the route he intended to take out of it.

'When you talk like this,' she said at one point, 'I can feel myself being screwed up like one of those debt letters you've been hiding in the kitchen bin under the potato peelings.' She stopped and looked at him as if she had never really seen him before, as if he had suddenly shed a skin to reveal the true monster.

Her anger had seemed shallow at first but towards the end of the morning it deepened, hardened, and finally it was as if he had been viewing a huge continent from its edge and, as it slowly tilted up into view, he felt its cold shadow looming over him.

They stopped talking. They had moved the problem nowhere. It had been like trying to move a large piece of furniture though a doorway, the two of them straining to co-ordinate their pushes and pulls, but their efforts working against each other. It wouldn't go through the gap, it just wouldn't.

He lay on the sofa. She sat at the table looking at the space where the Mac had been. She sat there for a long time. Eric missed the squelchy ticking of the keyboard; it was comforting, sensual. He tried to speak to her but she ignored him.

Upstairs, he put a few things into a rucksack, then left the house. Outside there was a watery light over everything.

WE ARE SOFT BARRIERS

Mrs Coan was sitting up in bed when I put my head round the bedroom floor. 'Here's some tea, Mrs Coan.'

Mrs Coan didn't look at me. She continued to stare out of the window at the thick snow that covered the garden. The snow hadn't let up since we'd got her out of the pond two days earlier.

Just in time it turned out. She went under for nearly ten minutes. But in extreme cold water the body does a strange thing. The people at West Cumberland Hospital explained that the extreme shock forces your system to completely shut down. It goes into a kind of suspended animation, so you don't drown. When they pulled her out she was alive.

'I hope you're feeling a bit warmer now.' I put my hand against the radiator. 'The heating's on full. Julie said to switch on your fan heater if you need it. It's there. Just ask me.'

Mrs Coan nodded.

'Just call out. I'm in Julie's room doing some revision. She'll be back later, but I've got a free morning today.'

I went over to the window. 'I've never known snow like this. Usually never settles, my dad says. Is it something to do with being near the sea? Well, anyway, it's dead cold. The schools might close for the rest of the week, they said. The boiler's struggling. A lot of the kids'll be happy. And the teachers.' I laughed.

I heard a creak from Mrs Coan's bed and turned to see her put her hand beneath her pillow and pull out a transparent tube. She shook a couple of capsules into her fist and inserted them into her mouth, hardly parting her lips to do so. She tucked the container back under the pillow, a child hiding sweets.

She seemed *half-buried-in-some-sediment-of-despair.*

'Like I say, Mrs Coan. I hope you don't mind me being here. It's just, well, with Mr Coan being. Anyway, Julie will be back later, like I said.'

Julie. I never used her real name, never really thought about it. Every one at school had called her Spangles since she'd had a packet of the sweets confiscated in primary school. I would always call her Spangles no matter what. The name Spangles was engraved within me. If they cut me open, there the word would be, in wobbly rusty-coloured letters, spelled out in every individual bone, even the tiny bones in my feet and hands: Spangles, Spangles, Spangles.

Spangles was killing me and I liked it; I was as *happy-as-a-dead-body-walled-up-inside-her*.

A key scratched at the door and I went to the hall. Spangles threw her combat jacket over the banister. 'Hello,' she called up.

'Up here.'

She ran up the stairs and threw her arms about me. We kissed. Kissing Spangles was like *falling-into-a-pool-of-cool-still-water*. I sighed.

'I think I'm, uh, getting to like you a lot. You know.'

She looked into my eyes. Tips of her dark hair clung to my face with static. 'Eric, not now. How's my mum? I'm sorry to do this to you, Eric, to leave you looking after her but, I just – the doctor said keep an eye on her. People, they, often, they sometimes . . .'

She went into Mrs Coan's bedroom.

I went downstairs and sat on the sofa, exactly where I had sat all those weeks ago when Dad had taken me there to treat what he'd thought were going to be pigs.

The soft burr of voices from upstairs, feet scraping about. I sat listening for a long time, looking out of the window. I could see the main road a long way away, and I watched the cars going by and thought about all the different people driving and all the different places they were going and all the different things they were going to do, and about how separate all these people were, locked inside their private canisters, and I was suddenly overwhelmed by the poignancy of moving traffic; gliding, lurching, nudging, never quite touching.

Over the weeks, Spangles and I became as one thing: there was no edge, no point at which I stopped and Spangles began. We cooked, we tidied, we cleaned. I virtually lived there. It was a fuggy nowhere land between adulthood and childhood.

We were fourteen.

Spangles' mother would get out of bed now and again and come downstairs, but mostly she stayed in her room. She moved soundlessly, and seemed tiny, so tiny, like a child. She did nothing; didn't read, didn't watch or listen to anything. I imagined that she looked out of the window at the distant moving traffic and thought about the poignancy of it, as I had. I wondered whether feeling poignant sent you mad.

One night we were curled up together on the sofa listening to 45 records played at 33, which recently was the only sort of music Spangles liked – she enjoyed the long growling vowels of the vocalist, the slappy loose bass and the swish swish of elongated cymbal sounds – when we heard a key at the door. We moved apart and waited. My heart thumped in my chest. I knew who it would be.

Mr Coan went straight over to the record player, switched it off and stood in front of us. When he spoke it was as if he were reading from a script.

'This is the best way,' he said. 'Some of those debt companies. Well, you know.' He spoke directly to Spangles as if I wasn't even there.

An older teenager skulked in behind him: Spangles' brother James, who stared at me but also said nothing.

'Debt, it gets everywhere in the end. Into every room – the living room, the bathroom, the bedroom, the kitchen – then soon, it's all around. Are you OK, Julie, darling? Come here.'

Mr Coan was short and squat with quiffed hair and a

polished-looking face. Julie went to him and they shared an awkward hug.

'Who is he?' He didn't look at me.

'This is Eric. He's the vet's son,' she said as if that explained something.

'I can speak,' I said.

'Sorry,' her dad said. 'She's been through a lot. I'll go up and see your mum. Is she asleep?'

'No.'

'OK. So. You got my messages?'

'Yes, I got them.'

'So are you ready? Are you packed? It's tomorrow we leave.'

'I know. I'll sort everything later on.'

I was horrified. What did they mean, *packed*?

'I was meaning to tell you, Eric. We have to go. To Manchester. We are all going. We couldn't see another way. No one must know where we've gone. We can start again down there. You've seen what those debts have done to Mum.'

She used clear and unvarnished language. There could be no misunderstanding.

I was astonished. How could she have kept this fact from me? I had become her husband almost. We were inseparable.

'But . . . how will I see you?'

'I don't know. We'll work something out. Let's talk later.'

Mr Coan stood staring at the record player, which was spitting static because he hadn't turned it off properly. He looked crushed by the weight of everything. His face had a *patina-of-despair*. He left the room and Spangles' brother James followed. I heard their feet going up the stairs, then the door to Mrs Coan's room opening.

I got up and began to put on my shoes. Tears were in my eyes. 'How could you not tell me?'

'I'm sorry. I hated to destroy, you know, us. The moment. You have to live in the moment, Eric. Not the past, not the future. The moment. You should learn that. BE STILL FLOWING.'

261

'But . . . You and me?'

My bones, her name written inside every one. The tumbling, streaming snowflakes exploding with our love.

WE ARE SOFT BARRIERS.

'Do you remember those factories in Maryport, all lit up?' she said.

'Yes,' I said.

'Me too,' she said.

Loss came down on me like a cage.

'I'm going,' I said, and set off to the door. I stopped. 'Was it because I wouldn't – the trepan thing – I wouldn't help?'

'I'll ring you,' Spangles said.

But if she kept my number she didn't use it.

Not until much, much later.

Four

38

Julie's room was silent, but for the constant introverted thrum of a TV from below: a week he'd been there and the couple from the flat beneath, elderly and deaf, hadn't once turned off the set. It went from breakfast TV to late-night chat, and on, and after that he slept right through it as if floating on a bed of sound. He had tried drowning it out with Julie's stereo but the music was too painful: it was like a tide running over him, giving up its memories, drowning other thoughts, so that he stopped listening properly and stood in the centre of the room, thinking of Julie, seeing her in front of him, not moving even when the CD whirred to a stop.

He hadn't been out during the days he'd been there apart from one trip to the paper shop for boil-in-the-bag fish and tinned potatoes, which he ate cold.

The police had made marks in chalk all over the room. They had indicated things that shouldn't be moved, but most of Julie's stuff had gone. The room smelt mousy, empty. The carpet had been taken up and under it, on the floorboards, was a damp-looking circular stain, a stain that Eric felt was somehow on *him*. The bedclothes had been removed and he had been sleeping on the mattress with his clothes on; the clothes he had been wearing when he left Charlotte.

There was still no proper electric supply but the neigh-bour had let him put the wire through the window like before. He had given her thirty quid, but was worried about money. He was well over his overdraft limit. His next salary would be swallowed and still leave a hole. He hadn't been able to get hold of Doreen to arrange any more funds. Since she'd met Bennett Lowe about the funding application for the skills and resource centre, she had been oddly quiet, not answering her phone, nothing.

He wondered where Charlotte thought he was. He had waited so long to call her he no longer had the courage to.

He snapped on the two-bar fire, toasted a slice of bread using a purple Afro-comb for a fork, spread the toast with Happy Shopper margarine and took it over to the window. At the doorstep of the porno-mag exchange shop a policeman was helping a man gather up his bedding and pointing him towards the city centre. Sleep-dazed, the man staggered in that direction. He would go to the bus station. Eric had seen him there.

He bit a corner off the toast and set the slice to rest on the window ledge.

He had looked everywhere for Julie. The barman in Corbieres hadn't seen her. The Temple of Convenience barman, however, filled him in. He bought Eric a large whisky and sat down with him at a table. Where had Eric been? Hadn't he heard the news? Was he all right? Eric had grinned at the questions but the barman hadn't smiled back. The barman had touched him on the shoulder. Why was he touching him? Why was he not smiling? When the barman told him, Eric had swirled the remains of his drink in his glass, watching the amber waves lapping at the rim for a time, then threw it down his throat and walked straight out.

He crunched down the rest of his toast, picked up his bag and left the flat.

At the bottom of Shudehill he tried to make sense of the A–Z. His mental map of Manchester was a circle with roads coming out of the centre like the spokes of a wheel: the A6, the A34, the A56. He imagined pictures of landmarks along each bicycle spoke – the Harp Lager brewery and the Toast Rack building, the university, the MRI, Old Trafford. These roads were like sheep tracks, worn away by the tread of traffic, a city divided into corridors. He knew the tracks by their bus-route names: the 50, the 192, the 11.

An 81 bus appeared and he got on. It was taking him to Julie's funeral.

All the time he had thought Julie was alive she had been dead. Nearly two weeks ago, she had been rushed into hospital and had lain there in a coma for three days. Her mother and father had sat by the bed, talking to her, playing tapes they had found in her flat. But she never came out. Her brain had died, they pulled the plug.

No one told Eric about her death because no one knew that he'd been back in touch. His relationship with Julie had been perfectly discrete, separate from each of their lives. It was as if she were a star, a star that burned in his sky but had died in the universe long ago.

He fingered the disc of bone in his pocket. Its edges had lost their sharpness; it was nubbled and smooth, with being in his back pocket.

It hadn't gone through.

That was the message she had left. *It hadn't gone through.* Now he knew what she had meant. The trepan. He took the disc from his pocket and held it near the light from the bus window. It was only a sliver.

Eric hadn't done the job properly, so she had decided to do it herself. An electric drill. The people from the next-door flat told him all about it. Showed him a red-top headline: 'Hole Drilled in Coma Girl's Skull'.

Now she was dead. According to the newspaper, her friends had been interviewed for hours in connection with the incident, but the inquest had gone with misadventure.

Coma girl.

Eric was uncomfortable on the bus. Since he'd found out

about Julie, he was hypersensitive to the world, as if every sensation was crammed into his brain simultaneously: the bus engine growling, the air brakes gasping, the seat trembling, the blowers blasting him with muggy air. Every sensation was defined by the fact that it existed while Julie didn't and would never again. Everything was not-Julie: not the triangle nose, not the black, black hair, not the larky smile, not the sulk, not his special word tattooed on her arm. The shape of things – like clouds and bicycles and phone boxes – became compelling. The way the trees had grown around the shape of the passing double-deckers was like a poignant caress of absence, and looking at these shapes, these gaps, these holes, his throat filled with blood and his eyes ached for her.

The church was not as old as the St Cuthbert's Centre. Brick built, it was part of a council estate and on the roof, a neon cross fizzed red in the dirty Manchester air. Next to the church was the six-lane Princess Road; the tyres made a constant fluttering noise on the damp asphalt.

Julie's mother spoke to him. She looked exactly the same. Now at the top end of her fifties, he'd guess. Back then, when he saved her from the frozen pond, she'd seemed just as old, older even. Her bony shoulders held up a dark suit that wasn't new.

'You were a friend of Julie's?'

'Yes. Do you not remember me, Mrs Coan? From West Cumbria? That time –' He stopped himself. 'I came down to see her a couple of days ago. I just found out –'

'Down?'

'Down from Cumbria.'

'She had a lot of different friends.'

'I didn't see her very often.'

'A lot of friends, friends who loved her.' Her eyes swam. 'A lot of friends, but never any time for us, it seemed.' She straightened her face and gave her head a firm shake, as if she were coming up from underwater. 'Some of her friends didn't help. We –' she nodded to short squat Mr Coan, with his familiar quiffed hair and polished face '– we didn't agree with the misadventure verdict. But no amount of arguing over words is going to bring her back.' She put her hand on Eric's arm and looked up at him. She was tiny, so tiny, like a child.

'Did you know about this head thing?' She flicked her finger against her forehead, hard, leaving a red mark.

'No. Nothing.'

The younger funeral attendees, Julie's friends, gathered in a dense group near the entrance to the churchyard. Julie's mother nodded in their direction.

'They were the ones,' she said. 'They call themselves friends – but that's not friendship.' She squeezed his arm, a drowner dragging down her rescuer. 'Julie wanted happiness and that's what *we* wanted for her, ever since she was little. Charlie says it was drugs that made her do it, but what are drugs nowadays? We all take drugs. I take drugs off the doctor. You can't blame drugs for this.' Julie's mum touched Eric again, on his hand. It was as if she were trying to pass the sadness into him, make him know.

A young man with another large Coan nose came up alongside them and put his hand on Mrs Coan's shoulder. She looked up at him and nodded fiercely, clenching her little face. 'This was her brother. James.'

'*Is. Is* her brother, Mum.'

'James and Julie were close when they were little. James used to walk Julie home from school.' James gave a small tight smile. 'Julie didn't like walking past this big dog and James used to take her past it. That was when she was small. Before me and Mr Coan split up.'

The undertaker came over and said something to James in a quiet voice. He spoke carefully through barely open

269

lips and his hands stayed linked behind his back. While James thought about the problem, the undertaker gazed at him, moving his head slowly up and down and creasing his brow. His lips stayed clamped shut, as if he was holding something in his mouth, something he was not allowed to swallow or expel but that had a flavour he was desperate to communicate.

James lowered his head. 'They need more people, Mum. For Julie. To carry her.'

The coffin couldn't be wheeled – it was muddy around the graves – so they had to sling lengths of webbing under it, lift each end and slide the gurney out from beneath. The box swayed dreamily between them as they walked. Eric slipped a couple of times under the weight. They rested the coffin next to the grave, where the funeral party had gathered and the priest said some more things. Then they lowered the coffin into the grave, giving out lengths of the webbing slowly, evenly. But none of them had done this before and the coffin began to tilt slightly at Eric's end and, though he tried to right it, he overcompensated and sent the weight on to Julie's dad, who lost his footing and, in his struggle not to slip into the grave, let go of his end altogether. The coffin fell the last couple of inches, landing on a slant. Everyone was quiet but the priest told them not to worry; if it was crooked they would sort it out later. Sometimes they had to saw off the handles to make them fit.

The freshly dug earth, dampened by the rain, smelt fetid. Eric looked at the box lying in its hole. He couldn't imagine Julie inside. He thought of how little he actually knew her. What had been her private thoughts, inside her white face, under the crest of black hair?

A squelching sound brought him back; the priest was squirting holy water from a plastic bottle into Julie's grave while he said more prayers, but the bottle was nearly empty and the priest was having difficulty forcing the fluid through the nozzle, patting the base as if it were a sauce bottle. He passed the bottle to Julie's mother and when she squeezed it, it made a farting noise. She passed the bottle to Mr Coan who held it upside down and sent a strong jet on to the coffin, a few drops ricocheting back on to his jacket. The priest showed Mr Coan how the cap twisted off, and he scattered the last few drops into the grave.

'Do you want me to get more?' the priest asked him. Mr Coan shook his head.

The party broke up into smaller groups. Mr and Mrs Coan hugged at the graveside looking down at the damp coffin. Rain began to fall, and Eric saw his chance. He sidled over near to Mr and Mrs Coan, nodding to them solemnly, walked to the edge, picked up a handful of earth and sent the earth and the bone fragment tumbling into the grave together. His eyes swam; he felt dizzy.

The next Carlisle train beckoned. He was missing Charlotte. He had grown around her the way the trees grew around the passing buses. He had a huge hole in him, a Charlotte-shaped lump knocked out of his middle, like a Henry Moore bronze.

39

Late that evening, when Eric arrived back at 32, The Loop Road, he couldn't get in. Charlotte had locked the door with the drawbolt and, if she was in, wouldn't even come to the door, no matter how long he knocked and implored through the letter box. He ended up sleeping in his car and waiting most of the morning there, hoping for a glimpse of her. She never arrived and eventually Eric left for his meeting with Bennett in the town hall.

Bennett shook his hand and steered him into a small white office, empty but for a black filing cabinet, black table, black computer and black phone. No sign of work, no papers anywhere. Bennett placed both hands on the top of the computer monitor, turned it on its ball and socket so that they could both see the screen and opened a file named Eric McFarlane. A heading said *First Investigatory Interview*, today's date next to it. Beneath that, blank.

Eric noticed that Bennett's pointy sideboards had gone; he had instead a narrow stripe of beard in the centre of his chin, giving him a devilish look.

'This is what we have to do, Eric. I have to investigate this matter of the expenses. That's all. You are suspended, remember, not sacked. I will send a report to your management committee and they will decide whether to take disciplinary action.' He paused. 'And that's it. So I need a statement from you, which I will type up here and now and we can both sign.' Bennett's face creased into a grin, showing his funny criss-crossed teeth, and Eric grinned back. It was still just the issue of his expenses fiddling, nothing had been added to his list of crimes. Bennett suspected nothing about the fictional Cleator Moor Skills and Resource Centre. Eric had got away with it. Doreen would have the first cheque by now. She would have banked it. But she wasn't answering his calls. His plan was to use the £100,000 – his share – to buy loads of presents for Charlotte. The first thing he would get her was the limited-edition green vinyl version of '14th Floor' by Swell Maps. He would buy her lots of other things, but he knew Swell Maps would clinch it, Swell Maps would bring her back.

'Any questions, Eric?'

'Yes. What font will you be using when you write up my answers? Please don't use Ariel 12, the council one; Charlotte hates it. She would hate it if I was sacked using a font like that.'

Bennett ignored him. 'So here we go. We have a statement that on the third of January 1993 you made a claim for mileage costs to cover a trip to Maryport Citizens Advice Bureau, a total of forty miles, to attend a meeting about county court practice in West Cumbria. The manager at Maryport Citizens Advice Bureau has no recollection of the visit. We are told that you were out of the office for a whole day for the purpose of travelling there and back and attending the meeting and that you claimed a lunch allowance and a small amount, one pound and sixty pence, to cover parking in a Maryport car park. There was no receipt for this.' He recited all of this without referring to any papers. It was in his head.

'Have you a comment on this?'

'They have an aquarium at Maryport now. The *Westmorland Gazette* say it's becoming an attraction.'

'The manager of the Citizens Advice Bureau says she has never met you.'

'They have this squid and if you tap on the glass it shits a cloud of ink and hides in it.'

'The deputy manager of Maryport Citizens Advice Bureau – I am sorry about this, Eric, I don't enjoy this aspect of the job at all – the deputy manager also says she has never met you at the bureau either, though she has met you at the monthly meeting of the North West Money Advice Group.'

'Did she say anything about the squid?'

Bennett put his thumb under his lower lip and curved his mouth downwards.

'I just put the numbers in the boxes,' Eric offered.

Bennett flicked his thumb out from under his lip. 'I was thinking maybe you had put the wrong Citizens Advice Bureau, maybe that was it. Maybe you had muddled up the venues.'

Eric was silent.

'No other Citizens Advice Bureau you might have been to?'

Eric shrugged. 'I've never even seen that squid, to be honest.'

Bennett and Eric watched the blank space underneath the heading, as if it would fill up with text if they stared for long enough.

'OK,' Bennett said. 'Well, the other angle is mitigating circumstances. You may have many reasons – health, personal, whatever – that can be taken into account. Any problems at home? Any domestic or emotional difficulties? Maybe you took a day off to sort out your personal life – maybe you made the claim to make it look like you were really at work?' Bennett scratched a finger at the new line of beard. 'Is there anything at all you want to say, anything you'd like to ask?'

'Just one thing.'

'Yes?'

'Was it the numbers that gave me away?'

'Numbers?'

'The numbers I used on the expenses claim form. Too many fives and sevens?'

Bennett shook his head. 'No, Eric. Nothing like that. It's not that detailed.'

Then the lights in the office went out. There were no windows so it was pitch black apart from the dusty green glow of the computer screen. Bennett grabbed the phone and tap-tapped a number.

'Not been paying your bills?' Eric asked, wagging his finger.

Bennett looked at the ceiling as he listened to the receiver.

'It's the way this building works. There's a code for the lights.'

'You can get little switches. We have them all over our house.'

'It's an energy-saving building. The infrared lights detect movement and the lights stay on. If there's no movement for a while the computer assumes the room is empty.' He tap-tapped again but nothing happened. 'We obviously weren't moving around enough. I'll go and get the code from security.' He grinned at Eric and left the room.

Eric moved across to the computer screen and looked for other stuff relating to his case, but it was password only.

He was looking through Bennett's electronic diary when the phone rang. He picked it up.

A man's voice: 'Is that Mr Lowe?'

On a whim, Eric said that yes, it was Mr Lowe.

'Mr Lowe, good,' the voice said. 'Now listen carefully, this is important. It's about one of your workers, one of the people you pay. Are you the person who deals with crimes, irregularities, things done against the council?'

'I don't know,' Eric said. 'Is it about one of the voluntary groups we fund?' He looked out into the dark corridor.

'That's it, funding. It's about Eric McFarlane.'

Eric felt his spine tauten. Something clicked in him. He recognized the voice. It was the caravan man, the phone caller, the stalker.

'This Mr McFarlane, I know some things about him.'

Eric lowered his tone to disguise his voice. 'Things? What things?'

'Things to do with money.'

'Well, he does advise on money problems.'

'No, no, no, no, not like that. Bad money. He's involved in bad money, mucky money.'

The lights came back. Bennett would be back any minute.

'There is an envelope on its way to you,' the voice went on, 'which has inside it a tape of a conversation between Mr McFarlane and a woman, Mrs Jackson. It's about the funding application for the Cleator Moor Skills and Re-source Centre. This tape will be enough to get you all you need to sort out that worm Eric McFarlane.'

Eric looked about the room for a post tray, for the envelope with the tape inside. But there were no papers in the room, nothing.

'Wait a minute,' Eric said, but the voice was gone. But it had tipped a cup that rolled a ball that sprang a lever that flipped a door that raised a hammer that rang a bell and made a flag shoot out. Eric knew the voice. He did a 1471. It wasn't blocked. He scrawled the number on to his hand just before Bennett's foot scrapes came towards the room.

Bennett went to the keyboard and put in the words, *Mr Lowe explained the situation, as already documented, to Mr McFarlane.*

If sacking a member of staff caused Bennett any kind of distress, he didn't show it. He printed out the sheet and handed it to Eric.

Eric's video club card got him past security and he went up to social services and sat down at a computer monitor. No one asked who he was or what he wanted. In fact, he did have permission to access the council database, but on a pre-arranged basis only. He put in his password and opened up Clients: Handle with Care. A green light flickered and the machine made its dirty buzzing sound as he scrolled through a set of data-fields with headings like *name, AKA, description, behaviour (such as threatens to kill people, carries a knife), recommendations (do not interview alone, etc)*. The voice had rung a distant bell. Mr Friday. He kept the mouse cursor scrolling and the text jittered down to the Fs. French, Frenez, Freudenberg, Frezza, Friar, Friedman. No Fridays. He hit find and rattled in *Shopaloan*. Nothing. As a side thought he tapped in Doreen Jackson. He was intrigued as to how she was involved with Shopaloan. She had a debt to him, but so had half of Cleator Moor. How did she know him so well? Of course, that time in the waiting room. And they both bore a grudge against Eric. Mr Friday dropping her off at the court that day. And Shopaloan needed money.

Da-dah! He found it. Doreen Jackson. *Behaviour: bangs desk, shouts. Threatened female employees. Set fire to a social services waiting area in 1976 when children taken into care. Recommendation: do not visit alone, interview with caution.* Doreen Jackson was not so Eden Valley as she appeared.

He closed Handle with Care and opened the council tax database. He searched the telephone field for the number scratched on the back of his hand and got an immediate hit. It was what he suspected: Mr Friday. Mr Friday lived at Lilac House – the sickly purple house! – in Ennerdale, Cleator Moor. Welfare benefits: income support, with the disability premium, council tax rebate 100%, 25% discount for living alone. Then he scanned the rent system. Mr Friday had lived previously with his wife on the Leconfield Estate. The Pedro abduction house. He left a year ago and still owed over £2,000 rent arrears. Eric also confirmed Doreen's address, via the small amount of housing benefit she received, to which she probably wasn't entitled.

He spent the next two hours in the pub, drinking quickly and wondering what his next move should be. When he left, full of purpose, he stopped to leave Charlotte a long, complicated message on their answer-machine, to tell her all he had discovered and all that he was sorry for.

40

Eric drove past Hen Beck and swung the car up a steep rutted lane. A sign said PRIVATE: NO THROUGH ROAD, LILAC HOUSE ONLY. A few yards away from the house was a sliver of a track where a high mound of grass grew between deep tractor troughs – and this took his car down to a muddy car park by the reservoir. He parked and got out. The root wad of a fallen pine stood six feet high next to the car. A sign near the edge of the water read DEEP WATER VERY COLD STEEP SIDES DO NOT SWIM. There was an orange lifebelt on a post. He crossed a field full of tree stumps, bent stalks and rock debris. Nearer the lilac house the field blurred into a garden where three old televisions cast reproachful eyes over drifts of cardboard by a near collapsed fence. The house was covered in wooden clapboards and the bright lilac paint, luminous and stunning from a distance, was not so impressive close up: it was the colour of a fading bruise and large chunks had fallen away.

He walked around the house. There was music coming from inside: Slade, 'How Does It Feel?' At the back of the house were two cars: Doreen's toffee-brown Austin Allegro, the other a dented and pockmarked Volvo. The one that had chased him. He looked in at the back window. A low table, papers all over. No signs of life. He decided to go in, talk to him.

The doorbell played 'Colonel Bogey', then there was silence. Around him were bare trees and scrubby grass. He scanned the hills for movement. On a ridge above the stiff rows of pine trees that covered the hills with gloomy blotches were two orange-clad figures. They moved higher as he watched, becoming silhouettes when they reached the summit. He strained to hear them – you could sometimes hear hikers talking: not the words, but the sounds, even from a long way away. But all he heard was the wind and the rumbling from the open-cast mine a couple of miles down the road. In the distance he could see the gleaming globes and towers of Sellafield. Then the door to the lilac house opened.

Mr Friday looked paler than usual. A line of sweat lay across the top of his narrow moustache. He was wearing socks with no shoes. The socks had Christmas trees and snowmen all over them. Doreen stood in the hall some way back.

Eric looked past Mr Friday to Doreen. 'Are you OK, Doreen?'

She just looked at him. Mr Friday was chewing a sweet. Eric tried to sound fierce and official. He was a council-funded employee, a qualified professional, a money adviser, a member of the caring professions, the voluntary sector, the not-for-profit butter-wouldn't-melt section of the working world, the workers who put up with conditions no other worker would tolerate because they were working for some greater good, to empower, to empathize, to em-this, em-that, battered-this and battered-that. He spoke haughtily to Shopaloan: 'Have you got something you want to say to me? I'm trying my best for you people.'

Mr Friday laughed a shrill hee-hee and wiped his mouth with the back of his hand. He had a few different laughs: the hee-hee, a grim ish-ish-ish he did to himself, which sounded like a toilet flushing, and a loud ack-ack-ack when something really tickled him.

'There's something I want to show you, Mr McFarlane. Eric. Something I've been wanting to show you for a long time. Come in.'

In the back room Mr Friday knelt behind a low table on which sat a Kwik Save crisp box. His stubby hands gripped the sides of the container as if an animal were trapped under it. Eric noticed Friday's fingers: short, bitten nails, with dark crescents around the cuticles. Mr Friday bobbed his head towards a Chesterfield sofa that looked as though it had been a bed for dogs, its plastic-coated arms almost completely flayed of their ˙skin. Eric sat down. Doreen lowered herself stiffly next to him and produced a sickly smile for Eric, her thin lips spittly. Mr Friday's clothes were strewn all about. The furniture was house-clearance-second-hand-store-landlord stuff. Cheap surfaces everywhere. On the floor was a tea tray with a semi-completed baked-bean jigsaw, pieces scattered all over it. Every piece looked the same, as if they would all fit in anywhere, as if it didn't matter.

Mr Friday lifted the box. Under it was a model of a caravan. An old caravan, a vintage caravan. Mr Friday sighed and rocked back on his haunches. 'The 1958 Eccles Coronet. That's what it's all about.'

Eric surveyed the pictures of caravans all over the walls of the room. Different types, many just like the pictures he'd had through the door. On the TV a video played silently, cars pulling caravans. He looked out of the window at the fellside and said, 'I suppose you want a share of the money and . . .' then trailed off as the whole story came together for him. He gulped and turned to Doreen. For once he saw her as his way out of the madness, his interpreter, his guide through a foreign land.

'We had a deal Doreen, didn't we? I helped you out?'

Mr Friday's short thick hands caressed the flanks of the model. Its cream and red roof had paler streaks over it, as if it had been stroked many times before. He opened its doors as tenderly as if he were moving a baby's foot on the hinge of its ankle. 'This used to be mine. Until he robbed it away.' His head was bowed, his curly hair glossy with oil. He talked into the model: 'He took it away from me when he took away my job.'

'I took away your job? How? Tell me exactly how I took away your job.'

But Eric knew how. It was true; he had taken away Mr Friday's job. That was clear.

'When I had the job, the business, I had an escape. That was the Coronet. Every weekend we would go to the caravan.' He squeezed the sole of his stockinged foot with his hand as he spoke. 'The Coronet wasn't like any old van. It was special. Those Fleetwood nights, linking her home from the pub, the little gas light showing in the Coronet window and us two stumbling and falling over in the dark – not drunk, mind you: it was the field, potholes everywhere, you could break your bloody ankle. She used to get on at the site manager, get some big lights, but it was all money, he said.' Mr Friday paused and looked across to the sideboard, where Eric could see a picture of a grimacing couple with a red truck behind them. 'You see, we weren't getting on before, not really. Not before we got the Coronet. When we were on the estate we used to argue a lot, fight. Once, when she locked me out, the neighbours had to call the police. But after I'd bought the Eccles, the Coronet, this beauty –' he patted the roof of the model '– everything was fine. All week we would look forward to our break, our Fleetwood weekend. In the Eccles. It was its smallness that she liked. A cute little ten-footer. She used to say it was like a fairy house – that's what she called it – she said it reminded her of a little house made out of a tree stump, like animals have in kiddies' books. She said she felt safe in it – she never felt safe on the estate. There were always kids, big kids and little kids, running about shouting and breaking things, name-calling. She felt safer in the van than in the house because she said that if you didn't like where you were you could move a van, but a house was a prison.'

Mr Friday plucked a wrapped sweet out of a tin on the floor near his feet. With the fingers of one hand he rubbed off the cellophane, allowed the paper to float to the floor and inserted the sweet into his mouth. He made smacking noises and moved his slippery lower lip in and out as he sucked. He looked directly at Doreen. His eyes were small, full of hate. 'I wanted him to know what he had taken away from us.' He stared off into the distance. 'You could go anywhere in the Coronet, before it went static.' His hand moved to his foot again and he pushed his fingers up under the curl of his stockinged toes. Eric wished that Mr Friday would put his shoes on. Music oozed in from the kitchen, an old track by Sparks, sounding like a one-note drone muffled by a blanket, a slurry of congested frequencies with the odd buzzing of plastic when a high note tried to break through the fog.

Mr Friday spoke again, quietly, into the model. 'Then it started. The job began to go wrong. I had a good route. A route of people who knew me, trusted me. Families. My father had served them before me. I was a one-man operation and I operated on goodwill. It seemed to me it started on one particular day, an Ash Wednesday.' Mr Friday did his ish-ish-ish laugh. 'I remember that because she had a grey smudge on her forehead, a cross of ashes, and I know, even though I'm not a left-footer, that you aren't supposed to rub it off. The priest puts it there with his thumb. I lent to Catholics and Protestant both, by the way, there was no discrimination ever. But the cross stuck in my mind. I can remember her face talking and me looking at the mark wondering how long it would stay on, wondering if Catholics ever washed them off as soon as they got home.'

Eric remembered Father Rooney, a stinking old fella, smearing a gritty grey-cross on to his own boy-soft skin.

'And she says to me I got no money. And I smiles and says, No money? Nothing in the house? How you going to eat? I'll take care of that, she says. That's nothing to do with you. And I was only being amusing like, being light-hearted. Then she goes, You can't have any money any more. And I says, What do you mean any more? That's what the man says, she goes. What man? I goes. She goes, The man at the money advice shop. Money advice shop? I turned round and said, What do they know? I've been doing this route for years. They've got all the books, she says, all the law. She says that I don't have a proper licence. And then she says my agreement's not properly drawn up. And I'm looking at the ash on her head and I'm thinking that's very Christian, that's very religious, entering into an agreement and then not honouring it. And I nearly said there's probably something in the Bible about paying back loans, and you there with your fresh Catholic mark on your head, but I didn't say that I just said, Tell you what; I'll come back next week and we'll see if you can catch up then, but she goes, No, not next week, not ever. I'm not to call again. It's harassment. Then she slopes off inside and digs out a leaflet which has a picture on it of a big man at a door – and I'm not a big man – and under the picture it says *Protection against Harassment*. She reads out a bit from it but I can't remember what it said. Then she says I'm to deal with her in writing only. She's not even going to give me one pound, not even coppers. Nothing. Writing, that's what she wants.'

Eric's eyes moved from the window to the door, planning his way out. Escape looked easy. Then he remembered Doreen had locked the door. He could use a chair and smash a window. But why worry? He could walk out any time he wanted. Just tell them, order them to open the door. He looked at Mr Friday. Psychological profiles of maniacs specify functional clothing – no concessions to taste or fashion. That was a feature of the sociopath. Mr Friday's clothes were indeed functional; many-pocketed, robust-looking garments. But the Christmas socks argued the other way. Was it possible the socks were worn for convenience only – an unasked-for present, the style, colour and motif irrelevant to him? Or, conversely, that the socks were a deliberate choice: perhaps Mr Friday imagined they advertised a bright, humorous and quirky personality. You could go either way with the socks. Near the sofa were Mr Friday's elaborately tooled cowboy boots. Now, you couldn't say that they were functional. No. This man was normal, he was no risk at all. He was definitely sad, a sad man. And he was used to being sad, vengeful, accustomed to hating and plotting. He wore his desperation like his own skin.

Shopaloan had shifted his sitting position slightly and was now cross-legged, one hand on each of the Christmas socks, fondling the balls of his feet. He leaned forward and smacked the table. 'But writing is no good.' His voice had gone raspy, used up. 'Writing doesn't get to the heart of a person. You can stick a letter behind the clock, scop it in the bin, wipe your arse with it – but you can't do that to a person, you can't do that to me; nobody, nobody wipes their arse with me! A letter from me is actually me. It's me you are holding in your hand. Treat that letter, those words, how you would treat me! But if I'm not there how do I know what's happening? I need to deal in skin and blood, voices talking, human beings. I need to see my customers' faces.

'So I said to her, I'm not big on the writing idea. Let's not get into writing. I'll come back anyway, just to see how you're getting on. Maybe you'd want another loan, I say, to pay this one off and to get a few things in for the kids. But she wouldn't have it. Turned round and said I was diddling her. I was a hook. That I hadn't put some payments down on the card. Now, I'm not a violent man normally, I never lift a finger normally. But when someone says something like that – that I'm dishonest – well, the blood boils over the top. I used to say I would cut off my hand if it ever struck a woman in anger, but that's what I did that day I'm ashamed to say. I struck her, in the stomach with my fist like this.' He made a jabbing motion. 'She bent over forward and went quiet for a while, not crying, not anything, just bent double. And then the whole thing went mental. She screamed, says I'm attacking her. And it was one punch, that's all! I wasn't going to hit her again, she could see that. She was overreacting. It was her fault; after all, she said I was dishonest, called me a crook. What does she expect? Then she tries to shut the door on me but I'm not having that because I've got a contract with her, a legal contract, and it hadn't been resolved and I told her that, and I said the same thing to the neighbour woman who had come out to have a look, I told her it was about a legal contract and that one party to it had not been doing her part and I said what she had called me and then the bloke comes running down the stairs and he's naked and all wet, he's been in the bath, and I start to walk away and he comes after me up the path, naked, in the bollocky buff, shouting things. And he grabs me by the hair and pulls my head down like this –' he made the motion of holding a head under his arm '– and he goes to wallop me and then there's all this laughing and he stops and looks up and the street's full of neighbours and they're all laughing cos he's got no clothes on and he pushes me away and runs in shouting, I'll get you for this and that type of thing.'

Mr Friday shook his head sadly, as if the conclusion of his tale had been reached, and gave his concentration again

286

to the model. He lifted away the upper part. Inside was a 1950s kitchen looking right out of a black and white soap advert, and you could see a bedroom and a tiny toilet. There was even a sink with taps. Mr Friday flicked at the bedcovers on the miniature bed. 'See what it was like inside? See how nice?' He replaced the crisp box over the model. 'After the incident on Ash Wednesday a lot of things got done in writing, a lot of people did a lot of writing. I didn't do much, but things were written about me, to me and for me to sign. I was bombarded. There were letters from you.' He stared at Eric. '*Dear Mr Friday, re this re that re written agreements, re Consumer Credit Act, under Administration of Justice Act*, then it's letters offering bus fare off hundred-quid debts, and then it's administration orders, individual voluntary arrangements, bankruptcy, and nothing in any of these things for me. I turned up at court for a public examination of one debtor and the judge, the *actual judge* was sitting there – no wig or anything, nothing like that – he's sitting there and he's laughing! He's laughing at me and he says to me, Well, I think you are going to have to whistle, Mr Friday! And I said, I thought you were the judge, I thought you were the law, I thought that you would see me right. I'm the one that lent the money they've had, money they've never paid back, and I says to him, If I leaned over this desk and put my hand in your pocket and took out your wallet and helped myself to your money, you'd say that was stealing, you'd call the ruddy police, I should think. The judge gets all stern then and says, That's enough, like he's some head-master, and I goes to say more and he says he'll have me for contempt. It was *him* treating *me* with contempt, I would have said, eh.'

He laughed his ack-ack-ack, bitterly.

'That day was my last day as a collector, I would say. A Thursday. Pay day, still pay day in many people's minds around here. A good day to collect, people still feel good about money on a Thursday; even though you're paid monthly, Thursday you feel like you've been paid. It must be something they put in the genes. So we tried to keep the Coronet for a while. But with me signing on we couldn't manage the service charges, the site rentals. One weekend we turned up and the site man says we can't come on. Says we've got to turn round and drive back. He's got a court order to exercise a lien on my goods – goods meaning 1958 Eccles Coronet. Until I pay the rent I can't see it. Even though it's mine. So we went home. Then I thought I'll just sell it. But I couldn't! It turned out you had to sell it to the site owner. So he got it for next to nothing. That was the best van I had ever had. There were others – I had a little 1964 Bailey Maru and before that a Cheltenham Fawn – but the Eccles, there was nothing like the Eccles. Its body was –' Mr Friday drew a caravan shape in the air, his eyes glittering '– perfection.'

Eric stood up. 'I've got to go, Mr Friday. But we need to agree something first. We've got to get in front of this. That money. The first cheque for the skills and resource centre. I think that the best result would be for us to give the money back. Just forget about it. Tell Bennett Lowe we made a mistake. He doesn't know anything yet. He won't have had that tape. Let me go to Bennett's office and inter-cept the tape. If you posted it today I can get to the council post room and retrieve it. Or I'll see Bennett, I'll get Ben-nett to forget it all. I know Bennett Lowe, he's a friend. He wouldn't want it to end badly. It would reflect on him. He should have done more checks. But he believed in it, in this whole skills and resource centre idea.'

Mr Friday swivelled his head to face Eric. 'I don't think you realize your situation, McFarlane. Look.' He snatched a Cumberland *Evening News & Star* off the floor and held it up. 'This came through the door earlier.'

'Police Probe Cleator Moor Charity Shambles'.

'No specifics in the article but they know they are on to something.' He ack-ack-acked, slotting his eyes against the chuckle, adding more thin creases to his squint lines, like tiny threadworms shooting out. 'Do you know what my lowest point was? Dressed as a bleeding lemon and you sauntering past with that tarty little piece, skirt up her arse.'

Eric shook his head with a small narrow smile and turned to Doreen. 'Where's the money, Doreen, the cheque?' Suddenly she was interested; this was something she knew about. She got up and went to the sideboard. Out of a drawer she pulled out a cheque and held it up like one of the giant cardboard ones they use for pools winners.

'It's not what we asked for. But fifty thousand quid for a feasibility study. Not bad, eh? I'll be paying it in tomorrow. Into the account you set up for us.'

She aimed her left eye into the middle of his forehead. 'Fifty thousand, Eric. For me and him. Not you.'

For the first time Eric began to size Mr Friday up physically. He was a little man, but broad about the shoulders. Thick arms. Eric had never noticed his bulk before, had always thought of him just as a short man. And you dismiss short people. You look over their heads, you get served at the bar ahead of them, you feel they are children, somehow happier not having to compete at our level. Shopaloan was small, but his body filled a space, it seemed to ripple with tension, a concentrated knot of gristle and bone, a thick little pig-man.

Eric scanned the room. Mr Friday seemed everywhere; in Doreen, in the furniture, in the walls, in the flabby 1970s music; everything infected with his vengeful malignancy.

The songs came round again, 'Costafine Town', 'Mother Earth', 'How Does it Feel?', over and over. He felt jets of adrenalin forcing through his blood. His head tingled and his heart clubbed at his chest. He had decided that he wouldn't be able to escape. He had decided that he would have to face whatever it was Mr Friday needed to do.

Mr Friday lifted up an old-fashioned sewing machine, SINGER written on the side in gold lettering. That was when he hit Eric for the first time, on the side of his head, with the base of the sewing machine. When Eric was on the floor, Mr Friday dropped the sewing machine on to his chest. Eric was winded, he couldn't get up. From his position supine on the floor he watched Mr Friday moving about the room. Then there was a stinging whack on the front of his head. As the object left contact with him he saw from its edge that it was a solid-bodied guitar. He greyed out for a time, fuzzy voices scudding around on the edges of consciousness, then black.

In the dark cupboard under the stairs the grey-eyed man listens to dripping and a thin hushing sound like escaping gas. He sniffs, gets petrol.

Apartfromtheobvious and Magnum are talking, but their voices sound so faint they seem removed in time as well as in space. He pushes his shoulder against the door with as much force as he can muster. The fridge, which is against the door, shifts slightly, opening up a narrow crack. He can see the woodchip on the hall wall. Ten steps would take him outside. He watches them moving in and out of the hall, going about quickly and silently with some obscure purpose. Apartfromtheobvious takes into the living room an armful of what look like aerosol cans. Then the video player and what looks like part of a car engine, then cartons of some sort of liquid, boxes of matches and newspapers by the dozen.

He goes to shout but can't, no moisture. His mouth tastes vile and his skin feels tight and flaky. He senses he is thin and weak. Not eaten for the two days they've had him there, and before that, a week of nearly nothing but toast and Happy Shopper margarine. Oh, and the soy sauce.

His head is light; he feels himself soaring upwards from time to time, a drunk, stoned feeling, frightening. He can't fix his thoughts to anything. It is like trying to hammer a tiny pin into a wall.

Christ, this petrol stink, this running around with equipment. Say they fucking killed him or something, say they fucking did it. Made him pay the ultimate debt, the debt of nature. Or say they left him to starve. He remembered a photograph of a starved Holocaust victim, so thin he had no buttocks and his anus stuck out like a stovepipe.

Through the crack he sees Apartfromtheobvious murmuring something to Magnum, before squirming into his coat and disappearing out of the door. Hears the whisper of car tyres on gravel.

He drifts into some sort of slumber, standing up, the way a horse would sleep.

A thunderous crashing noise wakes him, repeating and repeating and repeating from the front door. He looks out through the crack and Magnum appears in the hall to see a pair of thick arms pounding and pounding through the frosted glass, and chunks of glass clatter and skid on the floor-boards and the wooden frame is twisted into an antic shape, and the arms smash and claw at the air until, gashed and bloody, their fat fingers are able to fumble for a lock, which they don't find, and then what must be a heavy body barges at the door and the whole thing, door jamb and all, collapses and a large figure in sportswear and glinting gold jewellery enters and moves towards Magnum, laughing. He flops his large hand on to her shoulder.

'Sorry about the door, love. Where is he? Where is the little cunt? He owes me money.'

41

Doreen quivers and backs away from the overspill mayor, who is standing in the shattered doorway, breathing heavily.

'Cheeky robbin' cunt,' he says, pushing Doreen into the living room. 'Where is he?'

The mayor is angry. He is angry and he wants Eric and wants his money. But Eric paid the small man on the estate, the man with the bumfluffy goatee beard, the watery pink eyes, the milky breath.

Eric shoves at the cupboard door again, but it won't move.

He puts his foot against the wall and heaves. It moves slightly. He raps with his hand and his knuckles sink into the surface with a flat thunk. He can't pull his arm back far enough to punch, so he kneels and leans on the wall with his shoulder. It doesn't give.

Who would help him now? Charlotte would be furious. It was so long since he'd seen her, so long since he'd left the message on the answer-machine, drunken and rambling about Mr Friday, Doreen, Ennerdale and the lilac house: she wouldn't know what any of that meant. And even if she was worried, even if she cared, what could she do? Nothing. And Charlotte was all he had left.

The overspill mayor's Mancunian tones floated over: 'The last one, McFarlane's woman, she put up a right fucking fight. Declared she had no idea where the little fucker was. Didn't take long to hook it out of her.'

Charlotte. The mayor has been to Charlotte. Eric has to get to her. He stands, leans back and tries to kick his way out through the plasterboard wall, but there's not enough space to swing his foot. He is a trapped animal; so how would an animal escape? He remembers an unusually intelligent guinea pig Julie had; the rest were docile but this one could escape from anything. She'd called it Steve McQueen. This would not be a problem for Steve McQueen. Steve McQueen would gnaw its way out. Eric scrapes the wall with his thumbnail and gets some chalky dust. He scrapes again, like digging into sugar.

The board is mostly powder held in a sandwich of thin card. He picks and gouges a small hole big enough for his forefinger, which he inserts and then moves around. Pushing and scratching and waggling, his finger gets quickly through the board and, feeling across a gap of a couple of inches, he finds another board. He gets through that too. Then he is easily able to rip out an opening big enough for a fist and with thumb and forefinger grip the ragged edges and, moving it from side to side, tear out a big slit. From there on he rips, pushes and pulls and soon the hole is big enough for his head.

He can hear Doreen crying softly, the mayor saying, 'Come on, come on.'

But he isn't out. And as much as he heaves against the plasterboard wall, as much he tries to topple the whole thing, he hasn't got the strength or energy. He pulls his head back in from the hole and thinks. Lower. Try lower. He gets on his hands and knees and searches every inch of wall with his fingers. From down low he sees for the first time pin-ends of light from a ventilation grid. He can see that it leads into the kitchen. He puts his head against it and, with his feet against the door, is able to force the plastic grille out of its casing and, incredibly quickly and with little effort, is able to wriggle his skinny body through into air and freedom.

And fear. Fear creeps into him like cold water up a radiator. He lies for a few moments on the stone floor, panting, heart pumping in his chest. A sickly fluorescent light around him. He stands and goes to the hall. He listens. The overspill mayor is repeating the same thing to Doreen, over and over: 'Where's McFarlane? Where's McFarlane?'

But Doreen is clearly too stunned to answer.

He follows the loud sound of escaping air back into the kitchen. On the table is a video recorder, and on top aerosol cans are snagged together in a bundle with a dressing gown cord. The video timer is wired to a gas igniter – the type Julie used to fiddle the electric meter. Eric edges closer and can see each can is pinpricked with holes. Gas hisses out. Dry newspaper spread around. A line of tied-together rags go from the can to the edge of the petrol-sodden carpet. A part from a car engine sits in the middle. It is surprisingly well thought-out, Eric thinks. Above his head the smoke alarm cover is off, batteries removed. Eric edges closer again and unplugs the video.

Back in the hall, he moves towards the doorway. He is about to make his dash when he catches a look at Doreen over the shoulder of the mayor. Her eyes arc up and down, beseechingly.

The mayor has a Stanley knife in his hand.

Eric coughs, then rasps out, 'I believe that I paid your colleague.' It hurts to talk.

The mayor swivels his round pink head. '*I beleeeeve. I paaaayed. Your colleeeegue.* It's the Damon-Blur-boy. It is he. The one with the face of a twat. Nice up here, innit? I should have brought the family. Bit of hill walking.' He ambles up to Eric and presses his face into his, foreheads touching. 'Fucking delivery fee? Forty-nine ninety-fucking-five? Charge me a fucking delivery fee?'

Eric backs away but the mayor follows, keeping his head pressed against Eric's, like Siamese twins dancing. The mayor's forehead is cold against Eric's skin, pleasant, like finding a cool part of a pillow.

'Eh,' the mayor keeps saying. 'Eh cunt? Eh cunt? Eh cunt?'

Eric looks down at the mayor's chest, the thick gold chain gleaming against the Adidas top.

'Please,' coughs Eric. 'I've had a rough time. Please, mate. Give me a break. I need a drink.'

The mayor moves his forehead away, rubs the heel of his hand at the point of contact, then wrinkles his nose. 'You stink, by the way. Like something crawled up your arse and died in there. What you doing here? And who the fuck is this?' He turns just in time to see Doreen running off down the path, furry slippers flap-flapping.

The mayor smiles, 'I don't know what's been going on,' he says, 'but your little bird bones are going to be talcum powder if you don't pay back that delivery charge.'

Eric feels things around him suddenly spinning and begins to sag as if he were being demolished from within. He lurches towards the sofa, where he collapses, his face towards the ceiling. He feels the mayor's heavy body settle next to him, hears the man breathing. The mayor passes Eric a half-full bottle of Fanta and Eric gulps down the lot. It is slick and syrupy and warm and there's no fizz, but it works.

After a time Eric asks, 'Did you say my bones would be talcum powder?'

'Yeh,' says the mayor, flinging his blinding white trainers up on to the low table. 'I always say that. One of my lines. Patter, like.'

Eric leans back further into the sofa, enjoying the feel of his bones sinking into soft furnishing. He sucks in a long breath. He looks down at his hands, his fingers; milky enamel flakes on his nails, from Doreen's make-up and powder from the plasterboard. His side feels sore, ribs bruised from the fall from the attic. He closes his eyes for a time and listens to the sounds drifting in from the smashed doorway – the rumbling of the open-cast mine, the birds twittering, the wind. The stink of petrol is still everywhere. When Eric opens his eyes again he sees that the mayor is pointing the Stanley knife at him, the fingers around the handle speckled in blood from smashing through the glass door. Eric focuses on the mayor's feet up on the table; the translucent bug-eyes on the sides of his trainers stare back.

'You fucked up, indie-cunt,' says the mayor, softly.

Eric closes his eyes again.

'Indie-cunt. Speak to me.'

'I'm here.'

'Buddy, buddy, buddy. You took the piss charging me that fee, that delivery fee. Everyone heard about it. Every lender on every estate. My peers, *my colleeeegues*.'

Eric tries to get up off the sofa, but has no energy, and when the mayor's fat hand presses his knees down, his legs buckle under him.

'See that bag over there?' he says to the mayor. 'In there you'll find my cheque book and wallet.'

The mayor goes over to where the bag lies amongst other stuff Friday and Doreen were obviously planning to take away with them, extracts Eric's cheque book and wallet and hands them to Eric along with a pen.

'How much?' Eric says.

The mayor picks a needle-like fragment of glass out of his arm, puckering his lips at the pain. 'Refund of your –' he coughs '– delivery charge. Forty-nine ninety-five, if I remember. Plus my collection charge.'

'The same?'

'The same?' The mayor laughs, a short hideous bark. 'You cheeky fucker. This is outside city boundaries. Well past fucking Bolton. Gonna be double. Call it one forty-nine ninety-five altogether. I was gonna let you off. At first. Was only fifty quid after all. But a few other things happened. Fucking fucklaycard . . .' He stops, presses his fist hard into his forehead and whines long and slow in a creaky high voice. Then he pauses for a time, breathing slowly and deliberately. His knuckles have left white indentations on his skin.

'Fucking fucklaycard,' he goes on, slowly, enunciating every word, 'charged me twelve quid for going over me limit. Rang and gave them shit. But it was . . . unsatisfactory.'

'Did you say the talcum-powder thing?'

The mayor clenches his fist again, then relaxes. 'I did, but the bitches they have there still wouldn't give it back. Then those divs at the GasfartBoard charged me twenty quid for a late payment and after that *on the very same day* I had to send back some bastard tickets I got for my bird's birthday – Paul Simon, him out of Garfunkel – cos he cancelled, and they charged me a booking fee of three quid and I was walking out of GMEX thinking about the three quid to that short fat freak Paul Simon and the twelve quid to fucklaycard and the twenty quid to the Gasfart-Board, and right away I thought about you. You see?'

Eric nods. He scribbles the cheque and hands it to him.

'Number for the back?' the mayor says.

Eric slides his card from his wallet and copies the number on to the back of the cheque. The mayor checks the card against the cheque and returns the card to Eric.

Then he holds out his fat fist and opens it slowly. On his blood-sticky palm lies a shiny 5p.

'You made it out for one fifty.'

'Keep it,' says Eric.

'Take it, mister,' says the mayor.

'Keep it,' says Eric.

The mayor's hand doesn't move.

'It's five p,' says Eric.

'It's money.'

'Think of it as a tip. The exemplary quality of your . . .'

The mayor lifts the Stanley knife and Eric's eyes follow its gleaming tip.

'Take the fucking five p.'

Eric looks at the coin. The hand that holds it trembles. The other hand raises the Stanley knife higher. The two men sit for some time in that position.

The mayor takes out a cigarette and lighter. Eric thinks of the petrol stink and wonders if the whole place will go up, but the mayor fires up and nothing happens. Too far away from the cans. The mayor takes a series of long deep pulls, thinning his eyes against the smoke.

'Did you see Julie before it happened?' Eric asks.

The mayor expels a long rod of smoke from the side of his mouth. 'I heard about what happened, yes. I'm sorry, indie-cunt. Sorry to hear about that. I did see her. A few days before. Was round there for the rent. She had a bandage on her head. Maybe she'd had a fall, I didn't know. Something all stained under the bandage.' He makes a motion across his head, magician's spooky hand. 'All brown. Looked proper tired, pale. She was a bit behind with the rent, as you know, and I had a proposition for her, but she told me to fuck off. Had vim that kid. Liked her as a matter of fact. Sparkling girl.'

The mayor finishes his fag, nods to Eric and Eric removes it and places it in the ashtray. Its grey string of smoke sways with unseen currents in the air and they sit in silence looking at the smoke and the 5p in the mayor's blood-speckled hand.

A whisper of gravel announces a car and they watch through the window as Doreen's old Allegro pulls up next to Friday's Volvo, which has its bonnet open and looks half dismantled.

'Aye, aye,' says the mayor. 'Chucky returns.'

Friday pauses at the smashed door then looks to the window, sees the two men on the sofa and his face buckles in shock. He creeps backwards towards the car, nervously scouring the scene for clues, then stoops and picks something up, raises it to his face. One of Doreen's slippers. Turns and looks behind him, walks a few steps and picks up the other. Holds the furry slippers and looks at the bushes. Then he says, in a piercing whisper which they can hear even in the house, 'Mags. Mags. Doreen. Where are you?'

The mayor laughs. 'Fucking mong. Where does he think she is? Up a fucking tree?'

'Magnum.' Loud stage whispers. 'Come on. I'm here. Come on. We got to go.'

And sure enough Doreen appears from the bushes, brown leaves in her hair, dirt on her face, pointing towards the house and gibbering. Her fists mime smashing an invisible door, her hands Stanley-knife the air with upwards thrusts and Friday's eyes grow bigger and his body seems to shrink further towards the ground. He grabs at Doreen and pulls her into the car. But they don't leave. They sit for a time, arguing, heads jabbing, fingers stabbing, hands gesturing wildly, Doreen's head peck-peck-pecking at the space in front of Friday's face, her mouth ripping the air. Then finally Doreen's mouth widens and she seems to roar at him – must have made a fabulous noise – and Friday gets out of the car. Doreen drives away.

Friday stands for a time in the drive, then moves towards the house, enters through the smashed doorway and stands there, staring at Eric and the mayor.

'I'm Friday,' he says to the mayor.

'The arse end of the working week or the day before Saturday?' says the mayor.

'This is my house. This is – was – my door. That's my sofa. That's –'

'I'm getting the picture,' says the mayor.

'*He's* mine, too. He owes me.'

'Money?'

'More than that.'

'You in collection?'

'That was my line.' Friday sits down on the chair opposite. 'I had a good round, good customers, trust, everyone –'

'Don't fucking start all that again,' Eric says.

'Yes,' says Friday. 'I was very persuasive. Dogged, they said.'

The mayor stood up suddenly. 'Well, Mr Friday, this is lovely, I have to say, and I could sit and talk debt-collection techniques with you till my cock falls off, but I think it's time I was off. Thanks for the hospitality – tea and buns would have been nice, but still. And thanks for sorting out my little indie friend here. Looks like you pair of freaks have done my job for me.'

He looks at the 5p in his palm and with the finger of his other hand flicks it on to the floor.

'Look after the pennies –' says the mayor.

'And the pounds look after themselves,' says Friday.

The mayor looks at him.

'Can you give me a lift?' says Friday. 'Mr –'

'Fokse. Call me Fokse.'

'Mr Fokse. A lift to the station. Better still, Manchester airport? My car,' he waves towards it, disabled on the drive, 'my car is no good now. We needed it to make the clever little device in the kitchen.'

'You are, a fucking head-the-ball, but yes, buddy, a lift is the least I can do. I'm on my way back to Manchester right now. But what about him?'

Trussed up with masking tape and tied to the radiator again, Eric watches through the window as the mayor and Friday drive away. Shouldn't be long before someone finds him.

Charlotte knows where he is. The sky is reddening over the fells and Eric catches sight of his own dark transparent reflection in the window; he has a hollow look, his body looks an outline only. The radiator makes a ticking sound as it cools. Reminds him of the snow crackling past when he and Spangles were lying in the park, 'Dancing Queen' coming from the park keeper's radio.

He looks at the model of Mr Friday's caravan on the table. Perhaps, when this is over, Eric will buy a caravan. He can see the attraction. Be like rolling up into a ball, making yourself tiny. A shrunken world where everything is cheap and easy and you owe nobody and nobody owes you. But he would miss it. Miss the debts, the money madness. Hard to believe, but for Eric, debt is the sticky stuff; it binds. It is danger, it is chance. Without it, why would we speak, sing, fall in love? We owe everyone, always, all the time. We owe the world, and we owe it to ourselves. It is our job, our duty, our right to borrow, default, fall into arrears. Who wants to die with money in the bank?

He strains at the electric lead that binds his hands and manages to get himself flat against the floor. Then, with a caterpillar motion, he crawls, inch by painful inch, as far as his bindings will allow him. Only an arm's length away. He sighs. He can see it, smell it almost. Then, one extra push and he is there. He pushes out his tongue and touches it. Cold metal. Pleasant. One huge extra lurch of effort and the 5p is between his lips and, with a twist of his head, inside his mouth. The clack of it against his teeth, the vinegar tang of the mayor's sweat. He presses the coin against his palate with his tongue and closes his eyes.

Communion.

Everything is quiet for a long time. Then the sirens come.

About the Author

Photo: Jonathan Bean

DAVID GAFFNEY was born in West Cumbria, and now lives in Manchester. He has worked as a film studies lecturer, a holiday camp entertainer, a medical records clerk, a pub pianist, a debt counsellor in Moss Side, and now works for a shadowy government organisation. His short short story collections *Sawn Off Tales* and *Aromabingo* have been highly acclaimed.

Acknowledgements

Thanks to Luke Brown for his brilliant editorial input and to all at Tindal Street. Thanks also to Peter Wild for general writerly support; Martin Bax and everyone at Ambit for first putting me in print; to Jen and Chris at Salt for having enough faith in me to publish my short story collections; and to Mike Toms at the Eccles Caravan Owners Club.

Thanks also to all the debt counsellors, money advisors and welfare rights officers I've worked with in the past; to all the clients I've helped; and to all the banks and finance companies who've been getting a pound a month ever since.